Shadowing
IVY

JANELLE TAYLOR

ZEBRA BOOKS
Kensington Publishing Corp.
www.kensingtonbooks.com

ZEBRA BOOKS are published by

Kensington Publishing Corp.
850 Third Avenue
New York, NY 10022

All Kensington titles, imprints, and distributed lines are available at special quantity discounts for bulk purchases for sales promotion, premiums, fund-raising, educational, or institutional use.

Special book excerpts or customized printings can also be created to fit specific needs. For details, write or phone the office of the Kensington Special Sales Manager: Attn.: Special Sales Department. Kensington Publishing Corp., 850 Third Avenue, New York, NY 10022. Phone: 1-800-221-2647.

Zebra and the Z logo Reg. U.S. Pat. & TM Off.

ISBN-13: 978-0-8217-7892-0
ISBN-10: 0-8217-7892-7

First Printing: October 2007
10 9 8 7 6 5 4 3 2 1

Printed in the United States of America

*Dedicated to my wonderful husband, Michael,
for his love, support, and romantic suspense
during our forty-two years of marriage.*

*Also to Amanda Rouse
for all her help and support
during the past few years—
thanks!*

Chapter One

The bride, clutching a lacy white veil, sat sobbing on the stoop of a brick apartment building. She was rail thin, coatless, and looked like she might blow away in the harsh March wind. Her shoulders shook as she cried.

Ivy Sedgwick, one of Applewood, New Jersey's finest, and her partner, an idiotic blowhard named Dan, got out of their squad car and headed up to the woman.

"Oh, Lord. It's not like her fiancé dropped dead," Dan muttered under his breath, which smelled garlicky, as usual.

Ivy shot him a look, something she did on a regular basis since getting paired with the jerk last month. Her previous partner, a great guy named Tom, had been promoted up the ladder. Soon it would be Ivy's turn. Detective. Her dream. And then she'd never have to listen to Dan's mind-numbing rants or watch him stuff half a dozen stereotypical donuts down his throat.

"Laura Mylar?" Ivy asked gently. "I'm Officer

Sedgwick, and this is my partner, Officer Dan Wilmer. You reported a stolen wedding dress?"

The woman jumped up, her pretty blue eyes puffy and red from crying. "It was stolen right out of my car. I picked it up from the bridal salon, drove home, ran upstairs to install a hook on my bedroom door so the dress wouldn't drag on the floor, and when I came downstairs, the dress bag was gone! Who would steal a bride's wedding gown?" She slumped back down, burying her hands in her face.

Who, indeed. Ivy thought of the wedding dress hanging on a hook outside her own bedroom door. If it suddenly disappeared, Ivy would be uncharacteristically beside herself. She loved her gown, loved how she felt in it. Princess for a day wasn't Ivy's thing; she would have been happy in a fancy white pants suit, but her mother went off on one of her many speeches about waiting twenty-seven years to watch her daughter finally find happiness (as though Ivy wasn't happy before she and Declan got engaged!) and she simply had to wear a gown befitting a movie star.

Dana Sedgwick had dragged Ivy, kicking and screaming, to every bridal boutique within fifty miles, and Ivy had to admit, trying on dresses was more fun than she'd expected. She'd fallen in love with a simple white satin gown, strapless, with a row of delicate beading across the empire waist. When she'd looked at herself in the mirror the first time she'd tried it on, she'd been stunned by how . . . pretty she looked, how feminine. She had felt like a movie star.

Until she took it off and put back on her uniform

to head back to work. Ivy Sedgwick, movie star. It was laughable. Four years after graduating from the police academy and Ivy's mother still thought Ivy was "finding herself." Her mother was also under the delusion that after the wedding, Ivy would quit the force and stay home to "provide a lovely home for her husband."

"Did you see anyone running away from the car when you came back?" Dan asked, barely able to contain his boredom.

"If I had, I would have chased them down," Laura said, her voice cracking.

"Not in those," Dan commented on a laugh, glancing at the woman's three-inch peau de sois white pumps.

Laura let out a deep breath. "My mom told me to break them in, to wear them as much as possible before the wedding. But now I don't even have a dress. The wedding is next weekend. I'll never be able to afford another gown, no matter how many shifts I take on."

Ah, Ivy thought. *That's why she looks so familiar.* Ivy sat down next to her. "You work in Applewood Diner, right? I eat there all the time."

Laura nodded. "I've been working double shifts to pay for the dress and this veil."

Ivy and her best friend, Alanna Moore, had had breakfast at the busy diner just that morning. Alanna, fellow police officer at the Applewood PD, was working extra shifts to pay for her own wedding. She'd lost her mother years ago, and her father was who-knew-where. Alanna's fiancé was a resident at the local hospital and didn't earn much yet. Ivy had managed to save up a good nest egg, but her mother insisted on paying for her wedding, something Ivy very much appreciated.

As Ivy and Alanna had awaited their breakfast that morning, they'd been impressed at how well Laura had handled her tables—rude businessmen, disrespectful high schoolers, impatient elderly couples. But how she handled one table in particular was amazing—four-year-old triplets who were flinging scrambled eggs off their spoons at Laura and passing busboys. Instead of losing her cool, Laura got down on knee level and said in an excited voice, "Okay, guys, I want to see which one of you will be right. How many plates of breakfast do you think I can balance on my arms without dropping them?" Blessed silence for an entire half minute. Then each boy made his guess. Two! Four! Thirteen! Laura disappeared into the kitchen, the triplets silent as they watched her return with three plates balanced on each arm. "Yay, you all win," she said to their mother's relief, and handed them each a mini Rubik's cube, which she apparently kept a bunch of just in case. Everyone enjoyed a quieter breakfast after that, the triplets, their tongues out in serious concentration, twisting tiny colored boxes on their toys.

"I just wanted everything to be perfect for my dad," Laura continued, wiping at tears. "He has cancer and doesn't have much time left. It means so much to him that he'll get to see me marry a great guy and settled in my new life." She sniffled, then sobered. "I guess it doesn't really matter what I wear, right?" she asked, looking at Ivy. "My wedding is a celebration of love, and my friends and family will be there. That's what matters."

"Keep telling yourself that, honey," Dan whispered into an obnoxious cough. Dan was on his third wife. How he got anyone to marry him was beyond Ivy.

She would have jabbed her elbow back into her partner's beer gut if he hadn't moved suddenly to avoid getting run over by a group of skateboarding teenagers.

I just wanted everything to be perfect for my dad. For a moment, Ivy felt the familiar sting of envy. Her own father, the late William Sedgwick, had never been interested in fatherhood, marriage, or commitment to another human being. He'd married Ivy's mother in Las Vegas after knowing her three days, then annulled the marriage a week later because "he'd been drunk." He'd never had any interest in Ivy or her older half sisters, Amanda and Olivia.

Never had any interest until three months ago, that was. He'd surprised her early in the morning, before sunrise, on an ordinary weekday, by knocking on her door.

"Dad?" she'd said, so shocked to see him standing on her tiny porch. Her father had never been to her house, a tiny but adorable slate-blue Cape that she'd been so proud to buy.

The venerable William Sedgwick, chairman of Sedgwick Enterprises, which bought and sold corporations, wore a heavy black wool coat, a gray cashmere scarf wrapped around his neck, and an old-fashioned black hat. He'd always reminded her, physically, of the actor Sean Connery. He didn't smile, or step forward to hug her, or even offer a kiss on the cheek. There was no, *You're looking well, Ivy.* No, *What a lovely home.* Ivy had no doubt William

Sedgwick, whose primary residence was on Park Avenue, would turn up his nose at middle-class Applewood and its small, tidy houses.

Ivy glanced around him to the black sedan parked in front of her house. A driver sat reading a newspaper.

Her father looked directly at her. "There's a serious matter I need to discuss with you, Ivy."

Ivy laughed; she couldn't help it. He hadn't considered her appendix almost rupturing when she was fourteen a serious matter. He hadn't made an appearance at the hospital, even though she'd worked up the courage to call his office during her recuperation. His secretary had assured her she'd pass along the message. He hadn't visited, nor had he sent a card. When her mother had barraged his home and office with calls until he did respond, his answer to Ivy's mother was: *Is she dead? Then, it's hardly serious. If you continue to harass me, I will pass the matter on to the police.*

"A serious matter?" Ivy repeated. "What serious matter could you possibly—"

"Don't marry Declan McLean," he interrupted.

Ivy's smile faded. Declan had worked part-time at Sedgwick Enterprises—until he'd been abruptly fired a couple of days prior to her father's visit. Ivy's mother was an old friend, well, acquaintance, really, of Declan's late mother. A few months before she'd died in a car accident, Declan's mother had made use of the contact by calling William directly and asking about a job for her son. When he and Ivy met at one of her mother's many parties (Ivy never went to her mother's parties, but her mother had tricked her into going to that one specifically to meet Declan), and she'd heard he worked for her father's company, she'd been even more attracted. Her own six degrees of separation. Well, one degree. But she and her father couldn't be farther apart.

Ivy had shivered and wrapped her arms around herself; it was a cold winter morning and she was standing there in the doorway in only her uniform. "Come in," she said.

William didn't step forward. "Right here is fine. I'll only need a moment of your time."

Whatever, Ivy thought angrily. "How did you know I was engaged?" she asked. She certainly hadn't called him to share her happy news. Experience had taught her well.

"Your mother informed me, of course," William said coldly. "She wanted to 'rest assured' that I would pay for the wedding and even suggested The Plaza as a venue."

Ivy's face burned. As if she'd expect, let alone want, William Sedgwick to pay for her wedding! "I—"

He held up a hand to shut her up. "As I told your mother, I will not contribute one dime toward the wedding. Declan McLean is an unacceptable choice. You must not marry him, Ivy. You should end the relationship now."

An unacceptable choice. Right. Because he was still a student at thirty. Because he'd been working part-time at Sedgwick Enterprises in an entry-level capacity as a junior analyst and that wasn't good enough. Because he wasn't wealthy. Because he came from old money that had been lost generations ago. William was new money. He respected new money. And

Declan, with his part-time salary, barely had *any* money. He even lived in a dorm with a roommate. Declan had a new job almost immediately at another corporation in the same capacity.

William suddenly winced in pain and clutched at the lapel of his coat.

"Dad? Are you all right?"

Dad. She never called him that.

He regained his composure almost immediately, but Ivy could tell he was in pain. "Do not marry him, Ivy," he said again.

But as usual, there was no expression in his eyes. He might as well be telling her not to buy white bread, that wheat bread was healthier. But perhaps this was it, all there was to William. Perhaps there was no other dimension to his personality.

No, there had to be. He'd gotten three beautiful women—Ivy's, Olivia's, and Amanda's mothers—to fall madly in love with him. Not to mention countless others. Then again, he was rich as hell. Ivy loved her mother, but the woman valued money. Ivy had been surprised her mother had pushed for her to meet Declan, a struggling MBA student without a dime to his name. Until Ivy realized that her mother thought Declan's family still had money. Declan's mother had been too proud to come clean about the family's financial situation. Ivy still hadn't bothered to set her straight.

Based on how Ivy felt about Declan, how in love she was, she wondered how her mother could really have married William at all. She tried to picture her mother, so young, so beautiful, with William in some ritzy Las Vegas hotel, where he gambled without a care in the world and—according to her mother—slept with three other women, strippers, hostesses, whoever he found physically appealing. She tried to imagine her mother walking in on him with another woman in their hotel suite. William, annoyed, waving her out when she gasped.

Her mother still married him that very night! Just hours after he'd been having sex with someone else in their hotel bed, her mother's tears and William's bottle of scotch resulted in an impromptu wedding ceremony at an all-night chapel with a ridiculous name: The Gamble On Forever Wedding Chapel.

Sickening.

Seven months later, Ivy came along. Which was why her mother had married William despite everything. But he'd had the marriage annulled a week later. According to her mother, William Sedgwick had met Ivy for the first time when she was seven— seven!—and only because he instituted his annual vacation for offspring at his summer house in Maine. There, she'd met her older half sisters for the first time, the stunningly beautiful and impossibly kind Olivia, with her light blond hair and peaches-and-cream complexion. And Amanda, raised by a poor mother in one of the New York City boroughs, who carried herself with such self-respect, something Ivy had noticed immediately, even as a seven-year-old.

Ivy could recall being so excited to be invited to her father's summer house, to finally get to know him, to feel her hand in his, to feel his love. It wasn't until she was a teenager that she realized he *didn't* love her or her sisters. It had been Ivy's own mother who'd pointed that out, who'd angrily informed Ivy that her father didn't give two figs about her, that he only invited her and "those other girls" to the house every summer because his public relations manager told him it would look good for him when he interviewed with reporters from *Forbes* and the *New York Times* about his personal life.

Billionaire William Sedgwick is also a loving family man whose three daughters spend two idyllic weeks every year with him at his Maine cottage, where they boat and fish and barbecue. . . .

Right.

Girls, there's nothing like the fresh Maine air, William would say every morning. That was actually *all* he'd say for the day before going off to golf or lunch with an associate. Then he'd repeat it the next morning. Suffice to say, the Sedgwick girls did not get to know their estranged father one iota during the annual summer, two-week vacations. It had been something, though. Something to make Ivy feel "normal," like every other girl. She *did* have a father.

A father who didn't think she should marry her fiancé, yet wouldn't say why. Why was obvious, though. Declan, a business student, a low-level employee—whom he'd subsequently fired, of course—wasn't good enough for William Sedgwick's daughter. Only in the "Your daughter is marrying whom?" sense. The reality was that William Sedgwick didn't give a rat's butt whom Ivy married.

She'd faced her father, shoulders squared. "I am going to marry Declan," she told him, feeling the defiance in her eyes, in her tone. "I love him and he loves me and that's all I need to know."

He winced again, and the driver rushed from the black sedan. As William went back to his car, he turned again. "Do not marry him, Ivy."

That was the last time she saw her father. Weeks

later, he died from heart failure and complications from cancer that no one knew he had. He'd died just a few months ago, and Ivy was still waiting to feel grief. She often wondered if that meant she was cold, but the more she thought about it, the more she knew that she couldn't love, couldn't grieve a stone. And that was what her father was and always had been.

A car horn blasted Ivy out of her thoughts. She dashed over to her squad car and retrieved a heavy cardigan sweater, then ran back and draped it over Laura's shoulders.

"You're absolutely right, Laura," Ivy told her. "It doesn't matter what you wear. But I know where you can get an absolutely stunning white wedding gown for free—in three days."

Laura brightened. "Where?"

"I'm getting married Saturday night," Ivy said. "I won't need my dress on Sunday." She'd actually already offered it to Alanna, but Alanna had totally different taste and had her heart set on a Victorian-style dress with a high, lacy neckline and puffed sleeves. She had it on layaway and put twenty-five dollars down on it each week.

Laura's mouth dropped open. "You'd give me your wedding dress?"

Ivy nodded and smiled. "What am I going to do with it? Get it dry cleaned and store it in the back of my closet for twenty-five years until maybe or maybe not the daughter I might or might not have might or might not want to wear it?"

Laura bit her lip. "I can't believe you'd really give me your dress. That's so unbelievably nice. And I think we're even the same size," she added, glancing over Ivy's thin figure.

"Well, even if you have to do some fast sewing and altering," Ivy said, "you'll have a beautiful dress. I'll drop it off at the diner around ten Sunday morning."

"Really?" Laura asked again, the color returning to her cheeks. "I can't believe you'd do that."

Ivy smiled again. "I'm happy to."

And she was, though she wondered, for just a moment, if she was supposed to want to keep her gown tucked away in her closet for the daughter she might or might not have. Perhaps she just wasn't sentimental or nostalgic. Then again, family memories weren't big with Ivy's mom. Dana Sedgwick hadn't been particularly close to her own parents, and they'd died when Ivy was just a child. Sometimes Ivy thought she should work harder to change, to become someone with a hope chest, someone who treasured family heirlooms, especially of the homemade variety.

You are who you are, Declan said all the time. *And who you are is pretty great.* And that was good enough for Ivy. She would feel better about where she'd come from and who she was and where she was going. Which was, to her father's dismay, to a future with Declan McLean.

As she and Dan walked back to the squad car, Dan said, "I sure hope I don't knock into you on the dance floor at your wedding and spill my beer all over your gown. I did that at my cousin Annie's wedding. Man, was she pissed!"

Who put Dan on the guest list? Note to self: Avoid partner at wedding.

Chapter Two

"To the bride-to-be!" Ivy's bridal party toasted in unison, the four women raising their glasses of champagne. Ivy stood at the head of their big round table at Lulu's Bistro and clinked each glass.

"And it's all my doing!" Dana Sedgwick boasted, raising her hand triumphantly. "If I hadn't been friendly with Declan's mother—God rest her soul—and if I hadn't had that party, Ivy wouldn't have met Declan and wouldn't be getting married tomorrow. I just love that I, and I alone, am responsible for getting my daughter married. And to such a catch!"

Ivy's half sisters, Amanda Sedgwick Black and Olivia Sedgwick Archer, both married to "catches" themselves, shot Ivy "your mother continues to amaze me" good-spirited glances. Alanna, who'd grown up just a few blocks away from Ivy, had long been used to Ivy's mother.

Ivy shared a conspiratorial smile with her sisters. She still couldn't believe her sisters were really here, part of her life, part of the biggest, happiest day of her life. Just a few months ago, prior to William's death, she might have invited them to the wedding, but she wouldn't have been surprised if they'd made excuses and sent vases or a card with a check. Now, here they were, her co-matrons of honor, fussing over her the way sisters would. They'd even created this bachelorette party for her.

Previously, her sisters had been like strangers to her. But when they'd been called together for the reading of William's will last December, a relationship had begun to form. Who else could possibly understand what it was like to be a child of William Sedgwick except for his other children? Amanda and Olivia *knew*. And in the past few months, the three women had relied on each other for support. They had become real sisters.

Ivy's mother had been scowling and harrumphing at Amanda and Olivia all night. She'd also been criticizing them like crazy.

"Amanda, dear, you should really think about cutting off all that long brown hair—you're so bony, I mean, thin, of course, that your hair just overtakes you. You might try a short cut like Amanda's. Yes, a short, no-nonsense cut would suit you much better. And, Ivy, you should really think about growing out your hair. Look a little sexier, for heaven's sake. Now, Olivia, if I were you and had that peaches-and-cream complexion, I wouldn't use that sheer lip gloss. I would use a bright pink. I think you should try it."

Unbelievable. Her mother was trying to make her sisters as ugly as possible.

Dana Sedgwick had long been obsessed with looks. Disappointed in her tomboy daughter, her mother had tried to frill Ivy up, but Ivy would revert back to her T-shirts and jeans and unadorned hair. When Ivy was thirteen, her mother had forced her to attend a local modeling school, where you didn't so much need looks or height or a thin figure as the money to pay the tuition. The other girls, though, were local beauties, and they looked at Ivy with "what is she doing here" contempt. Still, Ivy spent six weeks walking back and forth on a four-inch-wide line with a book balanced—sometimes—on her head. She took lessons in makeup application, how to properly smile for the camera, and how to stand with one foot slightly forward at all times.

When Ivy told her mother she was quitting whether she liked it or not, her mother used what she always used to control Ivy. And for some reason it worked, as it always did.

You know, Ivy, I think the reason your father has nothing to do with you is because you're . . . well, not the glamour-girl type. I'll bet he makes a fuss over Olivia.

Of course, he didn't, which Ivy learned during their two-week summer vacations together. But as a teenager, Ivy had fallen prey to the idea that if she was just *more,* her father might suddenly pay attention to her. She wised up a few years later and began to accept herself. Something her mother never could quite do, which was fine with Ivy. She loved her mom, but her mother was nutty.

Take, for example, how the bachelorette party wasn't even finished with their main course when her mother got her worst dig of the evening into her sisters.

"It's funny how little Amanda and Olivia look like their father, don't you think, Ivy? You look so much like him. Then again, I suppose that because God knew you were the only legitimate heir—"

Ivy had dragged her mother outside at that point for a little chat. After promising to not say a single word about Olivia or Amanda for the rest of the night, Dana Sedgwick was allowed to stay at the bachelorette party. She'd headed back to the table muttering about how "touchy and insecure the illegitimate were."

And her mother had barely been able to keep her promise. Why? Because her sisters had received their inheritances from William, but Ivy—and let's all say it together—William's only legitimate child!—would receive hers tomorrow. Ivy's mother was a nervous wreck about what Ivy would get. If it wasn't bigger and better than the "illegitimate" Sedgwick girls, Dana Sedgwick planned to sue. *Good luck there, Mom,* Ivy thought with a mental roll of her eyes.

"Declan is quite a catch," Alanna agreed, blowing a kiss at Ivy. "Gorgeous."

"I understand that your young man is quite a catch himself," Ivy's mother said. She turned to Amanda and Olivia. "Alanna snagged herself a doctor."

Alanna blushed. "He's a resident at Applewood General. Wow, I can't believe that in just six months I'll be following Ivy down the aisle."

"Someone at this table won't be getting married," boomed a raspy voice.

The five women whirled around to find a diminutive woman, her head wrapped in multicolored jewel tone scarves, and her slight body draped in a full-length fur coat, staring at them, her expression as serious as her voice.

"Excuse me?" Alanna asked, barely able to contain a giggle.

The strange woman stared at Alanna for a

moment, then looked at each woman at the table before settling her gaze on Ivy. "You are the bride to be, no?"

Ivy had no idea who this woman was. "Yes, I am. And you are?"

"I am Madame Elena."

"Oh!" Ivy's mother said, jumping up. "This is the fortune teller I hired for your bachelorette party! Oh goodie that you're here."

The woman scowled.

"Mom," Ivy whispered in her mother's ear. "Tell me you didn't."

"Of course I did!" Dana Sedgwick said loudly. "I want to find out how many babies you're going have."

Ivy rolled her eyes, but had to smile. "Mom. Declan and I are not planning to start a family for at least two—"

"I will get started," Madame Elena interrupted. She had yet to crack a smile. She removed her coat and snapped her fingers at a waiter, who rushed over to take the fur. Then she positioned a chair between Ivy and her mother and sat down. "Everyone hold hands and close your eyes."

There were barely suppressed giggles, but a peek told Ivy that everyone complied.

"As I said," Madame Elena continued, her hands ice cold on Ivy's. "Someone at this table will not be marrying her fiancé."

Ivy opened her eyes; so did everyone else.

"We're looking for fun fortunes," Ivy's mother trilled with a glare at the fortune teller. "We're celebrating here."

"I only speak the truth," Madame Elena said.

Ivy's mother glanced from Ivy to Alanna. "Alanna, honey, don't worry." She leaned closer. "She can't really see into the future."

"Actually, I can't," Madame Elena said. "I can see into the past. And based on the past, I can see the future."

Alanna looked nervous. "My past with Richard isn't so hot. He broke up with me twice before we got engaged last year. He wasn't ready to commit." She bit her lip. "He's going to dump me, isn't he? I've been putting down money every week on that gorgeous wedding gown and he's just going to dump me."

"Alanna, absolutely not!" Ivy said. She turned to the fortune teller. The *liar*, actually. "I'd like you to leave now."

"There's been trouble among you," the woman said as she rose. "Danger. And it's not done with you yet."

"You can go now!" Ivy's mother shouted. "And I'll be calling my credit card in the morning to cancel the transaction!"

Ivy shook her head and turned to Alanna. "Honey, the woman is a nutjob. Don't give it a second thought. Richard adores you. He's crazy about you."

Amanda nodded. "I once had my fortune told. The lady told me that I'd become a movie star when I turned twenty-five. You haven't seen me in any movies, have you?"

That got a small smile from Alanna.

"And a fortune teller once told me that all my hair would fall out and that I'd be covered in boils because of something awful I'd done," Olivia said.

"I was thirteen at the time, so of course I believed it. I clearly looked guilty about something, and so she focused on it and told me something awful so that I'd keep paying her to tell me more."

Ivy nodded. "I'm getting married tomorrow and you're getting married in six months and we will both live happily ever after." She raised her champagne glass to her best friend. "Alanna," she whispered. "Trust me. My mother found Madame Weirdo in the Yellow Pages."

Alanna took a deep breath, then smiled. "You're right. I'm being ridiculous." She lifted her glass, then clinked and smiled. "To happily ever after."

Ivy stretched luxuriously in bed and squinted against the bright sun shining through the curtains. The forecast called for a high of fifty degrees, warm for March. Ivy was glad she'd chosen to be married on the first day of spring. It meant change. Rebirth. New. Her entire life was going to be different.

She was getting married today! This was the last time she would sleep alone in this house. The last time it would be *her* house. After she and Declan returned from their honeymoon, he would officially move in and commute to Manhattan. This would be *their* house.

She thought of Declan, of his tall, muscular body that made her mouth go dry on sight. Of his thick, chestnut-colored hair, his sparkling, intelligent blue eyes. The dimple in his left cheek. She wished he were here right now, making mad passionate love to her. But he was at the dorm, holding to tradition of not seeing his bride before the ceremony.

It had been fun, actually, to be separated from him last night. And after Madame Weirdo had left, her bachelorette party had been a blast. After dinner, they'd danced at a local club and then returned to Ivy's house for some serious girl talk. About men, about love. Alanna had been completely reassured that Richard was madly in love. And Olivia and Amanda were both so happy, both so in love with their husbands. Ivy and Alanna couldn't wait to use the words *my husband!*

The phone rang, and Ivy glanced at the clock: 7 a.m. She didn't have to look at the caller ID to know it was her mother. Today was more than just Ivy's wedding day. It was the day she had to pick up her letter of inheritance from her father's lawyer. The letter that she was not permitted to receive until today—her wedding day. William's way of controlling her from the grave.

Back in December, at the reading of her father's will, which Ivy hadn't even wanted to attend, she and her sisters had been shocked to discover that William had left them each an envelope, which they were to open on specific days. Amanda had received hers just days later. Olivia a month later. And Ivy was to receive hers on March 20. Her wedding day. Hardly a coincidence.

Ivy grabbed the phone. "Morning, Mom."

"I really think I should accompany you to the attorney's office, Ivy," Dana Sedgwick said predictably. "You really shouldn't have business on your mind on your wedding day."

"Mom, I'm sure the letter will inform me that I'll inherit Dad's bed-and-breakfast." The beautiful old inn was located an hour's drive from Ivy's town.

"And if I do inherit it, I'm sure Dad'll make me live in it for a month and instruct me to walk backwards through the rooms or some other ridiculous thing."

Ivy shook her head at the idea. Both Amanda's and Olivia's letters indicated that they would each inherit property if they followed his instructions to a T. After not opening certain doors or looking in certain mirrors and having to sit on a living room chaise for one hour a day, Amanda had inherited a brownstone in Manhattan, which she'd then donated to charity. It was in that brownstone that she, then a struggling single mother, and Ethan Black had fallen in love as he saved her from a crazy ex-boyfriend. And, before inheriting the house in Maine, Olivia had had to buy two items from local stores in Blueberry, Maine, where the girls had spent their summer vacations. And where Olivia had first met her husband as a sixteen-year-old.

"That inn is on the water, Ivy," her mother snapped. "It's a multimillion-dollar property. I could retire well, there."

Retire. As if Dana Sedgwick had worked a day in her life! The only woman who'd managed to get William Sedgwick to marry her, despite his having annulled the marriage a week later, Ivy's mother had won herself a tidy settlement. She was more than comfortable.

Ivy sat up in bed and leaned against the headboard. "Mom, I think you'd better be prepared for the letter to contain nothing but a tirade. Remember, I'm marrying Declan against William's wishes."

"You're his only legitimate child. He wouldn't cut *you* off."

Ivy rolled her eyes. Her mother had been saying

that for as long as Ivy could remember. No matter how many times Ivy retorted that her father had cut her off and out all her life, her mother still insisted that it mattered that for one week, she and Ivy's father had been married.

"Yet, he chose my wedding day to insist I receive and open his letter," Ivy pointed out. "I'm sure the letter says that if I go through with the wedding, I'll inherit nothing."

"I'll bet he not only left you the inn but a huge monetary settlement," her mother said. "You are his *only* legitimate child, Ivy," she added yet again. "And to make up for having compensating Declan so ridiculously poorly at this point in his career and then having the gall to fire him for no reason, William probably left you a fortune in cash."

Her mother was seriously delusional. "I really doubt that, Mom. And I don't want William Sedgwick's money. I've been telling you that for years."

"Nonsense! He owes you, Ivy!"

What Ivy felt her father owed her was his love, and he'd never given her that.

She threw off the blanket and stared at her feet. In just a few hours, her toenails would be a sparkly pale pink. It would be her first pedicure. "Mom, I need to get going. I'll call you later."

"Promise you'll call the moment you open that letter!"

Ivy promised, hung up, and headed into the bathroom for a long, hot shower. Her last shower as a single woman. Strange. She would probably be thinking silly things like that all day. Her last cup of coffee as a single woman. Her last meal. She'd just slipped on her bathrobe when the doorbell rang.

No way her mother could have gotten here *that* fast to continue their conversation. Ivy padded to the front door and peered through the peephole. Declan.

Her heart leapt in her chest, as it always did at the sight of him. God, he was handsome.

"Excuse me, Mr. McLean," she teased through the door. "But I don't believe you're supposed to see your bride on your wedding day before she walks down the aisle."

"I can't wait," he said in that delicious deep voice. "It was bad enough not waking up next to you."

She smiled and opened the door and jumped into his arms. Mmm, he smelled good. Like soap and spicy aftershave. Tall, muscular, and masculine, with that thick chestnut brown hair, those sparkling blue eyes, and that irresistible dimple, Declan was so good-looking. Ivy had been so surprised that he'd been interested in her in the first place. Her self-esteem was fine. But she wasn't a glamour girl like her sister Olivia or built with the sexy curves and boobs of her sister Amanda. She had the same boyish figure she'd had in high school, and the same short brown hair, albeit expensively highlighted, compliments of her mother for the wedding. She was a police officer in uniform. But even out of uniform she looked the same. Even with some makeup or in lingerie, neither of which she felt comfortable in.

Yet in her wedding dress, that gorgeous satin gown on the back of her closet door, she didn't look like plain old Ivy just playing dress up. She looked the way Declan made her *feel* all the time.

Declan, from the first moment, had looked at Ivy

as though she were a Playboy bunny. He'd barely
taken his eyes off her at the party where they'd met.
Though Declan was the son of a long-time acquaintance of Ivy's mother, they had never met before.
Once they'd been introduced, he'd stayed by her
side all night, asked for her number, and then sent
a dozen red roses to the precinct the following day.
He'd swept her off her feet. And Ivy had needed
some feet sweeping. Prior to Declan, she'd rarely
dated. A couple of guys from the police academy,
and a detective in a neighboring town. But nothing, no one, like Declan.

Now, he closed the door and pressed Ivy against
the wall, kissing her neck, her jawbone, nuzzling
open the lapels of the ivory silk robe he'd bought
her as a "just thinking of you" gift last month. What
timing—she was so glad she'd just taken a shower,
slathering on the delicious scented body cream a
girlfriend at the precinct had given her.

Ivy leaned her head back and moaned softly as his
tongue flicked over her breast, then the taut nipple.
His hand caressed her other breast, then traveled
down past her stomach and in between her legs.
She, Ivy Sedgwick, of the 32B bra and sensible flat
Merrells, might as well have been Pamela Anderson
for the way Declan responded to her. It was as
though just the sight of her made him wild with
desire. No one had ever felt that way about her. As
Declan's mouth moved to her other breast, his
tongue busy on her nipple, he brought her hand
to his zipper. He was rock hard. She slid down the
zipper and in moments he faced her against the wall
and was inside her, thrusting so hard she had to
brace both hands against the wall to protect herself.

"Let's move into the bedroom," she managed to say against her breath.

But Declan gripped her hips and continued to thrust, harder and harder. He liked sex this way, a bit rough. Every now and then she could get him to be more romantic about sex, but for the most part, Declan liked sex anywhere but a bed. And he liked to make love to her from behind. She would prefer to look into his eyes while they made love, but even when she was on top, he tended to busy himself at her breasts or his eyes were closed with pleasure.

The sex was amazing and nothing like Ivy had imagined sex could be. Not that she'd been a virgin when they'd met. She'd been with two other men, men she thought she'd fallen hard for, but neither relationship had lasted. Both men were much more romantic than Dylan in bed, but neither had actually ever brought her to orgasm, something that bothered both of them. And something that led to ridiculous fights for which she had no defense. How did she know why she couldn't reach orgasm? Did they want to hear that they were bad in bed, for which Ivy really had no real reference point? Perhaps she wasn't really in love with them. That was what Declan had said when she came back to life after climaxing with him for the first time. But she had had strong feelings for those two guys. Just nothing like she felt with—and for—Declan.

And orgasms she continued to have. Mind-blowing, bad-day-erasing orgasms. She supposed she was more a traditional type when it came to sex; she actually wished Declan would sometimes want to do it missionary style. But their sex was hot and passionate and incredibly satisfying, if not exactly sweet or romantic.

"Oh, baby, oh, baby," Declan was whispering in her ear as he exploded and thrust one last time into her, then slid down to the floor with her. He kissed the back of her neck, and they lay there for a moment, catching their breaths. "That was great, as usual," he said.

"You know," she said, turning to face him. "For our wedding night, I'd really like it if we made love slowly. In a bed. You facing me. I want good old-fashioned lovemaking."

He smiled and kissed her nose. "Your wish is my command, love." He glanced at his watch. "We'd better get to that lawyer's office for your inheritance letter."

She raised an eyebrow. "You don't have to schlep all the way to the city with me. My sisters both offered to go with me."

He sat up and took a breath. "I guess I just really want to be there when you get the letter. Your father hated me. What if the letter tells you not to marry me?"

She kissed his shoulder. "Declan, he already told me not to marry you. Am I listening?"

"But what if he threatens not to leave you the inn?" he asked. "You deserve something of your father's for the way he treated you your whole life."

Ivy didn't know about that.

"I think you should open the letter after the wedding," Declan said, "so that no matter what it says, we're husband and wife, a union."

"I think so, too," she said. "There's no way

William Sedgwick is going to interfere with my wedding day any more than he already has."

He smiled and looked at her for a moment, in that way that made her feel so beautiful, so special, and then he began to make love to her all over again, right there on the shaggy rug.

Chapter Three

"You should be at home, being fussed over by your mother and your sisters," Declan said as they arrived at the Manhattan law office of George Harris, attorney at law. "I hate being the cause of this."

Ivy took off her gloves and held Declan's hand. His eyes were shielded by his sunglasses, and his wool scarf was bundled almost up to his nose. Declan was always cold and buried under layers. She smiled. "You are not the cause. This is the happiest day of my life, and a twenty-minute trip into Manhattan won't take away from my primping time."

"Forty minutes there and back," he pointed out. He looked out at the traffic whizzing by. "What do you think is in that letter, Ivy?"

"I really don't care. I'm abiding by his inconvenient instructions to pick up the letter today just in case it contains something that will be valuable to me, like an explanation for why he was such a non-existent father."

"But he didn't leave letters like that for Amanda and Olivia," Declan said.

Ivy considered that. Her father had worked some strange magic from the grave with the letters he'd left for her sisters. He had handpicked the perfect man for Amanda. And he'd reunited Olivia with the child—and the man—she thought she'd lost. *That last one was William's doing in the first place,* she reminded herself. William was capable of the worst.

"Declan, I'm going to get the letter from the attorney, slip it into my purse, and forget about it until the last possible second."

He nodded. "But you're supposed to open it today or the contents are null and void. The attorney made that clear at the reading of the will."

She put her arms around her fiancé. "So, a minute before midnight, I'll read it and make a quick call. Whatever it says won't affect me because I'll be married to the man of my dreams. So let's just get the stupid letter and then forget about it till later, okay?"

He let out a breath. "I love you, you know."

"I know. And I love you, too." She pressed her lips against his and then pulled open the door to the building. In the elevator to the sixteenth floor, Declan looked like he was going to pass out. "Honey, don't worry. I want to marry you more than I want to know what is in that letter, no matter what it is."

He squeezed her hand. The doors pinged open, and in moments they were seated in the reception area, awaiting Mr. Harris.

Five minutes later, the attorney finally made his appearance. Giving Declan enough time work up a nervous sweat on his forehead.

"Miss Sedgwick, delighted to see you here." The attorney glanced at Declan and said nothing.

Ivy smiled at the man, despite his rudeness to her

fiancé. "We're crunched for time," she said. "As you know, Declan and I are getting married today."

"I am aware," George Harris said, his expression blank. He then led them into a small room with a table and chairs. An envelope, a plain white envelope, business-size, lay on the center of the table.

Ivy shivered despite the warmth of the room. She squeezed Declan's hand.

"I will leave you to it," George said. "But please note that your father's instructions are quite clear." He pulled out William's last will and testament. "According to your father's wishes, you must open the letter *prior* to the ceremony, or the contents will be null and void."

Anger rose up in Ivy. "Amazing that he's trying to control me from the grave."

"Ivy, it's okay," Declan said. "If those are the instructions, those are the instructions."

"If you do not call me to read the letter prior to your ceremony, Miss Sedgwick," the attorney said, "you will forfeit your inheritance."

"Which is?" Ivy asked, her eyebrow raised.

"You will find out everything you need to know when you open the letter," George responded. "Good day." And with that, he left the room.

"Why don't I just open it now and get it over with," Ivy said. "What's the worst it could say?"

"That I'm beneath you," Declan said. "Or maybe he'll make something up. Like that the reason he fired me was for stealing a paperclip from the office."

"He fired you because he wanted to break us up," Ivy said. She shook her head. "You know what? Let's just get out of here." She stuffed the envelope in her purse. "Maybe I won't open it at all."

"But what if it does contain an explanation of why he was such a bad father?" Declan said. "He finally did right by Olivia. Maybe he wants to do right by you now. Or maybe he left you millions, Ivy. We could start so many youth programs in Applewood with that money."

Declan dreamed of starting up a program for kids who had nowhere to go after school. He talked about his dreams for the future all the time. He had such a kind, generous heart. She knew Declan, and she had a cop's instincts. Whatever her father had had against Declan, it wasn't serious. If it were, William would have stated his reason.

"The ceremony isn't until six tonight," Ivy said. "We have all day."

He took a deep breath. "Let's just open it together right before the ceremony. If William has more venom to spew against me, we'll be too happy about getting married in five minutes to care."

She smiled and they sealed the deal with a kiss.

In the back room of the tiny church, Ivy sat before a lighted mirror and adjusted the white veil on her head, unaccustomed to the feel of a barrette digging into her scalp. She scowled.

Kayla Archer, her niece and flower girl, laughed. "It holds your veil in place, Aunt Ivy."

Ivy smiled. "It figures a thirteen-year-old knows that and I don't! Can I just throw the veil over my head?"

Alanna, her only bridesmaid, shook her head. "When Declan lifts it, he'll end up with it in his hands!"

"Oh," Ivy said, eyeing the tiny flower buds decorating the mother-of-pearl barrette. She wasn't used to seeing flower buds on her head.

"You can be girly for one day!" Olivia chided with a smile, fluffing the filmy material over Ivy's shoulders.

"You do look like a princess," Amanda said as she took a photograph of Ivy.

Ivy stared at herself and had to admit she did look like a princess. Olivia, a former fashion magazine editor and one of the most glamorous women Ivy had ever seen, had done Ivy's makeup. Ivy's complexion glowed, and her blue eyes, lightly enhanced by liner and mascara, were huge. Her lips, usually treated only to Chap Stick on these chilly March mornings, were a soft, glossy red. And her hair, a basic brown bob, had been styled by a former colleague of Olivia's, and now shone with highlights, fringy bangs swept glamorously to the side.

Once again Ivy was struck by how amazing it was that her sisters were her co-matrons of honor. It was ironic that it took their father's death to bring them together. When he died, just months ago, the three Sedgwick sisters had barely spoken in years. They'd been raised that way. As separate people, not family. And their father had done nothing to change it. Yes, he did invite them every summer to his house in Maine for two weeks, and while he golfed and lunched with his own friends, the three girls did spend time together. Not much time, but enough for Ivy to see that Amanda was kind and compassionate, and that Olivia was as lovely inside as out.

"Can I go show Grandma how I look?" Kayla asked her mother. "I know she'll see me walk down the aisle, but I can't wait!"

Olivia smiled. "Go ahead. And give your handsome dad a kiss for me."

"I'll show you where they're seated," Alanna said, and led Kayla out the door.

"Be back in five minutes, though!" Amanda cautioned, eying the clock on the wall. "The ceremony starts promptly at six."

When the door closed behind them, Ivy turned to her sisters. "What do you think is in my inheritance letter from William?" she asked, gnawing away her pretty red lipstick. None of the Sedgwick sisters referred to their father as Dad.

Amanda stopped fluffing Ivy's veil. "You haven't opened it?"

Ivy shook her head. "I'm supposed to open it before saying, 'I do.'"

Amanda stared at Ivy. "Before? That's a bit unnerving. What the hell is in that letter?"

"You don't think there could be any credence to whatever William might have had against Declan?" Olivia asked, her eyes gentle on Ivy. "Do you? I hate to even bring it up, Ivy. But, well, it was so unlike William to even care about anything the three of us did."

Ivy stared at her sisters. "What could William Sedgwick possibly have against Declan McLean? A graduate student. A former part-time, entry-level employee at his own company. It makes no sense."

"Maybe he wanted to pick your husband for you, the way he 'picked' ours," Amanda suggested, shaking her head.

Olivia put her hand on Ivy's shoulder. "Maybe. But, it seemed like William was trying, in his own twisted way, to right some wrongs of his from the grave. He left me the cottage in Maine so I'd find my way back to Zach and our daughter."

"And he left me the Manhattan brownstone just when I was desperate for a place to live," Amanda added. "He really seemed to custom pick Ethan for me."

"I have thought about all that," Ivy said. "I've thought about everything." She lowered her voice. "I know this will sound terrible, but I even did a background check. Just for peace of mind. And Declan McLean hasn't so much as been arrested for jaywalking."

"If William had a real reason for being against the marriage," Amanda said, smoothing the short train of Ivy's gown, "he would have told you what it was. He wouldn't let it get this far. I mean, you're getting married in a half hour."

"Agreed," said Olivia. She took Ivy's hand. "And enough of this. You're marrying the man you love. The man who loves you."

Tears pricked Ivy's eyes. She wasn't much of a crier, but sometimes, and especially now, before she was to walk down the aisle, she got so . . . *verklempt*, to use just the right word, about getting married. She still couldn't believe that she had found Mr. Right, Mr. Wonderful, Mr. Amazing. She, Ivy Sedgwick, the girl who sent away for detective kits in the back of old *Ellery Queen* magazines that she found in the library. The girl more interested in forensic science than in dating. When she was a teenager and would spend those two weeks at the Maine cottage with her sisters, Ivy could always be found with her nose buried in books—from mysteries and police procedurals to true crime. One year, Olivia had suggested that Ivy try out for the town's Inner Beauty Pageant, and Ivy had freaked out on Olivia. Ivy had assumed Olivia thought she would be a good candidate because she had inner beauty instead of outer beauty, like Olivia. But when she'd finally allowed Olivia to explain herself, Ivy learned just how much Olivia actually admired her as a person—and thought she was pretty, besides.

But Ivy never thought she was pretty. Middle school, high school, college—Ivy never seemed to attract men the way some of the other girls did. Girls with big boobs or long hair or the gift of flirtation. Ivy and a girlfriend, who was also guy-challenged, once practiced flirting techniques from magazines like *Cosmopolitan,* but her lines fell flat. She'd even found her old modeling school "text book" and tried the tips to enhance her looks, but guys just weren't interested.

And so she let herself be chosen by the few guys who were interested, which got her to the prom and college dances, and at twenty-one she lost her virginity to a perfectly nice man whose last name she'd forgotten. Not too memorable. She'd always told herself that one day, when she was more grown up, when she was working, she'd do the choosing.

And then she'd met Declan McLean at that awful, boring party. So handsome. So tall and muscular. He made her mouth go dry. She could barely speak for the first few minutes. That's the effect he had on her body. For the first time, Ivy understood what it meant to fall madly in love on sight. To be driven wild with desire. When they'd been introduced, Declan mentioned he worked for Sedgwick Enterprises as an analyst. She'd immediately felt a strange spark of envy; this total stranger was closer to her father than she was, since he worked for her father's company.

She'd expected Declan to make a few minutes of polite conversation and move on (there were some gorgeous women in killer dresses at the party), but he never did. He asked her questions about herself, seemed so impressed that she was a police officer, that she was a strong woman in every sense of the word. They talked a little about William Sedgwick; Declan had said he'd had the pleasure of meeting William just once and that he was one of his idols in the business world, that he was so lucky to be working part-time at Sedgwick Enterprises while he pursued his MBA full-time. And once they'd stepped outside on the terrace and he'd placed his suit jacket around her shoulders, Ivy had told him that she and father were estranged, that they rarely spoke, that he simply had never had an interest in his own children.

Declan had understood. He had a troubled relationship with his own father and he also had a half sibling whom he'd never been close to, an older brother who'd made his life hell. They'd talked and talked and talked, and then they'd kissed for just as long. That very night, Ivy had brought him home and they'd made love for hours, again and again.

The next day, Ivy had received red roses at work. She could hardly believe it was only six months ago; she felt as though she'd known him forever. She smiled at the memory of Declan proposing after their third date. She'd said, "Maybe after our *thirty-third* date," and he'd said, "Okay, I'll be keeping track."

On their thirty-third date, he'd proposed again,

with a beautiful diamond ring. Ivy accepted. The next day, William Sedgwick had appeared on her doorstep, ordering her not to marry Declan. Prior to that, she hadn't seen William Sedgwick in over three years. And she'd never seen him again.

To the end, she hadn't had her father's blessing. In any aspect of her life. He'd thought being a cop was beneath her. He thought a student was beneath her. But he didn't seem to think that not being a part of her life since birth was beneath her.

"Will your mom be walking you down the aisle?" Amanda asked.

Ivy shook her head. "I decided that I want to walk down alone. As a testament to making peace with never having had a father in the first place."

The three Sedgwick sisters held hands, and then there was a knock at the door.

It was Declan. He looked at Ivy and his mouth dropped open.

She jumped up. "Declan? Are you all right?"

He stepped back, looking her up and down. "You look so incredibly beautiful," he said. "My God, Ivy."

She almost cried. Not good for her mascara.

"Hey, you're not supposed to see the bride before she walks down the aisle!" Olivia teased.

He smiled. "I know. But I need to tell my beautiful bride something important."

"We'll give you two some privacy," Amanda said as she and Olivia headed to the door. They both turned and smiled, then closed the door behind them.

Declan took both of Ivy's hands. "I've been thinking. I'm so sure that the letter from your father says that if you marry me, you'll inherit nothing. Are you sure you want to do that? I don't want to deny you what's yours, Ivy. What *should* have been yours."

"Declan, I don't care about my father's money. I've never had it. Why would I want it now?"

"I just don't want to take anything away from you," he said, letting out a breath.

"Marrying you is all I want, Declan. I'm absolutely fine with forfeiting whatever he left me. Let's just not open the letter."

"Are you sure?"

"I'm sure," she said.

"Ivy, I need you for a minute," her mother called through the door."

Ivy rolled her eyes. "Give me a sec," she told Declan and stepped outside the room.

Her mother, remarkably beautiful in her fifties, was decked out in a pale peach beaded gown, her highlighted light brown hair swept up to reveal a lovely diamond necklace, the one thing William had given her during their week-long marriage.

"Aunt Jane says she won't sit at the same table with her cousin Barbara. Should I switch Barbara to the Petermans' table? Or just leave it? That old bat is lucky I invited her. Do you believe she had the nerve to tell me she hoped we're not serving salmon, that's it's too fishy, and—"

Oh Lord. Save me. Please. "Mom, I leave it all up to you, okay?"

Her mother threw up her hands. "Dear, it is *your* wedding."

"I really need to go, Mom. I'm getting married in like ten minutes!"

"Well, then, one more thing," her mother said, reaching behind her neck. She unclasped the diamond necklace and moved behind Ivy to place it on her daughter. "This covers a lot—something old, something new, since it's new to you, and something borrowed. You don't need blue."

Ivy almost cried, suddenly sentimental and nostalgic. Sometimes her mother could be so wonderful. "Oh, Mom," she said, gently touching the three round diamonds that hung from the delicate gold chain.

Tears shone in her mother's eyes. "You look so beautiful, Ivy. I'm so proud of you. And now I'd better go make sure your relatives aren't murdering each other."

Ivy laughed and watched her mother walk away on her four-inch heels. Again her hands went to her neck. She wasn't sure why the necklace meant so much to her. What was the history behind it? Where were the memories? It wasn't as if the necklace symbolized her mother's happiness with the father of her only child.

It represented hope, Ivy realized. And love. And possibilities. When her father had given it to her mother, it had meant something. That was what it stood for. What lay between then and now wasn't the point.

Ivy slipped back inside the room. Declan stood by the bank of windows, glancing out. She admired his profile for just a moment. He was so beautiful.

"Ready to become my husband?" she asked.

He turned to face her. "Can't wait."

Another knock on the door. "Places, everyone!" someone called.

Declan and Ivy squeezed hands, then stepped outside. Declan headed toward the front of the church. Ivy waited at the rear archway to the church. Her sisters joined her, and Kayla and Alanna came running over. Kayla would walk down first, then Alanna, and then her sisters, together. Declan's mother had passed away last year, but Declan's father and brother and a few close friends would be attending. Ivy was so excited to meet his father and brother. Apparently, they were long estranged, but Declan had invited them. The day he told Ivy that they were coming to the ceremony was the happiest she'd seen him in a long time.

To my new life, Ivy silently toasted herself. When her sisters began walking, Ivy awaited her cue. At the beginning of the "Wedding March," she slowly walked down the aisle. Floated was more like it.

She was heading straight to her partner, to the man who would stand at her side forevermore. She kept her eyes focused on him. He seemed nervous. Unusually nervous. The blood seemed to have drained from his face. Was he sweating? His forehead was slick.

Was he that nervous about saying, 'I do'?

He was staring at someone in the pews, Ivy realized. Who? Ivy followed his gaze to a handsome man in his thirties, a stranger to Ivy. The man returned Declan's stare. What was going on?

Declan tugged at the collar of his shirt. Ivy could see he was sweating profusely now. Declan started looking around wildly, then he glanced again at the man in the pews. He held the man's gaze for a moment. And then Declan started running.

He bolted right past Ivy, nearly knocking her over, and ran straight out the church doors.

Chapter Four

On her three-inch heels, Ivy ran after Declan. The stranger he'd been staring at was out the door before Ivy could even reach it. When she reached the top stone platform, the stranger and Declan were gone.

What the hell?

She was suddenly surrounded by people. Her mother pushed through to grab her hand. "Cold feet, honey. That's all. Let's give him five minutes, okay?"

She heard one of the officers at her precinct ask, "Can we arrest him for fleeing the scene of his own wedding?"

Words, sentences, thoughts buzzed around her. Ivy felt like she was going to faint.

Her sisters and Alanna made their way to her. "Come inside, Ivy," Alanna said. "You're shivering."

She let them lead her inside and to the back room, where not five minutes before Declan had told her he loved her.

They sat her on the chair near the window. Amanda cracked it to give Ivy some air.

"What the heck just happened?" Alanna asked, her pale brown eyes confused.

"Declan was staring at someone in the pews, the man who ran after him," Ivy said. "Who could it have been?"

"A henchman of William's?" Olivia suggested.

There was a knock on the door. Olivia's and Amanda's husbands checking in. Her sisters assured them Ivy was all right—as all right as she could be.

Ivy's mother burst in. "Don't you worry about a thing, Ivy. I announced to the guests that Declan was suffering from a case of nervous jitters and that he'd be back in a few minutes."

"Doubt that," came a deep male voice.

Everyone whirled around. It was the man Declan had been staring at. The one who'd pursued him. He was tall and muscular. Imposing. Darkly handsome. Intense. Ivy shot up. "Who are you?"

She sensed he was a cop. He *looked* like a cop. Like a detective, actually. Something in his expression, in his posture. In the suit he was wearing, despite the fact that every male in the church was in a suit.

He pulled ID from his inside pocket. Ivy studied it. He was from Homicide, New York City. Manhattan. The ID looked real enough, as far as she could tell. She'd have to check him out later. Right now she could barely stand.

"Name's Griffin Fargo," he said to Ivy. "I need to ask you a few questions."

"I need to ask *you* a few questions," she retorted.

Ivy's mother rushed over to the detective. "Is it a crime to get cold feet? I'm sure Declan will be back soon."

Oh, Mom, Ivy thought, letting out a deep breath. This was all just too much.

"As I said, I doubt that," the detective responded.

"I'm afraid I don't understand," Ivy's mother said, her tone getting huffy. "Just what is your business here?"

"I'd like to speak with you alone," the detective said to Ivy.

Alanna turned to the detective. "I'm a police officer with the Applewood PD and this is our jurisdiction." She waved her finger between herself and Ivy. "I'd like to listen in, see if I can help. Ivy just had quite a shock."

"Well aware of that," the man said, his tone not the least bit concerned. "I'm here on police business from *my* jurisdiction. And I'll need to speak with Miss Sedgwick privately."

Ivy turned to Alanna. "It's okay. I'll be fine."

Alanna squeezed Ivy's hand, and Olivia and Amanda helped shoo Ivy's mother from the room. "We'll be right outside," Amanda said.

Ivy nodded. God, she was numb.

"Have a seat, Miss Sedgwick," Detective Fargo told her.

"I'd rather stand," she said, staring him down. But her legs wobbled and she sat.

"Are you all right?" he asked.

"No, I'm not. The man I was supposed to marry just bolted out of the church."

"Yes, I caught that," he said.

"Why did he run at the sight of you?" she asked.

"Because he knows that I'm Manhattan homicide," he said. "And he knows that there was a homicide this morning. And he knows I wouldn't be here otherwise," he added.

"How about if you don't speak in circles?" Ivy snapped.

"Okay, how's this. Your fiancé is my prime suspect in this morning's murder of his other fiancée."

The blood drained from Ivy's face. "What?"

He said nothing for a moment. Just watched her.

"His other fiancée?" she repeated. "Declan doesn't have another fiancée, Detective."

"Actually, he does," he said. "Did. Her name was Jennifer Lexington. Their wedding date was two weeks from today. She's now dead. There was a suicide note beside the body, but forensics show she was murdered."

What? This was crazy! Another fiancée? A wedding date in two weeks? A woman dead? This was all insane. Some big mistake. A mix-up.

"Look, Detective, I really don't know why you think Declan has anything to do with this murder. I can assure you that he wasn't engaged to anyone else!"

"How?" he asked, his gaze steady on her.

Her mouth opened and closed. "Because I know."

"You don't sound much like a cop," he said.

"I'm not here on police business," she reminded him, her tone ice-cold. "Right now, I'm a civilian."

He leaned against the wall for a moment. "With a fiancé who bolted at the sight of me. How do you explain that?"

She really couldn't. Yet. Why had Declan run?

Because he was set up. That must be it. He'd been set up, maybe. By her father? Framed on the morning of their wedding so that there would be no wedding? Ivy's mind started whirling with possible explanations.

If Declan had run, it was because he'd been set up and got scared. Her father had that kind of power. And Declan clearly knew it.

"I was hoping to bring Declan in for questioning before he got a chance to leave the country for his honeymoon," Fargo said. "Of course, Jennifer didn't know him as Declan McLean. He used one of many aliases with her."

"Are you saying that Declan McLean is an alias?" she asked. *Ha!* She had him. It wasn't an alias. Couldn't be. Ivy's mother was a friend of Declan's late mother. They'd known each other, albeit not well, for many years.

"Actually, Declan McLean is his legal name," Fargo said. "Declan Noah McLean, to be exact."

Ivy relaxed. A bit, anyway. "So I'm the fiancée he was going to marry under his real name, yet he had others under aliases. That makes a lot of sense." She shook her head and smiled. "Come on, Detective."

"Actually it does, given the family history. Your mother is an old friend of Declan's mother's."

Ivy faltered. "How do you know that?"

"It's my job to know," he said.

Ivy had had enough. She let out a deep breath. "What the hell is going on? Tell me straight."

"I am telling you, Miss Sedgwick."

Miss Sedgwick. She'd been moments away from being Mrs. McLean. But, apparently, someone else had been two weeks away from being Mrs. McLean, too. Aka Mrs. McLean, that is, if the detective was telling the truth. She still hadn't figured out how Declan had been set up. By her father. From the grave. She buried her hands in her face, trying to block everything out for a moment. Nothing made sense.

"I did a background check on Declan," she said shakily, uncovering her hands. She looked up at Griffin Fargo, hoping, waiting for him to tell her this had to be some kind of mistake.

"A con artist like my brother has favors owed to him everywhere," he responded.

Ivy's mouth dropped open and she shot up out of her chair. "Your brother?"

He nodded. "Declan is my half brother. Younger. We have the same father. Declan took his stepfather's last name when he turned eighteen. He didn't have much respect for our dad."

Ivy just stared at him for a moment. Fargo looked nothing like Declan. Not even remotely. Fargo's eyes were dark, as dark as his hair, which was almost black. His complexion was fair, like Declan's, and they were both tall and muscular. But so were a lot of men.

"You look nothing alike," she told him.

Fargo nodded. "I look exactly like my mother. Declan looks exactly like his mother."

"Any other half brothers who look like your father?"

He shook his head. "Just me and Declan."

"Declan told me he invited you and your father to the wedding and that you agreed to come, even though you'd been long estranged."

Fargo shook his head. "It's true that we've been long estranged, but Declan didn't invite me to the wedding. And our father died six months ago,"

Fargo said, his expression unreadable. "After suffering for months from Alzheimer's."

Oh God, Ivy thought. This was all news to her. Why would Declan have lied about that? What else had he lied about? "He didn't mention any of that," Ivy said. "We'd just met six months ago. He said his father was alive and well in Florida, living in a Florida mansion, that he was too busy playing shuffleboard to visit."

"Six months ago would be the time he learned his father—who hasn't stepped foot in Florida—left him nothing," Fargo said. "Declan has long been leeching women for money, for rent, for meals, but I think he always expected Dad would leave him a windfall. He had some money. Not much, but a couple hundred grand."

Declan McLean, a leech? A man who glommed on to women for their money? That made no sense. Wouldn't she *know* if something was off about the man she was going to marry? The man she loved? She was a cop, with a cop's training, a cop's instincts, a cop's nose for *off*. Alanna had met him several times and thought he was as terrific as Ivy did. He'd come to a few police functions, a promotion celebration, a couple of birthday parties, and he was well regarded.

"Detective Fargo, Declan knew full well that I have no money and that my father wouldn't leave me anything. In fact, my father was against the marriage."

His eyebrow shot up. "What were his reasons?"

"He wouldn't say."

He nodded and jotted something down in a little notebook.

There was a knock on the door. "Yoo-hoo? Ivy? It's Mom. The guests are growing restless!"

Ivy glanced at Fargo. He said nothing.

"He doesn't have cold feet?" she whispered, hoping against hope this was all some nightmare from which she'd wake up. Any second now.

Fargo shook his head. He opened his mouth to say something, then apparently thought better of it.

"He's not coming back?" Ivy asked, hearing the hope in her own voice. "He's a suspect in a murder and knows it? That's why he ran when he saw you? My father *didn't* somehow set up Declan to be framed for murder on the morning of our wedding, a wedding he didn't want to take place?"

"I'd think if your father didn't want the wedding to take place, he would have made sure you knew about the other fiancée. He wouldn't have had her killed, Miss Sedgwick. Was your father that ruthless?"

"I really don't know," she responded. What the detective said made sense. Why would her father try to have Declan framed for murder of his other fiancée, when it was that other wedding he would *want* to happen? And if her father knew about another fiancée, he would have told her immediately. That would have ended her relationship with Declan in a heartbeat.

So William clearly hadn't known there was another fiancée. Ivy was just grasping at straws, trying to come up with anything that would explain why her fiancé, the man she loved, had run at the sight of a homicide detective. His own half brother.

"Everything you're saying is true about Declan? He had another fiancée? There's no mistake?"

Fargo nodded. "I'm very sorry, Miss Sedgwick. I realize today is your wedding day. But I'm also relieved that the wedding didn't take place."

Someone at this table won't be getting married. . . .
Score one for Madame Weirdo.

"How did you connect Declan to his alias? I
mean, how did you know you were looking for
Declan in the first place?"

"Pictures in the apartment of the victim," he answered. He glanced down for a moment. "I was investigating a homicide and from photographs all
over the home, I realized the victim's boyfriend—
and suspect—was my half brother."

"That must have been awful," Ivy said softly.

He didn't respond. The emotion she'd caught
a glimpse of was gone. After a moment, he said,
"Despite knowing who I was looking for, I still had
a difficult time tracking him here. He covers himself well."

"You are absolutely sure," Ivy said, holding his
gaze. "Absolutely sure that Declan is your suspect.
There's no mistake?"

"Trust me, Miss Sedgwick, I wish there were."

Ivy felt tears sting the back of her eyes. Some cop
she was. She pulled the comb from her scalp and
threw the veil across the room, then went to the
door and opened it slightly.

Her mother was waiting outside, her ear practically plastered to the door. "Mom, please tell everyone that the wedding has been called off and that
there is no explanation at this time."

"But what *is* the explanation?" Dana Sedgwick
asked. "Ivy, tell me what's going on! Does this have
something to do with your father's inheritance
letter?"

The letter. Ivy had forgotten all about it. *Had*

William learned about Declan's other fiancée? Why not just tell her, then?

"Mom, please. Just go tell everyone."

Shaking her head, her mother finally headed off, and Ivy went back inside.

Fargo was now by the window on his cell phone. He hung up when Ivy entered. "I do need more information, Miss Sedgwick. Can we talk at your house? At your station house if you'd feel more comfortable."

The station house. How mortifying would that be? "I'd feel better at my house. Privacy."

He nodded. "I'll take you in my car."

Ivy took a deep breath. From out of nowhere, Laura Mylar, the bride who was marrying next week popped into her head. She was supposed to deliver her gown to Laura tomorrow morning. A gown symbolizing love and commitment and the future. But the gown was clearly cursed, wasn't it?

That was silly. The gown wasn't a lying, cheating, possible murderer. Declan was. She had to keep blame where it belonged.

And maybe Declan wasn't a murderer. Ivy could live with being duped by Declan. But she couldn't live with having loved a man who would commit murder. There had to be some mistake there. Perhaps the woman really had committed suicide. Perhaps she'd found out about Ivy. Perhaps Declan had been waiting to decide until that morning whom he wanted to marry and had chosen Ivy—which clearly he had, since he'd shown up for the wedding—and the woman had been so devastated she'd taken her own life.

But Griffin had said something about forensics not backing up the suicide note.

Okay, so someone else had murdered the poor woman, and Declan had come and found her, knew it would look suspicious that he had two fiancées, and fled.

That would explain how he'd managed to not look the slightest bit nervous when he'd come to her house that morning, made love to her as though nothing was wrong, as though everything was just peachy keen.

He'd come to her house and made love to her as though nothing was wrong when he knew his other fiancée was dead? Maybe he hadn't known then. Maybe he didn't find out till later, till after they'd picked up the letter from her father's office. While Ivy had met Olivia afterward to get her hair done for the wedding, Declan had had some last-minute alterations on his jacket done. They'd been separated for most of the day.

Ivy could think about this a hundred ways and still nothing would add up. She was sure the detective had done his own detecting and would give her his own ideas.

"What time was the woman found?" Ivy asked Griffin.

"Eight in the morning," Griffin said. "The superintendent of the building had come up at eight, as promised, to fix the cold water tap in the kitchen sink, which didn't work. The door to the apartment was wide open. He found Miss Lexington on the floor of her bedroom."

Still, Ivy thought. *He might not have known then.* It wasn't as though the two lived together. Declan lived in a dorm, with a male roommate. Whom she'd met once. Only once. Declan had brought her by the room. Maybe he didn't really live there. Maybe he'd paid some kid to let him say he did. *Oh, God,* Ivy thought. *Please tell me this isn't happening.*

She was suddenly aware that the detective was watching her, and she knew how she must look. She was a cop, after all, and it must be clear to Fargo that she'd been thinking through everything, trying to see how the pieces added up, not that they did.

She took a deep breath, picked up the veil and smoothed it. "I need to change," she said to the detective.

His cheeks colored for just a moment. "Of course. I'll wait outside."

When he left, Ivy dug into her purse for the letter from her father. It was gone. So was the five hundred in cash she'd taken out of the bank when she'd been in the city. When had Declan taken the letter and the money? In the two minutes she'd stepped outside to talk with her mother right before the ceremony? Had he known the cops might be on his trail? Had he taken the money as a precaution?

Oh, Declan. Was everything between us a lie? Was everything you said right before I walked down the aisle a lie?

Apparently so. Time to face the truth.

Ivy stood in front of the mirror and slid out of her dress, the dress that represented her dreams. *Do not cry. Do not cry,* she repeated over and over to herself. She picked up the dress and slid it on the hanger and into the dress bag along with the veil. Despite the debacle, the gown was what it was: a beautiful symbol of love, of hope, of commitment. She would give it to Laura as promised.

Ivy changed back into her jeans and sweater and boots and wiped off her red lipstick, then opened the door. Her mother and sisters and friends and officers from the Applewood police department stood milling around. "I'm okay, everyone. Apparently, Declan is not who I thought he was. I'd like to leave it at that. Okay?"

There was a rush of questions, and she heard her idiot partner Dan crack yet another joke about arresting Declan for fleeing the scene of his own wedding. But there were nods and solemn squeezes of her hand from those most important—her family, her friends—and then finally everyone left.

Fargo stood waiting. "Ready?"

Definitely not, she thought.

Chapter Five

Griffin Fargo had been through his share of "worsts"—those god-awful moments you doubt you'll recover from. He'd been shot in the line of duty, for example. Partners over the years had as well. He'd seen women beaten within an inch of their lives at the hands of their husbands. Children having to deal with negligent parents, and worse, of course. On the personal side, he'd had his heart broken once or twice. And he'd lost his father.

But nothing he'd been through had been worse than that moment of recognition, when he realized the man in the photographs, the man who lived with the murdered woman in Apartment 3A, was his kid brother. Declan could change his name all he wanted. His hair color, too (and he had darkened it considerably from blond to a medium brown). But the face, the eyes—those couldn't so easily change.

Griffin wouldn't put it past Declan to use plastic surgery to alter his appearance. Between the murder, which Griffin believed had not been premeditated, and the wedding, Declan had very likely plotted his next steps. A honeymoon out of the country. Plastic surgery.

As he'd stood in that apartment and looked at the photographs, he'd felt sick to his stomach. There had been a time, albeit when they were very young, that Griffin had loved Declan, truly adored him. Griffin was going to show his kid brother the world—or at least as far as their backyard and its treasures of earthworms to dig up, tree forts to build, and T-ball to play. And until he was around seven or so, Declan was a nice enough kid. Spoiled, yes. Temperamental, yes. But a fun kid brother. And then he'd started changing. Stealing. Kicking animals. Getting into fights. Declan was the nine-year-old bully of his block, then the neighborhood. Now, an entire city. Actually, now he was bullying in two states, New York and New Jersey. Now he very well might be a murderer.

As Griffin pulled his car up to the house Ivy directed him to, he took in the small, neat Cape with its trimmed hedges and the pretty white picket fence. Interesting. He'd expected something flashier, not that Ivy herself seemed flashy. But Declan was.

She led the way into the house, her eyes downcast, her hands clutching the dress bag that contained her wedding gown. He was glad she'd changed into regular clothes; he'd had a hard time getting words out when he'd first spoken to her. She'd looked beautiful in the strapless satin gown. She still looked good.

He couldn't quite read her. She'd been quiet on the drive over. Because she was heartbroken and duped? Or because she was working on an angle? Were she and Declan *both* grifters? In cahoots to bilk wealthy women out of their fortunes? If what she said about her father cutting her off was true, perhaps she was Declan's partner in crime. And if she were a dirty cop, she'd be able to cover his tracks—and her own—quite well.

He was usually pretty good at reading people, but Ivy was tough stuff. The inside of her house gave nothing away. Tasteful furnishings, not too modern, not too old-fashioned. Sort of shabby chic. She gestured for him to sit on the sofa, and she sat across from him on a love seat.

What struck him about Ivy Sedgwick was that she seemed truly smart. He could see the wheels turning. So if she wasn't a player, how could she fall for a con artist? Maybe it was easier than he thought. Maybe Declan was that good. Maybe Griffin just hated to admit it.

They'd never lived in the same house, but they'd grown up in the same New Jersey town, just a few streets from each other. Griffin had lived with his mother, who hadn't remarried after her divorce from Griffin's father, who'd then married Declan's mother and had Declan. Declan lived with his mother and their father, until they'd divorced when Declan was seventeen. Griffin spent considerable time at his dad's house, not wanting to be left out, forgotten. His dad had done pretty well on that front, but Declan was such a teenaged delinquent that his father pretty much washed his hands of both boys, spending more and more time away from his own home, let alone swinging by Griffin's to take him out somewhere.

Griffin had tried to befriend his half brother again at that point, tried to be the good older brother, but Declan had a mean streak that Griffin couldn't stand. Once, when Griffin was sixteen and Declan only thirteen, Declan had bet Griffin he could steal away Griffin's then-girlfriend, a very pretty redhead Griffin had spent months working up the courage to talk to. The bet was twenty-five bucks, which Griffin figured for easy money. His girlfriend might be swayed by the captain of the lacrosse team, but not by some scrawny thirteen-year-old.

Three days later, Declan told Griffin he and Griffin's girlfriend were planning to hang out in the library, last row right after school. Sure enough, Griffin found them making out, Declan's hand under the girl's shirt.

It was crazy, but Griffin couldn't date another redhead for years after that. Of course, the next time he did, he got his heart smashed. Declan had been involved in that one, too. A warning to back off. The girlfriend's unmistakable underwear (she liked them personalized with her name across her butt) pushpinned to the front door of Griffin's apartment with a note: *Back off, big brother. Just a warning.* Griffin hadn't backed off, of course. Declan had been arrested several times, and several times the charges had disappeared because he'd used the my-big-brother-is-a-cop card. He'd been let off before anyone had bothered to check with Griffin. Because his crimes were considered petty, the victims considered too dumb to live. Sometimes, police work just plain sucked.

"Were you and Declan close growing up?" Ivy asked, as he took off his black wool overcoat and laid it next to him.

He snapped out of his memories. "Miss Sedgwick, I—"

"Call me Ivy."

"Ivy. What I was going to say was that I would prefer to ask you the questions."

She let out a breath and leaned her head back against the sofa cushions. "Understood. I'm just trying to understand what happened to my life. An hour ago, everything was in place for my future, the future I wanted. Suddenly, it's been blown to bits. You're telling me Declan isn't who I thought he was. That he was a con artist and a thief. You also have the unusual advantage of knowing Declan pretty well since you grew up together. I'm just trying to under—"

She broke down in tears then. She'd come at him so strong that the tears were unexpected. Was she a good actress? Or the real deal? His partner was interviewing just about everyone connected to Declan and Ivy, so the information would reveal itself soon enough.

His brother had good taste. Always had. Ivy was very pretty in a clean, wholesome way. No flash, no exposed skin. Just pretty features and a nice body and great blue eyes. When Griffin and Declan were growing up, girls were always hanging around Declan. He was a pretty boy then, like Brad Pitt.

The dead fiancée was pretty, too. And Griffin had no doubt there were more fiancées.

Declan had always been a grifter, always working an angle. But a killer—that was new. Didn't fit. But Griffin wouldn't put it past Declan to do what served him.

"I just still can't believe all this," Ivy said, wiping under her eyes. "It's bad enough that Declan had another fiancée, but do you really think he killed her? The Declan I know couldn't have killed anyone."

Griffin raised an eyebrow. "You knew him for what, six months?"

"We spent a lot of time together," she retorted, the blue eyes flashing.

"Not so much that he didn't have time to get engaged to someone else," Griffin said.

She shot him a deadly look, then she got up and grabbed a box of tissues from a sidebar, sat back down, and dabbed at her eyes. "If it's true," she said. "Maybe you're lying through your teeth. Maybe you're the dirty one. Maybe Declan has something on you and ran because he's scared for his life."

He stared at her. "Interesting theory. Would Declan have left you behind to deal with the likes of me, then?"

She shrugged.

"I'm telling you the truth, Ivy. I'm sorry it is the truth."

"Why?" she asked. "Why the hell would you be sorry?"

"Because there was a time when I really cared about Declan," Griffin said. "But he let everyone down, all the time. Said one thing, did another. Made promises, didn't keep them. On and on. Still, he could do no wrong in his mother's eyes. No matter what he did, she made excuses. Everything from he was born premature to he had to deal with a father who had another child."

She eyed him but said nothing. After a moment she asked if he wanted coffee. He did. She got up and headed into the kitchen. He followed. It was a good opportunity to look around. There were pictures of a toddler and a teenager all over the refrigerator.

"My nephew and niece," she said, then began making a pot of coffee.

He glanced around. Nothing suspicious.

"I think you're forgetting that I'm a cop," Ivy said. "I know you're looking for evidence that I'm Declan's partner in crime. Don't waste your time. What I want to do is find out for myself if what you say is true. If Dylan really did have another fiancée."

"Let's go," he said.

She took two mugs from the cabinet. "Where?"

"To Miss Lexington's apartment. I think your questions will be answered." He nodded at the mugs. "Got to-go cups?"

Jennifer Lexington lived in a brownstone apartment in Greenwich Village, near the New York University campus. The mailbox for Apartment 3A had a sticker with Jennifer's name and a Dennis McLaren.

"Who's Dennis McLaren?" Ivy asked Griffin as he opened the vestibule door to the lobby with a key.

"You'll see soon enough," he said. They took the stairs to the top floor. The detective's presence took up all the air in the narrow stairwell.

When Griffin opened the door to Apartment 3A, Ivy gasped. Her hand flew over her mouth. The first thing she saw, just standing in the doorway, was a portrait of a woman and Declan, an artsy rendering, but it was clearly Declan. She could imagine Griffin entering the apartment, seeing the portrait and realizing it was his brother, hoping against hope that it would turn out to be just someone who looked like Declan.

That was what she was hoping for. Even though she knew, in her heart, it wouldn't be the case.

Ivy stepped in, scared to death of what she was about to learn. She wasn't sure she had the strength for this.

"It's a lot to take in," Griffin said. "I'll understand if you want to leave, come back tomorrow."

Ivy sobered up fast. "Once I leave this place I never want to come back."

"Understandable," Griffin offered. "Come look around."

There was a coatrack near the door. Declan's favorite black leather jacket with the telltale plaid lining was hung on it. As was the multicolored cashmere scarf that Ivy had bought Declan for his birthday. Photos lined the mantel of the fake fireplace in the living room. Photos of a pretty young woman and Declan McLean. In some, Declan was kissing her. In one, an eight by ten, Jennifer was naked from the waist up and Declan's hands covered her breasts. A few of the photos were in those cutesy frames that said *LUV* across the bottom.

Ivy's shoulders slumped; her entire body seemed to slump, and her legs almost gave out. Griffin steadied her, and she didn't even have the wherewithal to look up at him. *Get your stuff together, Ivy,* she cautioned herself. *This is clearly just the tip of the iceberg of what you're going to find out about Declan.*

Or Dennis.

Declan McLean had another life. How the hell could Ivy not have known?

And he lived here? Not at the dorm with a male roommate named John? Declan had a cell phone, so Ivy had always only called that number. And she'd only visited the dorm once, when they first started dating. Declan's things had been there. Well, some things. The jacket he always wore. His briefcase for work. The leather backpack he used for school. A few stupid things placed around a room didn't mean he lived there. He'd clearly paid some college kid fifty bucks or so to let him pretend it was his room. Because he lived with another woman.

Declan was thorough, Ivy had to hand him that. She'd been duped because Declan was *that* good.

She walked around, the detective allowing her to lead her own way. A door was closed. Ivy put her hand on the knob, but Griffin put his hand over hers. "She was killed in there. CSI has been here, but we don't want anything disturbed just yet. You can open the door and look inside, just don't walk in."

She looked at him and nodded, then opened the door. A four-poster bed dominated the room. More photos of Jennifer and Declan on the dresser. "Where was she killed?" Ivy asked.

"On the side of the bed," Griffin said. "On the floor."

"Why do you think Declan—or Dennis, I should say—killed her?"

"The suicide note is clearly forged, for one," Griffin said. "He did a good job, but not good enough. Handwriting analysis proved that. He clearly had to work fast and he was unusually sloppy for the Declan that I know. She was knocked against the wall with such force, over and over. There's no way she could have hit herself backwards against the wall that way. I think she might have found out about you and threatened him, and in a rage, he bashed her head against the wall."

"I'm so sorry for her," Ivy whispered, closing her eyes for a moment to escape the horror of it all. "She looks so happy in all the photos."

Griffin nodded. "According to her family, she was very happy. Thrilled to be getting married to a resident at NYU Medical Center."

"A doctor?" Ivy asked. "Huh?"

"Declan's a really good liar, Ivy. Our father was a doctor. He knew the lingo well enough to get by in basic conversation. I have no doubt he had Miss Lexington and her family completely fooled, too."

That "too" included her.

"I think I'm going to throw up," Ivy said and ran for the bathroom, where she was stopped dead in her tracks. Taped to the mirror above the vanity was a note in Declan's handwriting: *7 a.m. Jen Babe, gotta head to the hospital for a double shift. Won't be home till tomorrow late morning, and then just briefly before I take off for the week-long seminar in Boston. I'm going to miss you so much!*

Romantic. What a pig. What a lying pig! He was going to honeymoon with Ivy in the Bahamas, then come home and marry Jennifer?

And had he written that note after he'd killed her? To throw off police?

Ivy froze. He had come over to her house that morning and made love to her as though he hadn't just killed another woman in cold blood. *Oh, God.* Ivy slid down against the wall and buried her head in her hands. "How could I have been so blind? So stupid?"

Griffin kneeled down beside her. He was so close she could smell his soap. "He's that good, Ivy. I've know him a long time. Trust me on that."

She took a deep breath and nodded and accepted

Griffin's hand to help her up. His hand was warm and strong and for a moment she wanted to collapse against him.

"I'm going to take you home, Ivy. And then in the morning, if you'd like, we can start from scratch on where you think he might be hiding, what resources he might have. I'd like you to come down to the precinct, if that's all right."

Ivy nodded numbly. Right now, she just wanted to go home.

"But I want you to be clear on something, Ivy," he added. "You're clearly a smart woman. I can see that. And you might be *that good,* too. You might be working me right now, for all I know."

Fury shot through Ivy. "You're saying you think I'm Declan's partner in crime? That I had something to do with that poor woman's murder?"

"I'm saying I'm a detective, Ivy. And a good one. That's all."

Ivy wouldn't have thought it possible, but this day *had* managed to get worse.

As Ivy exited Griffin's car and headed to her door, she could feel his eyes on her. He was watching her. Before she could even get to her porch he was behind her.

"I'd like to come in, search the house. For your own protection," he said.

She whirled to face him. "For my own protection? Or because you think my partner in crime is inside, hiding from you?"

"Either," he responded, holding her gaze, those

intense dark brown eyes steady on hers. She couldn't imagine Griffin Fargo ever faltering.

And she couldn't blame him for wondering if she were as guilty as Declan. She'd learned very well today that you couldn't trust anyone. Even the person closest to you.

She'd worked so hard to trust the people in her life. Especially her sisters. There was no way she'd allow Declan to destroy her faith in people. People weren't bad. *Declan* was.

Dr. Phil would be proud.

"I can protect myself," she said. "And given my day, I'd like some time alone, to process everything."

He nodded, glancing around the property. "Check the door to make sure it's locked."

She did, and it was. "Declan didn't have a key, by the way. He didn't stay here often."

He seemed to be mentally taking notes on everything she said. "I'm going to check the windows for breaks or entry," he told her. "Just as a precaution."

What would Declan possibly want with her now, anyway? It wasn't like she would be coming into any money. And he knew she was an honest person, that she would turn him in in a second. Ivy figured Declan was on his way out of the country, to fool some other unsuspecting women.

Just as she had no doubt that Griffin would spend the night in his car, outside her house. Watching. She followed him around the property, his gun at the ready. There were no signs of forced entry. No sign of Declan. Griffin walked her back to the front door. "I'll need you at the precinct tomorrow morning first thing. Nine a.m."

"You have my word that I'll be there," she told

him. "Though I'm sure you or your partner or some poor uniform like me will be stuck on all-night surveillance, to make sure I don't flee with Declan in the middle of the night."

"Good night," was all he said, and he turned back to his car.

The moment Ivy stepped inside, the phone rang. It had probably rung off the hook all night. She glanced at the message counter on her answering machine: fourteen messages. Twenty was the limit. She let the machine pick up. It was her captain. He wanted to reiterate from his earlier message that she was to use any and all of the precinct's resources in this difficult time.

Thanks, Cap. But she had no intention of calling him or anyone back. The moment the machine clicked off, the phone rang again. Alanna. "Ivy, honey, I'm just so worried about you. Can you call me back, just assure me you're okay? I know this is the fourth time I've called, but I'm worried sick." A few seconds later, it was Amanda. Then Olivia. Then another officer from the PD, then her mother. Then her mother again. And again.

What was there to say to anyone other than: My dreams not only went up in smoke, they turned into a nightmare?

Ivy took a deep breath and unplugged the phone, then took off her coat and hung it up on the coatrack, her gaze moving to the living room, where she and Declan had made love that morning. Again, Ivy thought of how perfectly normal he'd seemed, not the slightest bit nervous. Though now she understood why he'd bundled up the way he had to head back into Manhattan for the meeting at her father's attorney's office. The sunglasses. The scarf practically up to his nose. It had been cold, but not that cold. He'd been trying to hide his face.

Some cop I am, she thought, her legs shaking.

Declan's just that good, she recalled Griffin saying. She owed him that.

She peered out the living room window. Griffin sat inside his car. Those seats weren't too comfortable. But there was no way she was inviting him in. She couldn't handle it. Not tonight, anyway.

Ivy doubted she could sleep, but she headed like a zombie into the bedroom, peeled off her clothes, and grabbed a robe, a different one than the one she'd worn this morning. That one she'd burn.

She lay down on top of her bed and tied the sash of the short white terry robe, clutching the ends as if they were a lifeline. She was so, so tired, in every sense of the word. If only she could sleep, just make this entire day go away, if just for a little while.

Who was she kidding; there was no way she could close her eyes. She sat up, her brain working at warp speed, trying to think of something, anything that would clue her in about Declan. Something he said or did that seemed strange.

But there was nothing. He was that good. A good liar. And Ivy, so in love, had apparently wanted to believe anything he said. She stood up and glanced in the mirror above her bureau—and froze.

Someone had scrawled in red lipstick across it:

Tell that cop anything and you and your sisters are dead.

Chapter Six

Ivy instinctively raced for her gun, then remembered that she had locked it up at the station house for safekeeping until she returned from her honeymoon. She grabbed her baseball bat from under her bed, then her cell phone and called Declan.

In seconds he was on her porch, his six-foot-two-inch muscular frame filling the doorway. "Are we in agreement that nothing is to be put past Declan McLean?" he asked.

She stepped aside to let him in, pulling the sash of her robe tighter. She nodded, her legs trembling. She was suddenly very glad the detective had been outside. That he was inside now. She was so drained, mentally and physically. She needed someone else to be in charge.

"In the bedroom?" he asked, his gun drawn.

She nodded. "The mirror." She followed him into the bedroom and forced herself to look at the glass, shivering under the robe.

He stared at the mirror, then took in the room.

"I'll call in CSI and my captain for an order of protection for your family."

As he dialed, she nodded. "I have no doubt they'll both leave town right away. They both have children to protect. And I'll stay at my friend Alanna's tonight. She's the officer you met at the church. I'll feel safe with her."

He held up a hand as he spoke to his captain. Ivy wasn't even grateful for the reprieve from his questions. The moment his attention wasn't on her, Ivy felt . . . unsafe somehow. He clicked the cell phone closed. "Ivy, to be very honest, I'd like you to stay with me tonight. Declan is somewhere close by, and he was clearly brazen enough to break into your home and threaten you and your sisters. I live just a few blocks from my precinct. I've got a two-bedroom, and you're welcome to the spare."

She stared at him. "Am I bait? You want me to lead Declan to you?"

"I would never use you as bait, Ivy. I simply want to protect you. Declan has turned to murder, and he could come after you anytime."

"But why? I don't know anything. Clearly. I don't even understand what he thinks I *could* tell you."

He upped his chin in the direction of the mirror. "Declan clearly thinks you know something." Griffin stared right at her, taking measure of her. Waiting to see the wheels turning, she was sure. Did he still think she and Declan were working together?

"Tell me the truth, Fargo," she said. "Do you think I had anything to do with Jennifer Lexington's murder?"

"I'd be a bad detective if I said no, Ivy. You know

that. Of course I think you might be involved. You and Declan, grifting together, bilking women out of their money. You have no conscience, so you don't care if he sleeps with other women in order to marry them and get his hands on their fortunes."

"I have no conscience. Right," she snapped. "I'm a cop, Griffin."

He shrugged. "You've never heard of dirty cops? There's an entire division devoted to sniffing them out."

"So guilty until proven innocent?" she asked, eyebrow raised.

"I'm just following all leads, all possibilities," he countered. "That fair?"

"Fair enough," she said. "Just don't waste your time on me."

"I don't think any time with you would be a waste."

The comment was so unexpected that she glanced up at him, but he'd turned away.

She was suddenly aware of her short robe. "I'm going to change."

"Actually, I'd prefer if you didn't touch anything in your bedroom until CSI has gone through it."

She nodded and wished her robe were a little longer. It reached to mid-thigh, but that was hardly long enough when a stranger stood in your living room. A stranger. Huh. Griffin was hardly that. Had she married Declan today, he would have been her brother-in-law. Not that she and Griffin would have met. She had a feeling Declan would have made sure to keep his past a total secret.

I don't want to put a wedding announcement in the paper, he'd said. *Somehow that seems so public when my*

*love for you feels so private, so personal. I almost wish we
could elope to Italy, just the two of us. But I know it's important to you that your sisters come to our wedding.*

Just one of Declan's many supposedly romantic
statements. And she'd been suckered by them all.
Of course he didn't want a wedding announcement
in the newspaper. With his real name. Well, his real
name until he was eighteen. It would have made his
name searchable online, and Ivy had no doubt Griffin Fargo had been checking all the names he knew
Declan as.

"You might know more about Declan and his activities than you think, Ivy. And he also might have
hidden things in your house or via your name. And
then there's the matter of what your father had
against him. The fact that he wouldn't tell you
makes me think Declan threatened him. Perhaps
with something like that," he added, pointing at the
mirror.

Chills slowly crawled up Ivy's spine. "You think
Declan threatened to kill me and my sisters if my
father interfered with the wedding?"

"Maybe," Griffin said. He ran a hand through his
thick, dark hair. "I wouldn't doubt it."

"But why? Wouldn't Declan clearly know that
William would make sure he—we—got none of his
money?"

Griffin pulled on his plastic gloves and began
looking around the area by the mirror, searching
for clues. "Who knows what Declan threatened him
with? That we'll find out," he added. He stopped
for a moment and stared at her. "You know, Ivy, it's
also very possible that Declan did love you, for real.
He could have very unexpectedly fallen in love.

Perhaps Jennifer Lexington learned about you, learned about the wedding, threatened to tell you about herself, and he killed her to silence her."

"Is that supposed to make me feel better?" she asked.

He smiled ruefully, shook his head, and resumed looking around.

Ivy closed her eyes for a moment. "In a parallel universe, I'm supposed to be on my honeymoon right now. Making love. Swimming in the moonlight."

"Sorry," he said. "For that part. For the part that was supposed to be real and innocent and true."

She glanced at him, surprised he understood. "Yeah, me too. I just needed to feel sorry for myself for a second there."

Griffin smiled again, a genuine, if closemouthed smile, and for a second she felt . . . protected somehow, not so alone.

Right. Griffin was after Declan, plain and simple. Ivy was a means to that end. She'd do well not to forget that.

She stared at the dress bag on the back of her closet door. "I promised someone my wedding gown and need to drop it off tomorrow morning."

He glanced at her, surprise lighting his dark eyes. "I thought all brides kept their wedding gowns in their closets for a hundred years. Though I suppose I can understand why you wouldn't want to keep this one."

She smiled. "Actually, I promised it away before I knew any of this. A vic had her wedding dress stolen right out of her car a few days ago. Can you believe that?"

"I can believe anything, Ivy," he said, holding her gaze. "So you told her you'd give her your gown?"

She nodded and explained about watching Laura at the diner with those annoying kids. About what she'd said about her own father.

Griffin seemed to be taking her measure, thinking, making assumptions. She wondered what he was thinking. *Potential suspect and dupe Ivy Sedgwick is the type who falls for pretty-boy con artists and gives away her wedding gown to any crying woman on the street.*

"So why don't we stay here tonight," he said, "keep ourselves situated in the living room so that CSI can do their job, and then we'll head to the city first thing after you deliver the gown."

He was going to stay here? In her house? Were they going to sleep head to toe on her overstuffed sofa?

"I'll put on another pot of coffee," she told him.

"You know what," he said, "I'm pretty good in the kitchen. You relax. I'll make us something to eat, if that's okay. And I'll make the coffee."

"Be my guest," she told him, aware that he very likely wanted free rein to snoop in her drawers. "I don't know if I can eat anything, but my stomach is growling."

"How about a glass of white wine to start?" he said. "I see you have some in your fridge."

She nodded. "Sounds good."

"CSI will be here in a few minutes," he added, then disappeared back into the kitchen. She heard cabinets opening and shutting. Plates clinking.

A few minutes later, he had a hunk of cheddar cheese and crackers on a plate and two glasses of wine on the coffee table.

"Well, isn't this romantic," she said and burst into tears, then shot up from the sofa. "I have to stop doing that. Bursting into tears. I'm telling you, Fargo, I'm not the crybaby type."

"But your wedding day turned into a nightmare, and you're entitled," he said gently, reaching to squeeze her hand.

God, his hand felt good. Big and warm and strong, and for a moment she wanted to just collapse against his tall, muscular body and let him hold her.

But Griffin Fargo didn't seem like the holding type. And she was still a suspect in his eyes.

The doorbell rang, and Griffin let in the CSI team. Ivy took a sip of wine and tried not to follow them around. She wasn't a cop right now. They dusted for prints, spent considerable time outside around the perimeter of her house, and then took photographs. An hour later, they were gone.

Griffin sliced some cheese and topped a cracker with it, then handed it to Ivy. "Eat."

She sat down on the love seat across from him and did as she was told. She was about to cross her legs when she realized he would get an eyeful. She accepted the snack—she *was* hungry. They ate in silence, sipping at their wine.

"Did you love Declan like a brother when you were kids?" she asked. She wondered if he would answer or again tell her that *he* would do the questioning.

He let out a deep breath. "I did at first. I was three when he was born. Our father was having an affair with Declan's mother for months before he left my mother. Because he and Declan's mother were married for so long, I thought my father wasn't such a bad guy, that he just fell in love with another woman. But Declan would tell me about seeing our dad with other women in the house when his mother was at work. She was a nurse and worked the night shift for a while. I think he stayed married to her because she had some family money. Despite being a doctor, my father worked only sporadically, then just stopped practicing altogether. He just wanted to play golf and sail."

She looked at him for a moment, surprised he'd told her all that. "My father was a workaholic to his last minute on earth, apparently. But I guess not being a workaholic didn't mean your father spent any more time with you or Declan, huh?"

"Nope. Just makes them bad parents," Griffin said.

Ivy nodded and took a deep breath. She rarely talked about her feelings about her father with anyone, even her sisters. Any time she brought up her dad, her mother would just rant and rave instead of getting to the heart of what Ivy wanted, which was comfort. It just plain hurt to have a father who didn't love you, didn't care about you, didn't want to know you.

Ivy realized she was all hunched up on the sofa. Between Declan and thinking about her father, she'd twisted herself into a knot. She rolled her shoulders, trying to ease the ache.

Suddenly, Griffin was standing behind her, his strong, warm hands on the bare skin of her neck. He massaged her shoulders, not too hard, not too soft. Just right.

"If you really suspected me of being Declan's partner in crime, you would not be easing my pain," she said.

He bent down and whispered in her ear, "Or maybe I'm trying to gain your trust."

She whipped around, their faces so close she could lean forward and kiss him. "Don't play games with me. I'm telling you that right now. I won't be toyed with."

"Touché," he said. "And it's a deal." Then he continued to rub her shoulders.

Lean forward and kiss him. Where the hell had that come from? She couldn't possibly be attracted to Griffin Fargo, could she? Yeah, his hands were on her bare skin at the moment, which felt amazingly good. And yeah, he was very good-looking. Tall, dark with those intense brown eyes. Masculine. Not pretty blue, like Declan. He was more George Clooney than Brad Pitt.

What he was, was on the up and up. Honest. A man trying to solve a homicide. He was the good guy. Not the bad guy. And the man she'd given her heart to these many months, the man she'd dreamed of marrying, was the bad guy. No wonder she wanted to throw herself into Griffin's strong embrace and just be held for a while. By the good guy.

Or maybe I'm just trying to gain your trust.

She'd better remember that Griffin Fargo wasn't necessarily all good.

"I need to get to sleep," she said. "This has been the day from hell." She needed a break from Griffin, too. His questions, his intensity. His . . . masculinity.

He got up and disappeared into her bedroom, returning with two pillows and her comforter. "I'd prefer that we slept here, on the couch. I don't want to jeopardize any potential missed evidence in the bedroom. And if Declan comes back, I want to make sure you're three inches away from me at all times."

Three inches sounded way too close for comfort.

But Ivy was exhausted and her eyelids heavy. She lay down on the oversized, overstuffed sofa, placing the back pillows on the floor so that there would be more room. "I really don't want to smell your feet," she told Griffin. She scooted her body back against the sofa to make room for him. "So can we forget about the head-feet thing?"

He smiled and lay down, staring up at the ceiling. She could smell his soap. Ivory. She had to admit, she did feel safe lying there between him and the back of the sofa. She'd been about to marry the boogie man, and now he couldn't get to her. He'd have to go through Griffin first, and as demonstrated at the church, that was something he was too scared to do.

Ivy moved to lay on her back, instead of her side. Their shoulders and thigh touched and a strange spark zipped through Ivy. For a moment, well, longer than a moment, she imagined him turning, that strong body on top of hers, the heavy weight of him against her breasts. The thought obliterated reality for a moment, and for that she was grateful.

"Penny for your thoughts," he said, turning his head to face her.

She closed her eyes. "Good night," she said.

"Night."

But it was a long time before Ivy fell asleep.

For a woman who was engaged to Declan McLean, Ivy Sedgwick sure didn't know much about him. With the woman sleeping less than an inch from where he lay, Griffin stared at his pad, a few notes that gave him very little to go on. He took a sidelong glance at Ivy.

Damn, she was beautiful. Her skin, so soft and creamy, and those long eyelashes. Her lips were slightly parted, as was the lapel of her white robe. The curve of her breast was visible, and Griffin swallowed.

He turned back to his notepad, forcing his mind off her body and on to her brain.

Was she in cahoots with Declan? Were they a team? The only thing he bet she was guilty of was being conned. But he would reserve judgment on that. At the moment, he was trying to figure out how she could know so little about her own fiancé. How was that possible?

According to what Ivy did know, Declan wanted to run his own corporation one day. He'd talked about retiring to the Caribbean with the millions he'd make, running a tiki bar, sailing. He wanted to learn Japanese. He talked a lot about opening a children's center, where kids from broken or depressing homes could go after school to play ball, games, have counselors present. Oh, and he liked tuna steak and Nestle Crunch bars. Declan and Ivy saw each other once or twice during the week, rarely overnight, as Declan supposedly had early classes. He'd sometimes stay over on a Friday or Saturday night, leaving early for a "study group."

Griffin did recall that his half brother liked chocolate bars. Other than that, hell if he knew if any of the rest was true or part of the package Declan had created to snare Ivy. Griffin had barely spoken to Declan in the past ten years. Each instance they had spoken, Declan had broken the law. Or *a* law—of human decency. But Declan would play the "my big brother Griffin is a cop" card, and he'd be let off, just like that. Years ago, Griffin had alerted his precinct that his brother was a con artist, but Declan had gotten much more careful over the years.

One truth Declan had told, in part, was about his name. He had been born Declan Fargo, choosing to take his stepfather's name—McLean—when he was eighteen.

Declan had gotten into a huge fight with their father right before then, and that had been that. Their dad had long ago washed his hands of Declan, so the name change hardly broke his heart. It had bothered Griffin. Even though he and Declan were hardly close, the last name Fargo was their one connection; it seemed the only thing that had made them brothers. And Declan had gotten rid of it.

Another truth was the fact that Declan had worked briefly at Sedgwick Enterprises, very likely to find his way to a Sedgwick daughter. As Declan's mother was an old friend of Ivy's mother, that hadn't been hard. And it made sense that Declan would have to introduce himself to Ivy as Declan McLean. He'd had no choice.

The more Griffin thought about it, thought about what kind of person his brother was, how smooth he was at lying, at spinning a story, at conning everyone he'd ever met, the more he knew that Ivy had been set up. It was easy to see how she wouldn't have been able to stand a chance against Declan, no matter how good a cop she was.

A memory flashed briefly into his mind, of the

time right before Griffin's stepmother, Declan's mother, discovered their father in bed with a nurse from the hospital. Griffin had been devastated by his father's betrayal, his father's insensitivity. He'd believed in his heart that his father had left him and his mother to marry Declan's mother because he was so deeply in love, but here he was, making a mockery of that, in bed with someone else.

Declan had told Griffin about the terrible argument, involving lamps being hurled, that had followed. His father had been married twice already. Griffin wasn't nuts about his stepmother; she wasn't the most emotionally generous person in the world, but she wasn't out and out unkind. He felt for her. Declan's response to his mother finding his father in bed with a nurse in her own home? Laughter. And then: *What an ass. You'd think Dad would be smart enough to screw around in the chick's house or a hotel.*

Nothing much affected Declan. He didn't seem to have much of a conscience.

Griffin wondered if he was on his way to some non-U.S. island at the moment, traveling under what Griffin assumed was a wallet full of aliases and fake identification. Maybe. Or maybe he was close by, waiting to get his hands on Ivy. For what, Griffin wasn't sure. The threat on the mirror indicated that she knew more than she was telling. More than she knew, perhaps. Griffin would put his bets on the last one.

The memory of his father, able-bodied, of sound mind, strong and handsome, shook Griffin for a moment. Just six months ago, Frederick Fargo had been slumped over in a wheelchair by the window overlooking the concrete patio of his nursing home.

A few stone tables, each with a potted geranium, made up the view. His father would fuss, wave his hands around, until he was led to his spot by the window. And he'd just stare out.

Griffin had visited every day, despite the fact that his father had no idea who he was. Once, he'd mentioned Declan's name, and he could have sworn he saw a light go on in his father's eyes, but it had gone out a second later. He'd sat with his dad by the window for a half hour, then he'd go check in with Joey, the eighteen-year-old boy—young man— whose own father was also ravaged by Alzheimer's. A senior in high school, Joey would come every day after school, at four o'clock, and sit with his dad by another window and tell the man everything. Joey's dad, only in his early fifties, seemed unhearing and unseeing, but Joey would sit and talk regardless, sharing his day at school, how the basketball team did, that his mom's new husband wasn't so bad, even though he had a "stick up his ass." Turned out Joey's mother had divorced her father well before illness struck. Griffin wished he'd had that much to say to his own father, but he didn't despite being almost twice Joey's age. Griffin was thirty-two. And he knew more about Joey's father, more about Joey, than he knew about anyone.

Griffin shook off the past and stared at Ivy. How could she know so little about Declan? How could Griffin know more about a stranger in a nursing home—someone else's father—than Ivy claimed to know about her own fiancé? She knew nothing of his past, except the nonsense he'd fed her, and even that didn't amount to much.

Then again, what did he know about what made

people fall in love? Griffin had never been married, though he could imagine being married. He'd fallen pretty hard for stupid reasons—once he'd heard a woman singing and fell before he laid eyes on her. Another time, it was the way a struggling single mother had talked so lovingly with her toddler, despite having just been robbed. He'd loved and he'd been betrayed, too. People got duped all the time, by con artists and by perfectly nice people.

Ivy looked so fragile lying there in her robe. He could tell she was sleeping fitfully.

A noise, like a gentle click, startled Griffin, and he bolted up. The front doorknob was turning. Quietly, as if the person outside didn't want his presence known. With his gun at the ready, Griffin silently padded to the door, ready to face his brother again.

This time Declan wouldn't get away.

Chapter Seven

Griffin moved to the side of the door, quietly unlatched the deadbolt, and threw open the door, his gun pointed at . . . Ivy's friend, the cop. Alanna something. He lowered his weapon and replaced it in his holster.

"I apologize," he said. "But I can't be too careful."

He'd spooked her. Shaking, the woman took a deep breath to regain her composure. "Agreed," she said, her eyes wide. She peered around Griffin. "Is Ivy here? Is she okay?"

The lady in question rose from the couch, wide-awake now and alert. "Alanna? What's going on?"

Alanna rushed in. "I was just so worried about you, hon," she said, pushing her long, brown ponytail behind her shoulder. "You didn't answer your phone. I've called so many times. And I stopped by earlier and you didn't answer. I just needed to see you with my own eyes, see that you're okay."

"You stopped by earlier?" Griffin asked. "What time?"

"Around seven-thirty, a little after," Alanna said,

glancing between Griffin and Ivy. "Why, what's going on?"

"Declan was here," Ivy said. "He left me a threatening message on my bedroom mirror."

Alanna let out a breath. "I know. I heard about it from the station house. New York City Homicide informed them. That's one of the reasons I've been calling like crazy."

"When you stopped by, did you notice anything out of the ordinary?" Griffin asked Alanna.

She shook her head. "Certainly nothing that caught my attention, and believe me, my guard was way up. The front door was locked, just as it was now. I tried it then, too. But, of course, Declan had a key, right?"

Ivy shook her head.

"He very likely took her keys and had a copy made, letting himself in and out," Griffin said.

Alanna stood next to Ivy and took her hands. "You're welcome to come stay with me, Ivy. I'd feel so much better if you did."

Ivy ran a hand through her silky brown hair. "I really appreciate that, Alanna, but I've got a much bigger bodyguard right here." She gestured her thumb at Griffin. "He needs me first thing at the precinct to answer more questions, so it's best if we just stay here."

"And if Declan comes back," Griffin added, "I'll be ready for him."

"I got a taste of that myself," Alanna said, "so I know you're in good hands, Ivy. Call me when you can, okay? Anything I can do on my end, just let me know."

When Alanna left, Ivy sat back down on the sofa,

pulling her throw over her. "It's good to have friends," she said, those pretty blue eyes cloudy with worry and hurt.

"And there's no reason to think that you can't trust Alanna?" Griffin asked as casually as he could.

Ivy shot up, the throw falling to the floor. "What's *that* supposed to mean?"

"Do you trust her?" he repeated. "Unequivocally?"

"Of course I do," she shot back, sitting back down and tucking her legs beneath her. She settled the throw around her, covering up that beautiful glimpse of cleavage. "I've been close friends with Alanna since even before the police academy."

"Why was she skulking around outside?" Griffin asked. "Trying the doorknob? Why not just ring the bell?"

Ivy shook her head. "She explained that. She's been worried sick about me. And don't forget, she's not just a girlfriend, she's a cop. This is all her territory, Griffin." He apparently didn't look convinced, because she added, "Griffin, don't waste your time going down alleys that'll lead you away from the suspect."

"Thanks for the tip," he said, smiling. "But I prefer to rule out all possibilities."

"Wow, so you do smile," Ivy said, lying back down. "I wasn't sure."

Griffin groaned inwardly, shut off the lights, and lay back down next to her.

In the morning, when Ivy woke up, there was one wonderful moment of total brain fog. And then it all came flooding back. Mostly because of the smell of bacon and eggs wafting into the living room from the kitchen, and the sounds of plates and utensils clattering gently. A man was cooking in her kitchen, and if there was one thing Declan hadn't ever done, it was cook.

"Scrambled okay?" Griffin asked, setting down two plates full of food. He'd even made English muffins and poured orange juice. And made coffee.

Ivy stood and cinched her robe tighter. "Scrambled is more than okay. I'm impressed."

"I'm not a great cook by any means, but I've never managed to screw up a big breakfast." He sat and wolfed down a piece of bacon.

Ivy watched him for a moment. The early morning light coming through the dining room window behind him lit his dark, thick, shiny hair. And those dark, intense, intelligent eyes were alert as always, taking in everything. Her, she noticed suddenly. She'd been staring, and he caught her.

She ate, surprised she had an appetite. "You *can* cook breakfast," she told him. "And thanks, by the way."

He nodded and sipped his coffee, then opened up his notebook and began reading his notes. "We'll leave for the city in an hour?" he asked, glancing up at her.

"That's fine," she said. "I'll just need to drop off my dress at the diner in town first."

He nodded again and returned to his notes. She was now grateful for the reprieve. She needed to figure out what she was going to say to Laura when the woman asked how the wedding went.

But of course the phone rang, and Ivy wished she

hadn't plugged it back in before going to bed last night. Griffin thought it was a good idea, in case Declan tried to call. He hadn't left any messages last night. Not that she wanted to hear from him, but she wouldn't mind something. Just an: *Ivy, I'm really, really sorry.*

Right. A con artist murderer apologizing!

She appreciated all the support she'd gotten last night, the phone calls from her family and friends, and her fellow officers at the Applewood PD. But what she needed were answers. Did Declan kill Jennifer Lexington? Why? And why was he going to marry Ivy when it was clear that she would inherit nothing from her father? Had he loved her? Or did he think he could eventually get his hands on the money?

Why had he taken the envelope from her father? And why did he steal the five hundred bucks even before he knew New York City Homicide was an unexpected guest at their wedding? Had he seen Griffin arrive? Or was he just preparing in case the cops did catch up with him at the church?

So many questions and no answers. She wished she could call Alanna and tell her everything. Alanna could provide the relationship—or lack thereof, actually—analysis that Ivy was embarrassed to admit she wanted and needed, plus Alanna could do all that from a cop's perspective. But Griffin had asked her to keep his investigation confidential. Which was all well and good anyway. Ivy had no business dumping a debacle of this magnitude on her best friend just because said best friend was a cop. Alanna had enough to contend with right now. She was only twenty-seven, but was the sole support of an elderly aunt, the only family she had left, and was busy planning her own wedding and working her tail off. Ivy would let the detective work his own butt off on his own case. She wouldn't dump her problems on Alanna. She didn't want to take away from Alanna's joy at getting married just because Ivy's own wedding had turned into the wedding from hell. An understatement.

Ivy finished her breakfast, then cleared the table and washed the dishes as Griffin sat, reading, writing, and tapping that notebook. She knew better than to make small talk when a detective clearly was thinking, so she let him think.

One hot shower and change of clothes later, and Ivy felt ready to meet the day. Which she knew would not be pretty. She made three very brief phone calls—to her sisters, who had both left town last night, and to her mother, letting them know she was fine and working with the detective and not to worry.

Not to worry. Ivy was trying to convince herself of that.

She came back into the living room to find Griffin on the sofa, writing away in his notebook. He glanced up, as if surprised to see her in something other than that robe.

"I didn't touch anything in my room other than to grab these clothes," she told him. She wore black pants, a green wool turtleneck, and black, low-heeled boots. She sat back down at the table. "Griffin, I'd like to talk to Jennifer Lexington's family."

He glanced up at her. "Why?"

"They may feel that I might be able to shed some light about Declan. Or Dennis, as he was known to them. I might actually be of some comfort to them.

And maybe something they say about him will trigger something in me, something that will lead to another alias or where he might be hiding."

He looked at her pointedly. "I've talked to her parents. The victim was something of a black sheep, and they weren't close."

"Black sheep? You said the family was wealthy. I assume she wasn't cut out of the will?"

Griffin shook his head. "Why?"

"I'm beginning to wonder if this is Declan's MO," Ivy said. "Romance women who don't have much family connection. Women who feel alone, vulnerable. They're easier targets. *We're* easier targets. But women who stand to inherit a fortune."

"Sickening," Griffin said. "Jennifer Lexington was close to her sister, who lives in Manhattan, too. She was too grief-stricken to talk yesterday morning, but she may be ready now. And being close to Jennifer's age, she may be able to shed more light on the relationship between Jennifer and Declan."

"Dennis," Ivy said, struggling to think of him that way.

Griffin nodded. "I lead the investigation. I lead the interview. Clear?"

"Yes, sir," she said, eyebrow raised. "I'm a cop, too, remember?"

He stopped tapping his pen. "You're out of your jurisdiction, Ivy. And we don't know what we're dealing with. If Declan will come after you to keep you quiet. Remember, we don't know *why* he killed Jennifer. It's my job to keep you safe. I'm asking you to follow my lead."

She would do that up to a point.

"And pack a bag," he added, "since you'll be staying at my place for a while."

"How long?" she asked.

"As long as it takes," he said, looking at her pointedly.

With sunglasses on and a fuzzy wool hat, Ivy entered the Applewood Diner. Griffin waited outside. The last thing she wanted was anyone to recognize her. She saw Laura busy with a large table, waved, and hung the dress bag on a hook by the kitchen entrance. Laura grinned back at Ivy, and Ivy was out of there before Laura come even come over.

Good riddance, my beloved wedding gown, she thought. *May you bring Laura a much better wedding!*

As she headed back outside into the chilly March morning air, Ivy tried not to think about what today might have been like had her wedding not been interrupted by Griffin. Well, interrupted by Declan's lies catching up with him. And in the nick of time. Right now, she would have delivered the gown to Laura, as she'd just done, but she would have sat down in the diner, with Alanna, ordered a big breakfast to regain the strength she'd lost from making love to her new husband all night long, and chatted with Laura about her wonderful wedding. About her family watching her walk down the aisle to the man she loved, about how wonderful it was to have her sisters attend her. How they were all married now, how they'd all found love.

And Ivy and Alanna would have gossiped about the reception, a fancy affair at a ballroom full of miniature red roses, which Ivy loved. She would have danced all night, slow dances with her new husband, fast dances with her friends and coworkers. She would have celebrated her new life with everyone who cared about her. And then right now, she and Declan would be on a plane to the Bahamas for a week of fun in the sun.

And it would have all been a terrible lie. Ivy tried to imagine what would have happened had her wedding not been stopped by Griffin's sudden appearance. She would be married to a man who would marry another woman in two weeks.

Ivy settled back into Griffin's car and stared out the window for the twenty-minute drive into Manhattan. Griffin was quiet; she could tell he was thinking, as earlier, and she let him. She wondered if he was thinking about her. About what kind of cop could be so easily fooled by a typical con artist, the type of con artist he must see a lot as a Manhattan homicide detective. In Applewood, New Jersey, Ivy's collars were pretty much the wedding gown–thieving types. There were some burglaries, rowdy teenagers who went too far, traffic lights that went out in the few intersections. It wasn't exactly high crime territory.

"Don't blame yourself," Griffin suddenly said, glancing at her.

She stared at him, so surprised that he'd read her mind. He was either a very good detective, terrific at reading people, their silences, their body language, or he'd gotten to know her a bit. She figured it was a combination. She wouldn't be able to hide much from him.

She took in his profile, the strong nose, the sculpted chin with the slight cleft. "Have you ever been in love?" she asked. *Where did that question even come from?*

"I thought I was supposed to be asking the questions."

"Didn't mean to get personal," she said, her attention back out the window. Ostensibly, anyway.

"Not really," he responded after a moment. "Been in love, I mean. I've been infatuated, yes. But I've never felt what you feel when you ask a woman to marry you."

"Declan was my first," she said. "Love," she rushed to say, her cheeks turning pink.

He turned and smiled, and she relaxed a bit.

"Though it's strangely gone now," she said. "Because there really is no Declan, is there? My heart is broken, don't get me wrong. But it's broken because I miss what I *thought* I had. There was no reality there. Declan was a lie, our life was a lie. There's nothing tangible to still be in love with." She shook her head. "I'm not making a lick of sense, am I?"

"You're making total sense," he said, capturing her gaze for a moment.

There was so much understanding in those eyes, those intense, intelligent eyes. Again, she felt that spark of safety, that she was all right in his company. It was so hard to lean on him, to rely on him, to trust him. To trust anyone. Especially when she knew she was a means to an end to Griffin. He needed her to lead him to Declan. End of story.

After a couple of hours at Griffin's precinct to take her official statement and sign paperwork, they headed to Mara Lexington's apartment. Ivy had no idea what to expect. Griffin had told Mara that he and a female officer would like to talk to her, and his plan was to tell Mara about Ivy's relationship with Declan—with Dennis—when they arrived. Griffin felt that Mara would be less shocked by the news, and more comfortable, once she saw Ivy in person. Once Ivy wasn't some femme fatale left up to Mara's imagination.

Because it'll be clear that Declan was only interested in me because I'm a Sedgwick? She wondered if that was what Griffin thought. If that was the truth. If everything between her and Declan was a lie, then his interest was clearly a lie, too. Fury lit through her when she remembered the way Declan would look at her sometimes, the way he'd caress her face and just look into her eyes as though he thought she were the most beautiful woman alive.

Jerk. Liar.

Ivy was glad to be shaken out of her thoughts by their arrival at Mara Lexington's apartment building. Though only in her late twenties, Mara lived in a luxury apartment building near Central Park on the Upper West Side. Expensive, like Jennifer's. The kind of building that twenty-somethings could rarely afford on their own.

"Does her father own the apartment?" Ivy asked as they headed toward the front door, which a doorman, dressed in a blue and gold uniform, rushed to open.

Griffin nodded. "He also owns Jennifer's."

Jennifer and Declan's, Ivy amended silently.

The doorman used the intercom phone to let Mara know her guests had arrived, then gestured to the bank of elevators in the marble lobby. Mara lived on the twenty-eighth floor. Ivy had once been visiting a friend in a skyscraper apartment during a blackout and had had to walk up twenty-two flights of stairs. Not fun.

When they arrived at Apartment 28C, an attractive woman opened the door, her tear-streaked face angry. Mara looked a lot like the woman in the photos in Jennifer Lexington's apartment. They had the same curly light brown hair. "That jerk killed her, didn't he?" she asked, wiping at her eyes. "She found out about the other woman and they got into an argument and he bashed her head against—" She broke down in tears.

Griffin glanced at Ivy, and she nodded slightly to let him know she was fine, to go ahead. *I'm the other woman,* Ivy thought, nausea churning in her stomach.

"May we come—"

Mara headed inside the apartment toward the living room, and Griffin and Ivy followed. "She saw him with her, saw him kissing the slut with her own eyes, and he still denied it, tried to tell her she was being paranoid, crazy."

Ivy recoiled for a moment, then quickly regained her composure. *Kissing the slut?* Had Jennifer seen Declan kissing her somewhere? Where? How? Ivy rarely spent any time in Manhattan with Declan. If anything, he came out to New Jersey on a weekend night.

"Platinum-blond slut," Mara continued angrily. "Jennifer recognized her from some party. Laura Frozier. She's not on the deb circuit or anything, but she comes from a really wealthy family in Pennsylvania. Dennis tried to tell Jennifer that if Jennifer saw him kissing her, it was because he'd leaned over to kiss her hello on the cheek, and Laura was drunk and grabbed him and started throwing herself at him. Do you believe that?"

Ivy now believed Declan capable of anything. So there was a third woman. Ivy wondered if Declan was engaged to Laura Frozier, too.

"Miss Lexington, do you know exactly when your sister saw this occur?" Griffin asked.

"It was the night before she was found murdered," Mara said. "She confronted him, but he talked a good game, I guess. She came here and cried on my shoulder about it."

"Where did she see Dennis and Laura Frozier?" Griffin asked, his pad flipped open for notes.

"At the bar of Devini's, the new hot spot on the Upper West Side," Mara said. "At first she didn't even realize it was Dennis, because he was wearing glasses and dressed entirely differently. I mean, Dennis was always in scrubs and then dressed pretty casually, but he was all decked out in Dolce and Gabbana. But all of a sudden he laughed, Dennis's distinct laugh, and she knew."

"Did she confront him right then and there?" Griffin asked.

Mara shook her head, tears brimming in her eyes. "She was too shocked and the place was so crowded that she just walked out, like in a daze. She called me and came over. I told her she should wait a few hours and call Laura and ask her straight out, but Jennifer wanted to give Dennis the benefit of the doubt. So she went back home." Mara broke down, dabbing at her eyes with another tissue that Ivy handed her. "And that was the last time I saw my sister alive."

Ivy's heart squeezed for both Jennifer and Mara.

"Miss Lexington, I'm so sorry for your loss," she said gently, taking the woman's hand and holding it. "My name is Ivy Sedgwick, and I'm a police officer in New Jersey. I knew Dennis under a different name. We were engaged to be married, and Detective Fargo actually interrupted our wedding. In the nick of time. He was quite the con artist."

The woman's mouth dropped open. "Oh, my God." She shook her head. "But how—I mean, how could he not have been caught in a lie somewhere along the line?"

"Because he was very good at what he did," Griffin said gently.

"I can attest to that," Ivy added. "He had me completely fooled. I was about to marry him. Without knowing that he actually lived with another woman."

Mara took a deep breath. "My sister was living a lie. Everything about her life was a lie. And now she's dead," Mara said. "I want that bastard caught. Promise me you'll do everything to find him and prosecute him."

Griffin nodded. "I do promise you that we'll do everything to find him." He jotted notes on his pad. "Miss Lexington, your parents said that they weren't very close to Jennifer but they didn't elaborate. Would you happen to know if Jennifer was still in your parents' wills?"

"She absolutely was," Mara said. "My parents objected to her career choice, which was bartending and taking acting lessons. Jennifer was something of a rebel. And she and my parents never saw eye to eye, but they wouldn't have cut her from the will. They loved her. And I think my mother secretly admired Jennifer and how she followed her own heart."

"They must have been pleased that she was engaged to a doctor," Griffin said.

Mara nodded. "Oh, they were thrilled. But that made Jennifer upset. She wasn't good enough as she was, but because she was marrying a resident who planned to be a very rich plastic surgeon, she was more acceptable to my father."

And the very sad irony was that Dennis was a fake.

"Oh, my God," Mara said suddenly, looking from Griffin to Ivy. "Was Dennis even a doctor? Or was that a lie, too?"

"A lie," Griffin said.

"He told me he was a graduate student at NYU," Ivy told her. "Getting his MBA."

Mara shook her head. "Jerk. A jerk and a liar and a murderer!"

"Mara," Griffin said gently, "what makes you so sure Dennis killed Jennifer? Had you seen a violent side of him?"

She bit her lip. "No, but once at a party, another guy was flirting with Jen, and I noticed that Dennis was watching. He was boiling mad. He was so angry that he actually squeezed the wineglass in his hand. He was bleeding all over the place. There was something about that look in his eye. The anger. It was the first thing I thought of when I was told Jennifer had been killed. Especially after what happened the night before." She wiped under her eyes. "You have to find him. You have to make him pay for what he did to my sister."

"I assure you we will find him," Griffin said. "But

please remember, Miss Lexington, that at this point, we still don't know for sure if Dennis killed Jennifer. It looks that way, but we need to investigate all angles."

"And I'm working with Detective Fargo to find Dennis. Or Declan, as I knew him. Believe me, I want him caught as much as you do."

"Find him fast," Mara spat out. "And then castrate the bastard."

Chapter Eight

After making the necessary phone calls to set up surveillance on Laura Frozier, who, for all Griffin knew, might be working in partnership with Declan, Griffin and Ivy drove away from Mara Lexington's building.

"Where to now?" Ivy asked.

"My place," he said. "I need to do some research, make some more calls."

And keep you in my sights, he added mentally. As long as Ivy was by his side, she wasn't making her own phone calls to Declan, slipping him information while pretending to work with the detective assigned to bring him in. If she was working with Declan, she was one hell of a good actress. The way he saw it, there was only a one percent chance that Ivy was working with Declan. Less than one percent. But he'd be a fool to ignore it.

She nodded. "How are we going to find 'the bastard,' Griffin? And we *have* to find him. We have to find him and make him pay for what he did to

Jennifer Lexington. Could he be hiding out with this Laura Frozier?"

"It's possible, but I doubt it," Griffin said. "Sounds to me like Jennifer went home and very likely argued with Declan all night about Laura. A witness—a tenant walking his dog—remembers Declan leaving around midnight and coming back a few hours later. So maybe he stormed out, then came back, and Jennifer threatened to call Laura Frozier in the morning to ask her straight out. Maybe that's when he killed her."

Ivy nodded. "To stop her from ruining his good thing with Laura. Sounds like she was his only possibility at getting his hands on a rich wife since Jennifer would have likely dumped him. I wasn't a sure thing, given the fact that my father would have likely disinherited me. Especially because I didn't open the inheritance letter when I was supposed to. So the way Declan saw it, Jennifer was about to destroy his chance to marry Laura for her money."

Griffin nodded. "You'd make a good detective."

"That's my goal," she said. "Though I'm not sure my captain will think I deserve it after letting a common crook like Declan snow me."

"Wasn't your fault, Ivy," he said for the second time that day. "As I've said, Declan is a master con artist. Your captain would have been fooled by Declan just as you were."

She bit her lip and nodded and looked away. He was struck once again by how fragile she could look, despite her strength. He had the urge to reach out, squeeze her hand or something, anything. His dad used to do that kind of thing, lay a strong hand on Griffin's shoulder to let him know he cared, that he understood whatever it was Griffin was going through as a kid, a teenager. And that would always make Griffin feel better, less alone with his problems.

"You okay?" he asked. "I know it couldn't have been easy to hear there's *another* woman." Damn. He hadn't quite meant to emphasize *another* quite so much.

She glanced at him and offered a small smile. "I'm getting used to it. I wouldn't be surprised if there were more to come." She let out a deep breath. "So this is where you live?" she asked as they pulled into a parking space on his street. She glanced up at the row of brownstones.

"I don't own the entire brownstone," he said. "Just one apartment. But it's nice. With a garden out back." He grabbed her suitcase from the trunk and carried it up the few steps. After unlocking his deadbolts, he stepped inside, his gun drawn. Ivy behind him, he checked out each room. Declan wasn't lying in wait for him. Nor had he managed to break in. No calling cards had been left. But Griffin wouldn't put it past his brother to leave him a warning. Or try to get him out of the way.

"Nice place," Ivy said, glancing around. "Definitely a bachelor pad, but nice."

He smiled and led her down the hall. "My guest room," he said, placing her suitcase on the bed. "All yours."

She glanced up at him. "Thank you, Griffin."

The small bedroom was suddenly too small. He had the sudden urge to grab Ivy and lay her down on the blue blanket and touch every inch of her. With his hands, his mouth. He suddenly wanted to make love to her with such ferocity that he turned away.

"Something wrong?" she asked.

Yes, something's wrong. I'm attracted to you when I can't be.

His cell phone. Saved by the captain. He went into his bedroom and shut the door, filling his captain in on the conversation with Jennifer Lexington's sister and his next steps—to question Laura Frozier. He also informed his boss that he was safeguarding Ivy. Griffin then made a couple more calls, one to a snitch to check in, and another to set up a meeting with Laura Frozier for later today. The woman had her own personal assistant, despite not having a job.

The doorbell rang, and again, Griffin drew his gun. He put his finger to his lips and gestured for Ivy to stay put.

Declan? Possibly, but Griffin doubted his brother would be so bold as to come to Griffin's home. Declan was smart, but Griffin was smarter. And bigger.

He padded to the door and peered through the peephole. Not Declan. Not even close. It was Joey, his young friend he'd met at the nursing home.

He unlocked the door and Joey barreled in, fists clenched. He was pacing so fast that his mop of dark brown hair flopped into his eyes.

"I hate him! He's such a jerk. I hate his stupid guts!" Joey ranted, his cheeks flushed and his big hazel eyes filling up with tears. The young man glanced up and noticed Ivy and slid down the wall onto his butt, his face buried in his hands.

Ivy gestured to Griffin that she would make herself scarce, and she slipped into the kitchen.

Griffin sat down next to Joey, his knees up like his young friend's. "Hey, Joey, calm down and tell me what's going on. It's just us now."

Joey glanced up, looking around. He let out a deep breath. "I just hate his guts. He's such a bastard!"

"Who, Joey?"

"My stupid jerk stepfather, that's who," Joey yelled. "I was eating lunch in the caf at school, and he calls me and tells me I have to go to some stupid wedding in his stupid family next weekend in California. He knows I spend every Saturday and Sunday visiting my dad. And my girlfriend isn't even invited to the wedding."

Despite being six feet tall and one hundred sixty muscular pounds, Joey was barely eighteen, finishing up his last semester of high school, and still, for the most part, a kid.

"Did you tell him how you felt?" Griffin asked.

"Like he cares? My mother and Chip the Diphead both said my dad wouldn't even notice I wasn't there. How dare they? Are they doctors? No. So they don't know anything. They don't know what my dad knows and doesn't know. Maybe he does know I'm there. Maybe he does hear me."

Griffin understood how important it was for Joey to believe that. And it could very well be true.

"And my girlfriend isn't invited to the wedding because 'she's not family,'" Joey continued, mimicking his stepfather in a singsong voice. "But I know the real reason. Chip the Loser and my mother think she's 'inappropriate.' That's their favorite word. Well, I think they're the ones who are inappropriate!" He buried his face again.

"I didn't even know you had a girlfriend," Griffin said.

Joey lifted his head, his expression brightening a bit. "She's a little older. Nineteen. She has her own apartment, well, with two roommates. Mom and Chip don't like her because she's not in college and has a belly button ring."

Griffin smiled. "What *is* she doing?"

"She's a singer. Well, a waitress-slash-singer. She wants to try out for *American Idol*. And I'll bet she makes it. She's really good. And so pretty." He stared down at the floor. "Sometimes, she'll sing without any music, and she makes me forget what's going on, you know? Like my dad."

Griffin nodded. "Women definitely can make you forget your troubles sometimes."

"Hot chocolate can, too," Ivy said, setting down three steaming mugs on the dining room table. "Well, it can at least warm you up on a cold day."

Joey half smiled and popped up, wrapping his hands around a red mug. "Thanks. So, are you Griffin's girlfriend?" he asked.

Griffin caught Ivy's cheeks pinken as he stood up and took a seat next to Joey at the table. "She's a fellow officer," he explained. The word *girlfriend* combined with Ivy filled Griffin's mind with images of kissing her, feeling those pretty red lips against his.

"Cool," Joey said. He sipped his hot chocolate.

Griffin forced thoughts of Ivy's lips from his brain. "You know, Joey, I'd be happy to visit your dad for you when you're away at the wedding. If you decide to go, that is." Joey was legally an adult and could do what he wanted, but he clearly respected his mother and stepfather's authority. He was a good kid.

Joey glanced at him. "Really? You'd really go see him? Talk to him?"

Griffin nodded. "You bet."

"Well, that makes you a lot cooler than my mom and Chip the Dipshit." He glanced at Ivy and bit his lip. "Sorry."

"It's okay," she said with a smile. "I hear a lot of curses in my line of work."

Joey laughed. "Yeah, like which ones?"

"I'll spare you and Griffin," she said with a smile.

"Anyway, Joey," Griffin said, "when I'm faced with a situation like yours, what I like to do is really think it through. Think through both sides and decide what's best, what's right. With a cool head—not a hot one. Know what I mean?"

Joey smiled. "I can get a little hotheaded sometimes. But that jerk makes me so mad!"

Griffin smiled. "Well, if you ever need to talk about anything, you can always come to me."

Joey nodded and bit his lip again. "I'm gonna go think." He glanced up at Ivy. "Thanks for the hot chocolate. You make it really good."

Ivy smiled. "No problem."

When Joey was gone, Griffin moved into the living room, and Ivy sat down next to him on the couch. "He's a good kid. Going through a lot."

Ivy leaned her head back, revealing the beautiful long column of her neck. "That's wonderful of you to visit his dad. Assuring him of that really seemed to take the pressure off him."

"He's a great kid," Griffin said. "It killed me to see him at the nursing home every day, never taking his eyes off his dad for a second just in case there would be some flicker of recognition of his son. Seeing my dad the same way took a huge toll on me and I'm an adult. Imagine what it's like for a kid in high school."

"I'm so sorry for what you went through," Ivy said. "For what your dad went through. Were you close?"

Griffin shrugged, an image of his father floating to the surface. His father, once so big and strong, once so brilliant, had been reduced to a shell. Frederick Fargo would be walking down the street and would suddenly turn to a stranger and bark orders as though he were in the hospital talking to an intern. And then, for a while, he thought he was a teenager. Griffin wasn't often scared by anything; he was always prepared for the worst. But he'd been scared to death by what happened to his father.

"Not too close," Griffin said. "We never were."

She glanced at him and nodded. "Sounds like Joey was very close to his dad. I hope you know what your support must mean to him. When I was a teenager, I used to wish I had someone to talk to about my dad and how bad I felt about it."

This time Griffin did reach over and squeeze Ivy's hand. She glanced up at him with a gentle smile, and before he even knew what he was doing, he leaned over and kissed her on the mouth. Not a friendly kiss, either. He felt her surprise, her momentary hesitation, but then she kissed him back. Tentatively, at first. And then passionately.

He pulled away to look into her eyes, to give her a moment to decide. She leaned closer, her lips barely touching his. It was an invitation. And that was all he needed.

He pressed her down on the couch while deepening the kiss. Her soft, cool hands were around his neck, in his hair, her back arching up. He slipped his own hands under her sweater and quickly disposed of her lacy bra. Interesting. He'd expected plain white, but this delicious piece of lingerie was pale pink and sheer with tiny rosebuds along the straps. And it smelled faintly of perfume, of Ivy.

He inched up the sweater until his hands covered her full, round breasts, then he practically tore off the sweater to get it out of his way. She smiled, and he kissed her, and she surprised him once again by sitting up and then pushing him down on the opposite side of the couch. He felt those breasts against his chest, her thighs against his thighs. She inched down a bit and began unbuttoning his shirt, and suddenly the zipper of her pants was in line with his. He groaned and grabbed her hands. Their eyes met then, and he knew she knew what he was trying to tell her.

This was it.

Either she stopped him now and they very quickly started discussing the case and murder victims and former fiancés who were also estranged half brothers, which would be the equivalent of a few cold showers, or they made love.

I have to make love to you.

Instead of putting a stop to this madness, and it *was* madness, Ivy unbuttoned his shirt, her gaze on his. The moment her hands touched his bare skin, his last rational thought left his mind and he simply *felt*. Felt her soft, full breasts crushed against his chest, her lips on his, his erection straining against his zipper. In seconds he had both of their pants off. He braced himself up to admire her curves. She was an innie. And her panties were as sexy as her bra. Pale pink and sheer. He pulled them down and lay naked atop her, teasing each rosy nipple with his tongue. She moaned and that was all he could take.

He slid inside her, gently at first, his gaze on her beautiful face. She opened her eyes and kissed him, then closed them again against a moan that escaped her lips. He thrust into her, his hands, his mouth enjoying her breasts. When she began moaning fast and furious, he knew he wouldn't be able to wait any longer himself. Griffin exploded, the pleasure intense, and lay against her, her heart beating like crazy against his.

"That was amazing," he whispered into her ear.

"Yes, it was," she breathed back.

They lay like that for at least a half hour. Griffin didn't want to move, didn't want to break the spell. And clearly, neither did Ivy. But then she wriggled underneath him, and he moved aside to give her room to get up. She grabbed the chenille throw on the arm of the sofa and wrapped it around herself, then headed to the bathroom. Without looking at him.

"Ivy," he said, having no idea what words would follow.

But she didn't turn around.

Stupid. Stupid. Stupid, Ivy berated herself as she stared at her reflection in the mirror above the sink in Griffin's bathroom. How could she have let that happen? For God's sake, she didn't even know if she could trust Griffin Fargo. If she was simply a means to an end.

The face that greeted her in the mirror looked so unfamiliar. The blue eyes were sparkling. Her complexion was glowing. And a warmth enveloped her, despite the fact that she was standing naked in the bathroom, the throw folded neatly on the rim of the tub.

That felt so good, she thought, closing her eyes against the memory of being underneath Griffin's rock-hard body, of looking into those gorgeous dark eyes. For the first time in a long time, a man had made love to her and actually looked at her. She'd almost forgotten what that connection felt like. And now that she'd felt it, had shared it with Griffin, there it was. Which was why she was hiding in the bathroom.

There was a knock at the bathroom door. "Everything okay in there?" came Griffin's deep voice.

It took Ivy a moment to find her voice. "Everything's fine. I'm just . . . washing my face." She quickly turned on the water. She could imagine him smiling on the other side of that door.

She wrapped the throw around her and then pulled the door open, and in fact he was smiling. His hands were braced on either side of the frame. He wore a pair of jeans and nothing else. God, he was sexy. He swooshed up all the air in the bathroom. "I'm . . ." She faltered. "I have no idea what I am, actually."

"I do," he said. "You're beautiful. And you're not sure if we should have done that."

"Yup," she said.

"I don't think either of us expected that to happen, Ivy. But I don't regret it."

"You might," she said.

He stared at her then, his eyebrow going up. "Are you admitting to something here?"

"Like what? That I'm a no-good grifter? That Declan and I are working together?"

"I don't believe that, Ivy."

But she didn't believe *him*. He was a detective first and foremost.

"Detective Fargo, I think we both lost our minds for a while there. And from now on, I think we should keep our mouths to ourselves."

He smiled, and then she did, too, adding a grimace to let him know she was angry at him, though she wasn't sure why.

"I'm serious, though, Griffin," she said. "Sex, whatever it means, will complicate things here. And things are complicated enough."

"Agreed," he said, pulling on a black T-shirt over that incredible chest. "How about I make us some coffee?"

"Great idea," she said. "And then we can discuss what we'll do next."

"We?" he asked on the way to the kitchen.

"We," she repeated. "Are we going to see Laura Frozier?"

"Ivy, *I* am going to investigate the murder of Jennifer Lexington. I have an appointment to question Laura later today at five o'clock. I'm not sure if your presence will get Laura talking or enrage her. We don't know how she's going to react."

She followed him into the kitchen. "But you allowed me to accompany you to question Mara Lexington."

"This is different. Laura is romantically involved with Declan. She may not take kindly to meeting you. Mara Lexington was a murder victim's sister. To her you represent someone who can help find Declan."

"I know, but—"

"But we want Laura to talk, not clam up, Ivy. And, you're here in the first place because I want to keep you safe. Not because you're a New York City homicide detective. You're not on the job here, Ivy."

"Well, I'm not on my honeymoon, either," Ivy retorted, watching as he calmly set about brewing a pot of coffee. He was infuriating. "Griffin, I'm not about to sit around when I can be of service. Remember, I know Declan."

He turned and stared at her for a moment. "No, Ivy. You don't."

Bastard. But it was true. Who was she kidding? She didn't know Declan McLean. Not at all.

"Look, I didn't mean—"

"Yes, you did, Griffin. You did mean to make me face up to the truth. Never a bad thing. A hard thing, though." *Idiot, idiot, idiot,* she berated herself. "Anyway, what I really think is that I need to get dressed. I'm sort of at a disadvantage with a throw wrapped around me."

He nodded, and she escaped into the guest room. She shut the door and locked it and leaned against the back of the door, taking a long, deep breath. Her mind was whirling in so many different directions that she sat down on the bed and forced herself to think of anything but Griffin, anything but Declan. Anything but multiple fiancées. And murder.

She glanced around the room, which was nicely furnished. The bed was covered in a sage down comforter that looked remarkably inviting. There was a wood bureau with a round mirror and a bookcase full of hardcover and paperbacks, from classics to best-sellers.

Ivy stood and walked to the window, which faced the row of brownstones across the street. She twisted the wooden blinds and looked out at the glittering city. People strolled on the sidewalk, despite the cold weather. A woman walked a beagle. A couple stood kissing under an awning. Everything seemed so normal out there. But it wasn't.

Declan, where are you hiding? she wondered. *And what are you trying to do?* She still couldn't figure it out. He had been moments away from marrying her, when it was ninety-nine percent certain that she would inherit nothing. And how had he been planning to juggle so many wives, anyway?

Perhaps the same way he'd juggled fiancées and girlfriends. She hadn't suspected a thing.

"Ivy?" Griffin called from the other side of the door.

She wasn't quite ready to face him. She wasn't even dressed.

She walked back over to the bed and opened her suitcase, removing a pair of comfortable jeans and a cream-colored sweater. Considering that her underwear and bra were buried somewhere in Griffin's couch, she grabbed fresh undergarments and got dressed.

What she needed right now was her best friend. She was desperate to talk to Alanna, tell her everything, get her perspective. Tonight, she'd ask Alanna to meet her in Manhattan for coffee. If Griffin gave her a hard time about her safety, she'd remind him that Alanna had a gun and knew how to use it.

Ivy glanced in the mirror and again was struck by how . . . alive she looked. She brought her fingers to her lips, tracing the imprint of Griffin's lips. A tingly heat warmed every inch of her body.

"Ivy? Are you all right?"

Even his voice did strange things to her nerve endings.

She hurried to the door and opened it, and there he stood, all six feet plus of him, his thick, dark hair tousled by her own fingers.

"Your coffee awaits," he said.

She followed him into the dining room, where two mugs of coffee, milk, and sugar rested on the table.

He sat and flipped open his pad, taking a sip of his coffee. "I'd like to ask you some questions about the people in your life, peripheral and otherwise, who might have been seduced by Declan."

She froze, her own cup of coffee midway to her mouth. "Seduced by Declan? What?"

"Ivy, I think we should explore the possibility that Declan may have been romancing someone you know. A friend, even one of your sisters."

She shot up. "How dare you? Are you telling me I don't know my own friends?"

"I'm just saying that Declan may have gotten to someone in your life—even an acquaintance. Like the receptionist at the Applewood precinct."

Mary Beal flashed into Ivy's mind. Barely twenty-one, Mary was a part-time student at a local community college. She was on the plain side, shy, and wasn't dating anyone, as far as Ivy knew.

"And Declan is romancing Mary because?"

"Access," Griffin said. "Passwords into the computer system, for example."

"So, every day when I walked into the precinct for work, I said a cheery hello to the woman who was having an affair with my fiancé. Is that what you're suggesting? That Declan and Mary made a complete fool of me without my knowledge?"

He laid his hand over hers. "It's possible, Ivy. That's what I'm suggesting. *Someone* left you that threatening message on your bedroom mirror. Maybe Declan. Maybe a partner of his. Maybe someone close to you."

Tears came to Ivy's eyes and she blinked them back hard. "I hate this. I hate all of this. Damn it, I'm supposed to be the smart one, you know? The Sedgwick sister who didn't get the gorgeous looks like Olivia or the amazing body like Amanda. I got the brains. And a good heart. And what was the damn point?"

"Ivy," Griffin said, "you were conned by the best."

"That doesn't make me feel better. I should have known. I should have sensed something was off. God, was I that desperate for love? For—" She stopped, aware that she was actually speaking out loud, actually telling Griffin all this. The man she'd just made love to. No, correction: the man with whom she'd had sex.

"I've said this before, Ivy. Declan may well have loved you. If your father was disinheriting you, Declan wasn't marrying you for your money."

"Great. A lying, cheating, murdering con man loved me." Ivy buried her face in her hands.

"We'll get to the bottom of this," Griffin said. "I promise you that."

Ivy uncovered her face. "You said *we*. We."

"We," he repeated. "You're a cop and you're in this deep. I need your help to find Declan."

"You've got it."

"But it's going to mean accepting some things you don't like. Such as the receptionist being a double-crosser. Or someone else in your life."

"Like?"

"Like your friend and fellow officer, Alanna Moore. Like any of the female officers at the Applewood PD. Con men have their worker bees all over the place, Ivy. They do favors for people and call them in. Or, if they're very good-looking and even better liars, they romance their helpers."

"I'm planning to meet Alanna, my *best friend* and a good cop, for coffee later," she said. "I'm going to talk to her like the best friend that she is."

Griffin shook his head. "That's a mistake. You should talk to her like a cop, Ivy. She could have fallen prey to Declan."

Ivy rolled her eyes. "Alanna is engaged to be married," she reminded Griffin. "She's madly in love. And she's a terrific, honest person. She would never betray me."

"I don't think you can honestly say that, Ivy. About anyone."

"So there's no such thing as trust. As faith?"

He glanced away for a moment. "There is, of course. But with the ability to accept that people aren't perfect."

"That's just cynicism, Griffin."

"It's reality."

Ivy shrugged. "I know about reality. I was raised by reality. And apparently so were you."

He nodded. "Fair enough. But do you think

you'll be able to keep an open mind when you see Alanna—when you speak to anyone in your life?"

An open mind about her best friend or the kind, Applewood PD receptionist being her ex-fiancé's evil lover? Ivy doubted she could be that open-minded. But she would be more careful from now on. Of everyone and everything. Especially Griffin Fargo.

Chapter Nine

At three o'clock, Ivy sat along the counter at the large windows in a midtown Starbucks, aware that Griffin was somewhere nearby, watching. She wouldn't be surprised if he'd planted a bug on her to eavesdrop. If he truly thought that Alanna could be working with Declan, there was no way he'd leave Ivy alone with Alanna, even in a public place like Starbucks. There was such a thing as drugging someone's latte and pretending to help them outside to a waiting car that would lead them to a lonely stretch of road in the woods.

Ivy hadn't come to that nugget of wisdom herself, of course. That was Griffin's contribution. And so he was somewhere nearby. Watching. Maybe listening. Which meant she couldn't exactly talk about him. Griffin. And what had unexpectedly happened earlier this afternoon in his living room. On his couch, for heaven's sake.

Then again, Griffin had also cautioned her to be natural. To be herself. To share what she'd always share with Alanna. Which at this point, was everything. She could even mention what Jennifer Lexington's sister had shared. After all, it was nothing that Jennifer herself hadn't shared with Declan. It wouldn't be news. And if Alanna were in cahoots with Declan, and it were news, well then, it just might lead to some interesting developments.

Ivy felt an incredible sense of relief as she saw Alanna walking up the street toward Starbucks. Alanna, her pace quick, her expression worried, hurriedly entered the café, and Ivy waved. Alanna rushed over and hugged Ivy, and all Ivy could think about for a moment was the first time Alanna had hugged Ivy, in eighth grade, when Alanna had moved to New Jersey from somewhere in Ohio. Alanna, who'd been so pretty at thirteen, but with thick glasses, and so thin and tall, towering above her male classmates, was a bit awkward and shy then, and she'd gravitated toward another awkward, shy girl in several of her classes, Ivy. During Alanna's first week at school, in English class, before the teacher came in, a few popular girls were rating the girls in the class, and they loudly declared Ivy and the "Stringbean" a negative two. There'd been laughter. After class, Ivy had apologized to Alanna; if Ivy hadn't befriended Alanna, Alanna might have a chance at popularity and an actual decent time in middle school. Alanna had hugged Ivy and insisted she'd rather have one good friend than a bunch of fake ones.

That was the first of many instances in which Alanna had shown Ivy just what a good friend she was. How true-blue she was. After middle school, there'd been high school and then college and the police academy. Together. There was no way Alanna was remotely connected to Declan.

"I've been so worried about you," Alanna said. She took off her scarf and coat. "Are you all right? What's going on?"

Ivy offered a rueful smile. "I need a latte first. I'm okay, though. Really."

Alanna searched Ivy's face. "You sure?"

Ivy nodded, and the two friends headed to the counter to order lattes and one brownie to split.

"What in the world is going on?" Alanna asked. "Was Declan in some kind of trouble?"

"Apparently, Declan was leading a double life. Possibly a triple life. For all I know, a quadruple life. He had at least one other fiancée, with whom he lived, and she was found murdered the morning of our wedding. Detective Fargo is investigating the murder." *Oh, and I slept with him. And it was amazing.*

"Ah," Alanna said. "But how did Declan recognize Fargo as a cop? Had Declan been in trouble with the law?"

Huh? Am I not supposed to reveal the familial connection between Griffin and Declan? She supposed there was no reason not to. "Declan is Detective Fargo's half brother," Ivy said. "The minute Declan saw him in the pews, he knew that the police were on to him."

"Ivy, I'm so sorry," Alanna said, taking Ivy's hand. "I know how much you loved Declan."

Ivy wrapped her hands around her latte, the warmth warding off the chill that crept up her spine. "It's as if someone—Declan, actually—poured a bucket of cold water on anything resembling emotion for him. The feeling is gone, for him, at least.

How could I be in love with someone who didn't exist? Declan McLean wasn't real."

Alanna nodded, her expression hardening. "That bastard."

"You know what hurts the most, Alanna? That I'm not good at what I do, what I love: being a cop. How could I ever hope to make it as a detective when I couldn't tell that my own fiancé was a con artist?"

"Ivy, you can't think that way. You had no reason to suspect Declan. My God, he was practically handpicked by your mother. He came with a seal of approval."

Alanna was right. Ivy had almost forgotten that. Her mother would be thinking about that. Ivy would call her later, reassure her that she was okay. And that she should pay Madame Elena *double*.

"Ivy, I also wanted to let you know that if the idea of being in a wedding or having anything to do with a wedding makes you want to throw up, I understand. I'll postpone the date."

"Oh, Alanna," Ivy said, throwing her arms around her friend. The woman was willing to postpone her own wedding to make Ivy feel better. That was friendship.

"You will do no such thing," Ivy said. "I can't wait to be your maid of honor. And I can't wait for my dress fitting and your shower and the wedding itself. Weddings are about love, and it'll make me very happy to celebrate yours."

"If you're sure," Alanna said, tears in her brown eyes. "I mean, I was so upset when I thought that fortune teller was talking about my wedding. But I never wanted it to be your wedding that wasn't going to happen."

Ivy smiled. "Then again, thank God it didn't. Can you imagine if Griffin had come fifteen minutes later? I would have married Declan."

"Maybe you should pay Madame Fortune Teller a visit," Alanna suggested. "Who knows what else she may be able to tell you?"

"She said she could only see into the past, though," Ivy pointed out.

"Whatever that means," Alanna said. "Whose past? Whose past did she see when she looked at all of us? How could she see Declan's past?"

"Maybe she felt his womanizing, lying, cheating spirit or something," Ivy said.

On that somewhat lighter note, the two friends parted. Alanna had to hurry back to Applewood to meet her fiancé's parents to choose between salmon or swordfish for the fish entrée at the reception. And Ivy had a girlfriend of Declan's to meet.

She waited for a moment for Griffin to jump out from behind a ficus tree, but he didn't. When Ivy left Starbucks, however, he appeared at the door.

At least Ivy knew she'd been right about another thing: Griffin would always be watching. It was both comforting and discomforting.

Laura Frozier lived on the Upper East Side in her parents' town house. The Froziers were on safari at the moment, yet a household staff attended to Miss Frozier's every desire and whim. There was a butler and a housekeeper. And the personal assistant, who met Griffin and Ivy in a formal sitting room. Miss Frozier would be with them shortly, they were assured.

"Shortly" was practically twenty minutes. Griffin did not like to be kept waiting.

"I am so very sorry!" trilled an attractive young woman as she entered the room. She was flashier than she was truly attractive. "I was getting a massage in our spa room. I am so stressed!"

"Oh?" Griffin asked. "Is there something in particular that's causing you stress?"

"Try my fiancé was totally cheating on me," Laura said, flipping her long blond hair behind her shoulders.

Meet fiancé number three, Griffin thought, mentally shaking his head.

"I was taking a little catnap when all of a sudden, my phone rings, and it's some crazy woman screeching in my ear that her sister caught her fiancé kissing me in a bar and now her sister is dead. I mean, I didn't even know what the hell she was talking about! And then I get a text from Devin—that's my fiancé— telling me that 'it's all lies and not to worry,' and I have no idea what he's talking about, either."

"Is this your fiancé?" Griffin asked, holding up a picture of Declan.

"Yes, that's Devin."

Fifteen minutes later, Griffin and Ivy had gotten an earful from Laura about her wonderful fiancé, Devin McDoren, an investment banker on Wall Street. Right. They'd been engaged for two weeks. They'd been dating for four weeks. Laura had kept the engagement a secret from her parents, since they'd surely "freak" about the short period of time she'd known him. That had been Devin's suggestion. He wanted time for her parents to get to know him and love him.

Right again.

Another fifteen minutes later, and Laura Frozier got an earful about how *not* wonderful her fiancé was. She was sobbing uncontrollably, except to mention that she had to call her guru for an immediate meditation session. And her therapist.

"Laura, may I ask you a personal question?" Ivy said as she and Griffin began putting on their coats. At Laura's tearful nod, Ivy asked, "What made you fall in love with Devin so quickly? What was it about him that made you accept a marriage proposal after knowing him only four weeks?"

Laura sniffled. "He swept me off my feet. That's the only way I can explain it."

After promising to call Griffin if Declan attempted to contact her, Laura fled upstairs in tears, and the butler appeared so he could let Griffin and Ivy out.

"Do you think there are other fiancées?" Ivy whispered as they headed to Griffin's car.

"I can't imagine one man spreading himself that thin," Griffin said. "But as I've said, I wouldn't put anything past him. In any case, now that he has no fiancées, I'm sure he's romancing someone else to fund his ability to disappear for a while."

"So where does the investigation go now?" Ivy asked, buckling her seat belt.

"I have a few ideas," Griffin said. "One is to canvass all the wealthy single women in New York City and to check recent engagements for grooms-to-be whose initials match Declan's standard MO. Another is to question some of the relatives or friends of the fiancées—see who knew about Declan's relationship with Jennifer Lexington."

"For what reason?" Ivy asked.

"Let's say, for instance, that your mother discovered Declan was leading a double life or if she just thought he was having an affair. She might have gone to Jennifer's apartment to confront her, demand she not see Declan anymore. And Jennifer ends up dead."

Ivy shook her head and let out a bitter laugh. "So now my mother is the murderer?"

He took her hand and held it. "Just possibilities, Ivy. It's my job to look at every angle, no matter how outrageous or even unlikely. I need to consider motive. Means. Opportunity."

She stared at their entwined hands and pulled hers away. "Or Declan is the killer. As you originally thought."

"He is the prime suspect, Ivy. But there's no physical evidence connecting him to the crime. The suicide note was in his handwriting, though he attempted to disguise it. And he could have likely written the note in a panic because he would *seem* the likely suspect. Even if he hadn't killed her."

Ivy leaned her head back against the seat as Griffin pulled out onto the street. "I'm exhausted, Griffin. What I wouldn't give to just take a long hot bath and sleep for a million hours."

"I can arrange the bath and we can both hope for a good night's sleep," he said.

The thought of Ivy Sedgwick, naked and soapy and wet in his bathtub, flashed through his mind. It was going to be a long night.

Chapter Ten

Griffin had kept his word. Ivy lay soaking in a deliciously hot, mind-numbing—which was the object—bubble bath. The bubbles were made of shampoo, since Griffin was a bachelor and didn't actually own bubble bath, but it was still good. Ivy closed her eyes and tried not to think, but of course she did think—of the pretty young woman in the photographs at Jennifer Lexington's apartment. Of Mara Lexington's grief. Of Laura Frozier's tears, dramatic as they seemed. Of her own tears. Declan had hurt so many people. Not just the women he'd deceived, but their families, their friends.

And his own family. Declan and Griffin were all that was left of their families, and they didn't even have each other.

There was a knock at the door. "Need anything?" Griffin called.

A repeat of earlier, Ivy almost said. "Actually, I would love a cup of tea."

"Coming up," he said. And within five minutes he was back with a tap on the door and a cup of what smelled like Earl Grey. He set it down on a small stepstool within her reach, then turned to go.

"Will you stay?" she asked, without meaning to. She felt her cheeks burn. "I don't mean in the tub, of course. I just mean, will you—"

He smiled and sat down on the tile floor, facing the tub.

Ivy scooped up a handful of bubbles and let it fall down. "This is what I did the night before my wedding—my almost wedding, I should say. I took a bubble bath. And I lay there and fantasized about my future. I was so excited to change my last name. To finally get rid of the Sedgwick that meant nothing to me. Ivy McLean. I must have repeated it to myself hundreds of times, written it out on napkins while having my morning coffee. Guess I'll be stuck with Sedgwick after all."

"The way I see it," Griffin said, "your name is what you make of it. Not what someone else has already made of it. Declan didn't know that. He thought he had to change it to escape from a family he didn't like. He didn't need to change his name to do that."

"But my name is so connected to my father's. I can't even say the name Sedgwick, see it written, without thinking of William. And how little the connection of the name meant to him."

"Yet he must have cared about you," Griffin said. "He came to warn you about marrying Declan."

Tears sprang to Ivy's eyes. "And I dismissed him. I told him I would marry Declan. And weeks later he was dead. Maybe it pushed him over the edge."

In moments, Griffin was sitting on the edge of the tub. He took her hands, bubbles and all. "Hey.

Your father's death wasn't your fault, Ivy. He was very sick. And you said that he wouldn't tell you why you shouldn't marry Declan. He wouldn't give you a reason."

"What *was* his reason?" Ivy asked. "I keep trying to figure that out. It had to be something related to Declan working at Sedgwick Enterprises."

"Well, why don't we pay a visit to some of Declan's former coworkers?" Griffin suggested.

"And I can go see William's lawyer to get another copy of the inheritance letter my father left me. It's null and void, since I didn't honor the conditions of the will. But I want to know what it says. Declan took the letter before I walked down the aisle." Ivy closed her eyes; all of this was too much.

"Let's take a break from the case," Griffin said. "For the rest of the night, let's not even talk about it."

Ivy nodded, her chin full of bubbles, and Griffin laughed. He reached over to wipe the soap away, but his fingers lingered on her jawline, on her cheeks. She caught his gaze.

"I lied before," she said.

He stared at her. "About?"

"Wanting you in the tub. I mean, I do want you in the tub."

He smiled and slowly removed his shirt, as if waiting for her to tell him no, that it was a bad idea. And it was. In every way but one. The one that was burning for him. And then his pants were on the floor. And then he stood naked before her. Drop-dead gorgeous. Every inch of him.

He slipped into the tub behind her and positioned her so that she sat between his legs, her back and head resting against his chest. He began massaging her shoulders, his strong hands easing away the knots. And then his hands reached around her to cup her breasts, gently massaging the fullness. She moaned softly, then turned herself around so that she was straddling him. She reached down amid the bubbles to find his erection, her hand caressing the rock-hard length of him.

He groaned and pulled her against him, crushing her mouth with his. And then Ivy lifted up to slide down upon him. Griffin grabbed hold of her slippery hips and thrust deep inside her as she rocked against him, wave after delicious wave of sensation pulsating through her entire body. He scooped up water with his hands and let it pour down her breasts, then teased her nipples with his tongue until Ivy screamed.

And then she couldn't take it anymore. She rocked against him until they both exploded. She lay against his soapy wet chest and then Griffin drained the tub and turned on the shower, the bubbles pooling at their feet. He stepped out of the tub and grabbed a thick blue towel and wrapped it around her, then took another and carefully dried her hair, his gaze never leaving hers.

But how do I know if this is real?

The thought flashed through her mind so suddenly that it startled her, the towel dropping into the tub. Griffin got another and wrapped her in it, tucking the ends into her cleavage.

Can I trust my judgment? she wondered. *Why can I believe in this? What makes this any different?*

She'd believed in Declan without batting an eye. And she'd been a big fool. She could well be making a big fool of herself again.

He leaned forward to kiss her, but Ivy inched away, suddenly scared. *If I can't trust myself, who can I trust?* She had no idea what it would take to get that back. But right now, she needed to be alone. To sleep alone.

"I—" She faltered. "I'm just not . . ."

"You don't owe me anything, Ivy. You've been through hell. Just take care of yourself."

She nodded and headed to her room, bereft as she shut the door behind her. She missed him already.

Ivy's cell phone rang. She grabbed it from her purse and checked the caller ID. She didn't recognize the number. But she did recognize the voice.

"Stay out of my business, Ivy. Or I'll kill you and my brother."

Griffin spent two hours at the precinct with the best experts in technology, but there was no way to trace the call. Declan had rigged it so that the call seemed to originate from several different cell phone towers. The guy was either self-taught in advanced subterfuge or he had his hooks in everywhere.

What was clear to Griffin was that Declan was watching them, was aware of their investigation, knew they'd been in contact with Laura Frozier. He'd clearly been in contact with someone they'd spoken to today.

Ivy had been waiting all this time in an empty interrogation room. Not the most comfortable or comforting of places to rest and recover from a call that had spooked her, but Griffin hadn't wanted to leave her in his apartment alone. When he tapped on the door and walked in, he found her bent over the table, writing furiously in her own little notebook.

She jumped up the moment the door opened. "Were you able to trace the call?"

He shook his head.

She sat back down. "I've been making a list. Of everyone I can think of whom Declan had contact with. Anyone who might be helping him. And I used the Internet to develop a list of wealthy single women he might be targeting."

Griffin had no doubt Declan was doing exactly that—victimizing some rich woman at that very moment. He shook his head. There was a time, albeit when Griffin was ten or eleven, that he thought Declan would be president of the United States. Or a five-star general. As a young kid, Declan Fargo had been a leader, fearless, coming up with the crazy, fun ideas that made other kids say, "Yeah, let's do it!" Griffin's favorite was when Declan had organized marches against his—and most of the other kids'—eight-thirty bedtimes. Twenty or so neighborhood kids with their posters and pickets, walking down Main Street.

But then Declan started taking his stunts to a dangerous level, climbing trees to jump into too-shallow rivers, standing on train tracks, a train bearing down on him, and leaping off at the last possible second. And then throwing rocks at cats and dogs had begun. And worse.

He shook off the memories. "Let's take it back to my place and do what we said we would earlier—forget it for tonight. You need a good night's sleep, Ivy. We'll start fresh in the morning."

"Did you say a good night's sleep?" she asked,

running a hand through her silky brown hair. "I can't imagine even managing to close my eyes."

"I'll tell you some really boring stories," he said. "You'll be asleep in no time."

She offered a small smile and stood up, slipping her notebook and pen into her purse. As they walked to his car, she said, "Somehow I can't see you having a boring story to tell."

"Oh, trust me," he told her, opening the passenger door for her. "My senior-year trip to the Grand Canyon, painstakingly detailed about the history of the place, the rock formation. You'd be snoring in two seconds."

She laughed, seeming to surprise even herself. "Maybe so."

Twenty minutes later, they were back in his apartment. But Ivy didn't go to the guest room. Instead, she went into his bedroom and lay down on his bed, fully dressed. He felt something shift inside of him, just slightly. Okay, more than slightly. Something in his chest.

She needed him. And he hadn't been needed— this way—in a long time.

He lay down beside her, and she spooned against him. "So, about those rock formations."

He smiled. "The Grand Canyon is seven thousand miles wide and forty-seven feet deep," he said in his best monotone, having absolutely no idea what the true measurements were. "Every year, tens of thousands of visitors . . ."

He went on and on, and within five minutes she was fast asleep, her rhythmic breathing irresistible. He felt himself drifting off, his last memory the fresh scent of her hair and her hand tightening around his.

* * *

Ivy awoke to a pounding headache and the smell of sizzling bacon, which strangely seemed to help the headache. She slowly sat up, vaguely aware that she was in a strange bed. A man's bed. For a moment, she had no idea where she was. And then Griffin's face came into focus in her mind, those gorgeous dark, dark eyes, the strong nose, those lips. The jaw with the hint of five o'clock shadow.

She'd fallen asleep in Griffin's bed. In his arms.

She smiled, despite herself and the headache, as a memory, in the dimmest recesses of her mind, came to her. Griffin telling her about the size of the Grand Canyon.

And then another memory came to her.

Stay out of my business. Or I'll kill you and my brother.

She pressed her hands to her temples and rubbed. Ivy hadn't quite been able to process that Declan was a killer. She knew, intellectually, that he was very likely Jennifer's murderer. But the part of her that had loved him, that had been dreaming of a future with him—with the man she'd *thought* he was—couldn't quite take it in. Until she'd heard his voice. Threatening her. Threatening Griffin. His own flesh and blood.

She closed her eyes, letting herself sink into the memories of how it had felt to be wrapped in Griffin's arms last night. Safe. It had felt so safe. To lie there, fully clothed, those strong arms tight against her—Ivy had felt protected. And that was something she'd never felt before.

As a girl, she'd quickly learned—and accepted—that she wasn't going to be "Daddy's little girl," which was fine with her. Well, sort of. She'd minded there for a while. Until she realized there was no Daddy. No father figure. No consistent man in her mother's life to make her link the word *man* with safety. Security. Strong arms. Declan had meant a lot of things to her, but she'd never thought of him as a safe haven. She'd never, honestly, felt a need for one.

So between growing up with no father and a mother who was more concerned with lunching with the ladies than her daughter's "petty" concerns over mean girls or teasing boys or her problems with having to write essays in which she didn't feel comfortable telling the truth about herself (like her summer vacations, for example), Ivy had relied on her friendship with Alanna. That friendship had gotten her through just about every crisis, big and small and every kind in between.

She'd learned self-reliance and a new kind of reliance—the reliance on friends. In middle school, which Ivy still winced to think about, a group of boys would say, "Hey, Ironing Board Chest, are you sure you're even a girl? Let's see!" and grab at her crotch. The old Ivy would have burst into tears and curled into a ball. But the new and improved Ivy began to think of them as criminals, mini thieves and murderers in training, and she started to get interested in police work, ridding the world of the grown-up versions of these tyrants. By high school, she'd buried herself in books, both fiction and nonfiction about police procedure, and she knew she was headed for a career in law enforcement. So by that time, she thought of her tormentors—those mean, vicious girls and the nasty boys—as assailants, then

herself as the cop she'd become. The girls she'd
ignore. The boys who'd dared to touch her, she'd
surprise by springing up with a martial arts move.

And as an adult, with four years behind her as a
police officer, she was self-confident. She hadn't
been expecting the man she chose to marry to be
hiding a dark side. She wasn't used to needing to
be protected. Wanting to be protected. But damn,
it felt good.

As her headache began to recede, she sat up
against the headboard and glanced around Griffin's bedroom. It reflected him. All clean lines. Masculine. She wouldn't mind just lying back down and
pulling the covers over her head for the rest of the
day. She'd never felt like she could do that before—
let someone else take care of things. But Griffin was
a take-care-of-things type of guy. And, from the delicious aromas wafting into the room, he could
cook, too.

She threw off the covers and padded into her
room, then took a quick shower and put on some
makeup, just a little pressed powder to help the
smudge of dark circles under her eyes. She added
a bit of blush to replace the wan, pale cheeks with
a bit of color. And a few brushes of mascara to
open up her eyes. Satisfied that she looked a little
more alive than she felt, she chose black pants and
a fitted, button-down white shirt and her comfortable black boots, then followed the delicious smell
of bacon.

"Good morning," Griffin said, sliding scrambled
eggs from a skillet onto two plates on the dining
room table. "Hope you're hungry."

"I am," she told him. "Surprisingly." And that was a

good sign. That she was getting back to herself. That the events of the past couple of days weren't controlling her. That Declan's threats weren't controlling her. "Thank you," she added as she sat down. He'd made coffee, too. And there was a glass of orange juice by her plate and a small bowl of red grapes.

"Sleep okay?" he asked, sipping his coffee.

"Thanks to you, yes," she said.

He stared at her for a moment, as though he hadn't expected her to say that. Something personal. She took the moment to study him, the way the light from the living room windows lit his dark hair, how good he looked in his dark green sweater, a tiny bit of a white T-shirt peering out of the V-neck. He wore jeans this morning. Faded. Sexy. And dark brown leather work boots. He was so startlingly handsome that Ivy had to look away.

It was time to get down to business. She'd had a night in his arms, a night to forget her troubles and sleep. But the bright light of morning meant facing reality.

"Griffin, what business does Declan want me to stay out of, anyway? His love life? Or could he be talking about something else?"

He took a bite of bacon. "His love life seems to be his only business," Griffin said. "My captain thinks we should lay low for a couple of days. Let Declan think he's scared us into backing off."

"Giving him a false sense of security," Ivy said, nodding. "It won't be easy to just do nothing. Not that I know what we're supposed to do. But I can't say I'm not relieved."

There was a knock at the door, and again, Griffin bolted up, motioned for Ivy to move to the living room, and padded to the side of the door, gun in hand. "Who is it?" he said.

"The happy couple!" came a perky male voice.

Griffin put his gun away and shrugged at Ivy with a questioning expression. He opened the door, and in walked Joey and a pretty young woman with platinum blond pigtail braids and very short, choppy bangs.

"We're engaged!" Joey announced, holding up his and the woman's entwined hands. A metallic ring glinted on her finger.

Engaged? Joey wasn't even out of high school! He was barely eighteen.

"This," Joey continued, his arms around the woman's thin shoulders, "is Julianna. My fiancée. Man, I love saying that. My fiancée. My fiancée."

Griffin and Ivy glanced at each other. Griffin let out the deep breath that Ivy was still holding in.

"And you two are the first to know," Joey continued, his mop of thick brown hair making him look even younger than he was. "We didn't even tell our parents yet. I love having this juicy a secret."

"It's nice to meet you, Julianna," Griffin said, shaking the girl's hand. He introduced Ivy, and after more handshaking, the two were invited to sit down to breakfast. They practically jumped into the chairs.

Ivy would bet that neither Julianna nor Joey cooked much. Or had much money for the coffee shop. Or groceries.

"Isn't the ring great?" Julianna said as she picked up a piece of buttered toast that she topped with a heap of scrambled eggs and a slice of bacon. "We got it on the street for only twenty bucks."

Ivy's gaze focused on Julianna's strange hair, the

short, choppy white-blond bangs that didn't move. The pigtails. She wore several layers of clothes, too, on her slight frame. She was pretty in an exotic way. But the *exotic* might have been eyeliner.

"And once I get a good job, I'll replace it with a real diamond," Joey added. "A whole carat." He scarfed down a piece of bacon. "Wow, this is really good. Guess we'll both have to learn how to cook now that we'll be living together," he said to Julianna, leaning over to kiss her on the cheek.

"Living together?" Griffin said. "Didn't you say Julianna had roommates?"

Joey nodded around a mouthful of scrambled eggs. "Yeah, but we're only going to crash in her room until we find our own place. We're thinking a nice one-bedroom with an exposed brick wall."

"I think those are going for twenty-five hundred minimum," Griffin said. "Without roaches, that is."

Julianna grimaced. "I hate bugs."

"Don't worry," Joey said. "Once I get a job and we combine our income, we'll have enough to get a studio. A really nice one. No roaches."

Not in this city, Ivy wanted to say, but held her tongue. Joey and Julianna would discover the reality the moment they opened up the real estate section of the newspaper. She wanted to jump up and shout, *For God's sake, kiddos, are you crazy? You're like twelve years old! Date. But stay in school, Joey! And forget the engagement until you're . . . thirty!*

"A part-time job after school might not pay much," Griffin pointed out, barely able, Ivy could tell, to contain himself. "Maybe you could postpone the engagement and the living together until after you graduate, Joe."

"Oh, I don't have to worry about school," Joey said, scooping more scrambled eggs onto his plate. "I'm dropping out."

Griffin froze. "What?" he shouted. "With three months left to graduate? No way, Joey. No. Your father would not want this for you."

Damn. He'd surprised himself. He hadn't expected to play the father card, but in this case, it was true.

Joey's cheeks flushed. "Um, Griffin, I totally respect you, but you don't know what my father wants. I think he'd want me to be happy. And Julianna makes me happy. I'm eighteen and can do what I want."

Griffin held the boy's gaze. "You *can* do what you want, Joe. But being an adult means making grown-up choices. Not choices that can destroy your future."

Joey shrugged and threw his fifth piece of bacon on his plate. "I'll be fine."

Griffin glanced at Ivy and shook his head, then turned back to Joey. "Did you go home last night?"

Joey pursed his lips. "Nope."

"Your parents must be worried out of their minds," Ivy said.

"Worried about *themselves*," Joey said. "They don't care about me. Or my father. *I'm* my dad's next of kin. And I'm eighteen. So I'm going to decide what's best for him. And what's best for me."

"Meaning?" Griffin asked.

"Meaning that my dad is going to come live with me. Us," he added, squeezing Julianna's hand.

Ivy watched Joey's fiancée turn white. She also put her bacon back on her plate, her appetite clearly lost. Ivy had no doubt that the lovebirds' engagement would last only until they hit fresh air.

That aside, from the moment Julianna had walked

in and sat down, the girl-woman had seemed more interested in the drama the situation was creating than the situation itself. Joey was in for some more drama over exactly where his father would or would not live. Once Julianna tired of that, she'd tire of Joey. And that would be that.

"We're going to tell my parents now," Joey said. "Right after we leave here. They're going to freak, but oh well."

Griffin let out a breath. "Joey, that doesn't sound like you."

"I'm a new man," Joey said. "So we'd better go, Jules."

"You won't get a decent job without a high school diploma," Griffin added. "You can forget about a decent apartment, too. Or eating. Or anything."

"I can get my GED," Joey retorted. "And go to college part-time. It might take a little longer, but—"

Griffin shook his head. "Joey, have you heard the expression 'cutting off your nose to spite your face'? Don't ruin your future to make your mother and stepfather angry. It'll be you who gets hurt most of all."

"Oh, man," Joey said. "I thought you were on my side." He stood up, grabbing another piece of toast. "Come on, Jules. Let's get out of here."

Julianna smiled at Ivy and Griffin. "Thanks for breakfast."

Once they left, Griffin rolled his eyes heavenward. "Well, she's talkative. 'Thanks for breakfast'? That's all she had to say?"

"She did mention the ring was only twenty bucks," Ivy put in.

"He's not dropping out of high school," Griffin said. "Over my dead body."

Ivy couldn't contain a little smile. "You really care about this kid, huh?"

He dropped down on the sofa and leaned his head back against the couch. "Yeah. I sure do."

"Well, I don't think you'll have to worry about Joey dropping out of school or running off to Las Vegas. Did you see Julianna's face when Joey said his father would live with them?"

He stared at her. "Now that's good police work."

She smiled. "She'll break his heart. Very soon. And these grandiose plans he has for his father are going to go up in smoke, too. He's going to be hurt, Griffin. And really need you."

Griffin nodded. "I'll be here. As long as he doesn't drop out of school. I couldn't take that." He let out a deep breath. "Declan dropped out of high school. Did you know that?"

Now it was Ivy's turn to shake her head. "He told me he was runner up for valedictorian. And that he'd graduated with honors from NYU." She took a seat next to Griffin on the couch, leaning her head back and staring up at the ceiling. "I just believed everything he said, like a total fool. Since I believed he was getting his MBA, and he did work for Sedgwick Enterprises—at least for a little while—I had no reason to think otherwise."

"He dropped out his senior year, early on," Griffin said. "I was in college, commuting and working part-time. I tried everything to get him to stay in school, even offered to let him live with me for the rest of the year. But I guess he thought he could scam his mother and stepfather easier than he could scam me.

He stayed put there, fooling his parents into thinking he had some amazing job writing software and working for IBM and Microsoft."

"Meaning that he was bringing money home?"

"He started out as a middleman for a loan shark, then for a car theft organization. Then he discovered it was easier to live off the money of unsuspecting wealthy women."

Ivy flinched.

"Hey, I didn't mean—"

Ivy offered a rueful smile. "Well, I know you couldn't mean me, given that I'm far from wealthy and never will be. Not on a small-town cop's salary."

"So you're sure your dad disinherited you?" Griffin asked.

Ivy nodded. "I'm sure. But I would like to go see his lawyer and find out what was in that letter I didn't open."

Ivy's cell phone rang. Alanna. "Ivy, I've got some bad news."

More bad news? She mentally braced herself. "I can take it."

"Your house was ransacked," Alanna said. "Torn apart. I'm so sorry." She hesitated, as if she'd started to say something and changed her mind.

"And?" Ivy said.

"And there's another message for you. This time, it was a piece of paper pasted on the wall, typewritten."

"What did it say?" Ivy asked, closing her eyes against what she was about to hear.

"I think you should just come out here. You and the detective."

"Alanna, what does it say?" she asked, her voice wound as tight as she felt.

Alanna hesitated, then said, "'I didn't think sleeping with brothers was your style, Miss Priss. But your whoring will make it easier to kill both of you in one shot.'"

Chapter Eleven

Hell, Griffin thought as he followed Ivy into her house, *someone sure wants to get a point across.* And that point, he knew, was that Ivy's life would be systematically destroyed if she didn't stop poking into Declan's life. This vandalism, so soon after the phone call, was Declan's way of assuring Ivy he would come at her rapid-fire. And that she herself would be next.

So was it Declan who was behind this? Or a girlfriend doing Declan's dirty work?

The note, typed on plain paper, gave little away. Someone knew he and Ivy were spending a lot of time together—that they were sleeping together was a bluff, Griffin would bet on it.

Would Declan be so brazen to come to Applewood, where people knew him, where the entire police department was on guard for him? If he showed his face in Applewood, he'd be in jail in two seconds. Then again, Declan wouldn't show the face everyone knew and had grown to hate. He would be in disguise.

Griffin glanced at Ivy, who stood in the middle of the wreckage. He could see she was trying to keep it together, to not break down. Again.

The sofa had been slit open, white stuffing everywhere. Two bookcases had been knocked over. Lamps, plants, everything had been overturned. But there was something unusual that struck Griffin, something he didn't often see in this type of large-scale damage: small, personal items had been destroyed. A music box that sat on the mantel had been smashed, for example. Pictures of Ivy and her sisters were flung across the room. Yet, more ordinary, less personal knickknacks were left alone. Which told Griffin that this was very personal. And potentially another woman. The *other* other woman. One who didn't like that Declan had been planning to go through with the wedding despite the fact that Ivy would likely inherit nothing. *Would* inherit nothing, as she'd ignored the instruction of the will by not opening her inheritance letter before the ceremony.

Declan had loved Ivy.

Griffin knew it now as surely as he knew his name. Declan had truly loved Ivy. There was no other reason to marry her. She had no money. And she was so honest a cop that she would never have breached her ethics to support his cons. She would have dumped him in a heartbeat had she known the truth about him.

So, Declan loved Ivy. Another woman in his life, either a victim or a grifter, didn't like it. Someone who knew Ivy, too, very likely.

So why had Jennifer Lexington ended up dead and not Ivy? Perhaps Jennifer had been killed by

Declan because she'd threatened to go public with his infidelity, ruin his good thing. His money machine. And perhaps this vandalism was simply aftermath, another woman so incensed by Declan's love of Ivy, despite her lack of money. And incensed that she was working with New York Homicide to trap Declan.

Maybe. There were a lot of maybes. Too many. Too many different scenarios and possibilities.

As Ivy picked up a smashed frame containing a picture of her and her sisters, trying to salvage the photograph inside, Griffin walked into the bedroom, already knowing what he would find. The bed would be slashed, perhaps covered in dirt or even pig's blood.

Bingo. Dirt. Which told him that he was on target about a jealous lover. Declan's cohort was spitting mad. Perhaps they'd gotten into a fight, and Declan had confessed to loving Ivy. Perhaps Declan was very upset that Ivy was staying with Griffin, and that had prompted the fight. Whatever it was, Griffin was sure he was looking for two people now. Declan and his inside lover.

He could feel Ivy's presence behind him, and when he turned around the look on her face almost killed him. She seemed to be . . . heartbroken. Her gaze was on her dressing table, and she moved in slow motion over to it. She covered her face with her hands and dropped down to her knees and sobbed.

Griffin rushed over to her and wrapped his arms around her. "What is it, Ivy?"

It took a minute for her to finally speak. "When I was seven, I met my father for the first time. Can you imagine that? Knowing you have a father out there, being aware of that, at four, five, and six, but being told that your father is scum, a word no young child should know, by the way, and that he wants nothing to do with you?"

"I'm so sorry, Ivy," Griffin whispered, stroking her hair.

"And then I finally got to meet him when I was seven. He decided to let his three daughters spend two weeks at his summer house in Maine. And that first day, he gave each of us a shell he'd picked up on the beach, a shell that he said reminded him of each of us. I remember thinking, 'But how could anything remind him of me when he's never met me till today?' But then I remembered that my mother inundated him with photographs of me, report cards from school, art projects, that kind of thing. And he put a shell in my hand and said, 'I picked this one for you because you can hear the ocean the loudest in it.'"

Griffin continued holding Ivy and gently wiped away her tears. "Why do you think he picked that one for you?"

She shrugged. "I don't really know. And I never asked him. I always had the sense that one day I would just know what it meant. And as I got older, I started thinking he meant that if I put it to my ear and listened, I would *feel* his love. That the roaring of the ocean inside the shell would say loud and clear what he couldn't." She glanced up at Griffin, her eyes shining with tears. "Stupid, huh?"

"Not at all, Ivy. And I think you're absolutely right."

"It was the only thing he'd ever given me."

His heart squeezed in his chest. "It's destroyed, isn't it?"

She shook her head. "No. That's the strange thing. It's not. It's the one precious thing to me that wasn't destroyed in this house."

Griffin stood up and stared at the shell on Ivy's dressing table. "Who knew about the shell and what it meant to you?"

"My sisters and I talked about it, about their shells, too, in the past few months. And I told Alanna about it, a long time ago, though. And Declan knew, of course. I also wrote about it a lot in my diary. The last time I wrote in it was the night before I was supposed to get married."

"I think you'd better look for it," Griffin said. But he had a feeling it was gone.

The drawers to the dressing table were already open, their contents strewn about. Ivy looked inside one of them, then shook her head.

"It might have been stolen before today," he said. "By the person who left you the note on your mirror. I'm not sure if it's Declan or the woman he's working with or both."

"Ivy!"

Griffin turned around to find Alanna rushing toward Ivy, tears in her eyes.

"I am so sorry about this," she told Ivy, wrapping her in a hug. "I went back to the station house to file the report. I was driving by when I saw the door open, and when I checked on the house, I saw the wreckage."

He stared at Alanna, at her worried expression, at the protective way she hugged Ivy. Why was he so suspicious of the woman? There was no reason to suspect her, other than his gut instinct that first night, when she'd been prowling outside Ivy's house. Yeah, her explanations had made sense, but still, something nagged at him.

"I need to get out of here," Ivy said. She scooped up the shell and put it in her purse.

"Ivy," called an Applewood police officer from the living room, "would you mind just answering a few routine questions? And then we'll clean up for you."

Ivy nodded and woodenly walked over to the group of officers.

Alanna was surveying the damage in the bedroom, shaking her head. Nothing on her face remotely registered guilt.

"So, Officer Moore," Griffin said, "I'm thinking that Declan has an accomplice. A female accomplice. Someone who likely knows Ivy. Is there anyone you can think of who might have fallen prey to Declan?" If it was Alanna herself, he wanted to catch her reaction. And if it wasn't her, perhaps she could be of help in determining who it was.

"Please call me Alanna," she said. "Ivy is surrounded by good people. People who really care about her. Could it be that other fiancée?"

"Perhaps," he responded, unable to read beyond the straightforward answers, the concerned expression. Either she was as good as Declan at lying with a straight face, or she was true-blue. He had no idea which at this point.

For Ivy's sake, Griffin hoped for the latter.

The next morning, Ivy pulled open the imposing double doors to her father's attorney's office in midtown Manhattan, her heels clicking on the polished marble floor. She remembered the first time she'd come, back in December, with Declan beside her for the reading of the will. Now, as she would read the letter her father had left for her, Declan's *brother* stood beside her. Bizarre.

Last night, she'd again slept in Griffin's arms, fully clothed. Griffin seemed to know that she was numb. He simply laid down with her, put his strong arm across her stomach, and stroked her hair until she finally fell asleep. And when she woke up this morning, there was a full breakfast again and a pot of coffee.

She could get used to that. To sleeping curled in Griffin Fargo's arms. To the comfort. To the breakfast.

He'd understood about the shell. Despite the fact that Ivy had no relationship with her father, despite that there was no good reason why a shell from a beach should mean so much to her. Griffin understood. And he'd let her feel what she'd felt last night, asking her questions about her dad, about their short summer vacations together at the house in Maine. Griffin had suggested they go see her father's attorney first thing in the morning and get to the bottom of what was in the letter.

Ivy tried to imagine having to do this alone, be here, in this impersonal office building, her heart hammering, her hands shaking, trying to form sentences with a lawyer she'd met only once before. If she was supposed to feel her father's presence in the building, she didn't.

Thank you for being here, she said silently to Griffin as the elevator carried them upward. They rode in silence, and Ivy appreciated how Griffin always seemed to know when she needed quiet, when she needed to be alone with her thoughts, her fears.

"He has no idea what he threw away," she said, surprising herself. She hadn't meant to actually say the thought aloud.

He glanced from the row of floor numbers lighting up above the elevator door to Ivy. "I think he does. I think he did love you, Ivy."

She bit her lip. "I wasn't talking about me, Griffin."

He glanced at her, clearly confused.

"I was talking about you," she said. "How Declan has no idea what he missed out on by being such a crummy person and having no morals or values. I would have loved to have had a brother like you when I was growing up. Not that I think of you like a brother," she added quickly. And immediately felt like a fool.

Those dark, dark eyes lit for a moment. "Thank you."

She held his gaze, feeling like her heart might burst, and then thankfully the elevator doors pinged open.

In moments, Ivy and Griffin were ushered into a wood-paneled reception room, then led into another reception room. Ivy tried to stop tapping her foot and crossing her legs and sighing audibly. Griffin, to his credit, let her fidget.

"Miss Sedgwick."

Ivy glanced up, and there stood George Harris, her father's attorney. "Mr. Harris, this is Detective Griffin Fargo of the New York City Police Department."

The attorney shook Griffin's hand, then said, "I'm sorry you came all this way, Miss Sedgwick. But as you know, the letter and its contents are null and void, as you didn't open it per the terms of the will."

"I understand that," Ivy said. "But I would like to read the letter. I'd like to know what it said."

What was in that letter? Would it tell her why her father had been against the marriage? Or would it tell her that she was a disgraceful daughter for not heeding her powerful father's warning?

"Don't you have the letter?" Mr. Harris asked over the rim of his glasses.

"I'm afraid it was stolen," Ivy said. "By my former fiancé."

The attorney's expression remained neutral. "Ah. I understand completely. Please follow me."

They were led to a very small room with two chairs and a desk. He left briefly, returning with an envelope. "This contains a copy of the original that you received." He nodded, then left Ivy and Griffin alone.

Ivy turned it over, closed her eyes, and then said, "Here goes."

Dear Ivy,
Declan McLean is not worthy of you. I cannot reveal why. If you marry him, however, I bequeath you nothing upon my death.
All best, your father, William Sedgwick

All best? Ivy crumpled the letter and threw it on the floor.

Griffin picked it up and read it. "You okay?"

"All best," Ivy repeated. "What kind of closing is that?"

There came a knock at the door, and the attorney entered. "Miss Sedgwick, in the event that you did not marry Mr. McLean, your father instructed me to leave you another envelope, separate from the one you picked up on your wedding day." He handed her an envelope, then left the office again.

Ivy stared at Griffin. What was in this one? She ripped it open.

> *Dear Ivy,*
> *In the event that you do not marry Declan McLean, I bequeath to you my secret property in Manhattan. You may not like it in spirit, as it is where I had my dalliances, but it is where I felt the most love, however brief. I was not one for monogamy and had many affairs, but I loved each woman that I spent time with, however briefly.*
> *Your father, William Sedgwick*

A secret property? Ivy realized there was something else in the envelope. She slid it out. It was a key. Taped to the key was a tiny piece of paper with an address in lower Manhattan.

She handed the letter to Griffin. "This is the first I've heard of a secret property."

"I wouldn't be surprised if your father intended it as a safehouse for you, Ivy. Somewhere that no one, except for his attorney, knew about."

"And his girlfriends," Ivy pointed out.

"Let's go visit this secret apartment," Griffin said.

Ivy understood why the apartment was secret. It was practically a bunker. The building itself was a brownstone with an elegant storefront, a jewelry shop. The key opened the door to the right of the jewelry shop, and then two more steel doors. Down a flight of stairs was yet another steel door.

"He was either expecting to survive World War Three or a few jealous husbands," she said as she unlocked the door at the bottom of the stairs.

There, all similarities to a bunker ended. They stepped into utter luxury. It was small, with just one bedroom, and the two tiny windows with a view of people's feet barely let in light, but the apartment was like an opulent harem.

The living room held an overstuffed cream-colored sofa with throw pillows and a love seat. A thick, expensive-looking wool rug in soothing shades covered most of the floor. On the wall across from the sofa was a fifty- or sixty-inch flat-screen television. A beautiful antique desk held a computer. The walls were painted a pale salmon, one of Ivy's favorite colors, and there were beautiful paintings and sculptures.

The kitchen was fully stocked. Ivy opened the refrigerator, which was full of fresh food. The carton of milk wouldn't expire for a week. The attorney had explained that William's private instructions had left provisions for a weekly housekeeper starting on the day Ivy was to be married.

"And if I had married Declan?" she'd asked Mr. Harris.

"The apartment would have gone to someone else," was all the attorney would say.

"The Internet connection works," Griffin called from the living room. "You know, this is an ideal place for us to do our 'laying low.' As long as we have a computer with Internet access, we can do our research."

Ivy walked back into the living room and sat down on the sofa, which was plush and inviting. "It's so sickening to think of Declan romancing some unsuspecting woman, making her believe in something that's a huge and terrible lie. How can he not care what he does to people? To women with whom he has such intimate relationships?"

She felt her cheeks burning. She didn't exactly want to call attention to the fact that she had had many an intimate moment with Declan. She wondered if it bothered Griffin.

If it did, his expression didn't show it. "Preying on wealthy women is the only way he can survive— the only way he wants to survive, I should say. And we know he has to be laying low himself. So we'll find him by finding her. Between the list you already made while at the precinct and others we'll find, we'll find him."

Ivy nodded. "How many wealthy single women do you think there are in New York City? I'd say we have quite a few to weed through." She let out a deep breath. "Good thing we have a stocked fridge."

"You ready to get to work? Or do you need some time to yourself?"

"I'm ready to work," she said, her appreciation for him and his thoughtfulness growing by the nanosecond.

Two hours later, they had quite a list of names. They'd started with the Lexingtons, the Froziers, and the Sedgwicks, culling guest lists from recent fundraisers and parties, then researching who from that list was single. Griffin figured that in Declan's desperation to latch on to someone quickly, he would choose a woman whom he'd met before, someone who'd potentially recognize him from a society party yet not be able to place him. He would change his hair color, of course. And colored contacts would take care of his baby blues. Glasses, a certain cut of clothes. And Declan McLean could become whomever he wanted. And whom he wanted to be was the husband of several rich women.

This time, Declan very likely didn't have the luxury of waiting for someone's rich father to die.

"There are over twenty names on our list," Ivy said, rolling her neck to get out the kinks of the past two hours. "Who should we start with? And how exactly are we supposed to find out if any of them are involved with Declan—especially when we don't know what name he's using."

"Easy," Griffin said, tapping his pen against the thick sheaf of papers he'd printed out. "Old detective trick. We call, say we're reporters doing a story on how the rich and famous wed these days. Those who are engaged or planning to marry will yap away with details. And we'll ask pointed questions. We'll be able to cross off most with one phone call. And any who say they're engaged or might become engaged, we'll investigate further. Perhaps one will even announce her fiancé's name. Someone with the initials DM."

Ivy let out a deep breath. "And then we let her lead us to him."

"We let her lead him to *me*, Ivy. I don't need to remind you how dangerous he is."

He was right about that. She nodded, then stood up and stretched. "I could use a break. How about I make you lunch?"

"Can you cook?" he asked, a teasing glint in his eye.

"Not as well as you, but I can make a great tuna fish sandwich. And I saw some Portuguese bread in the breadbox."

"Sounds delicious," he said, poring back over his notes.

Ivy headed into the kitchen, aware that she'd started humming. Humming. She felt oddly comfortable in this strange apartment. *Because I feel safe,* she realized. *And because Griffin is here.* Her father hadn't cut her out of his will after all. Had he left her a poem or another shell, anything whose value would be strictly sentimental, she would have been just as pleased. She wasn't quite sure why it mattered so much to be remembered, to be included by William Sedgwick. But it did matter to her. It made her feel as though he was trying to do from the grave what he couldn't do in life. Share something of himself. Even if it was the place where he'd romanced the many women in his life.

She was also able to hum a happy tune because she and Griffin had a plan. It allowed Ivy to feel a sense of control.

She set about making lunch, adding fresh lettuce and cucumber and tomatoes to the sandwiches. Whoever did the shopping knew their produce.

She set down their plates at the small dining room table that was set off from the living room. A tiny blue glass vase held daisies, Ivy's favorite flowers. She wondered if that was coincidence. She doubted it.

"I'm trying not to imagine William Sedgwick and his lover of the day here," she said, placing a pitcher of iced tea on the table. "Sitting at this very table eating a sandwich together."

Griffin sat down. "I know something about fathers and their affairs. It's pretty sickening. I just can't even imagine loving someone enough to marry them and then cheating on them."

Ivy smiled. "Me, too. Your brother, however, stands for the other side."

"I wouldn't think Declan would have the energy to keep all those balls in the air," Griffin said. "Remembering who he said what to, remembering where he was supposed to spend the night. Three fiancées? Three families to meet. Three sets of friends."

She nodded. "Does seem almost impossible. But he never gave me any reason to doubt him. Maybe because I didn't see him all that much. Maybe because I didn't want to question anything."

"You said before that Declan was your first big love."

Again Ivy's cheeks flamed. "Maybe if I'd had more experience, I would have realized something was strange about the way he conducted our relationship."

"Two other women didn't seem to," he pointed out.

That was true. But then again, maybe they had. Maybe they fought often about where Declan was when he wasn't with them. But Ivy supposed Jennifer Lexington believed that her resident fiancé was sleeping on a cot at the hospital after a grueling shift. And Laura believed similar lies. Declan was clearly very good at keeping his lies believable.

Griffin took a huge bite of his sandwich. "This is delicious. You can cook."

"Well, I can mix," she said. She put her sandwich down, suddenly not hungry. "God, you must think I'm a moron."

"Ivy, that's the last thing I think. You fell in love.

Nothing wrong with that. And I remember how charismatic Declan was, even as a teenager. He stole a girlfriend or two of mine."

An important girlfriend? she wondered. *A serious girlfriend?* "Do you hate him?" she asked, holding his gaze.

"I hate what he does to people. What he might have done to Jennifer Lexington. I hate what he did to you."

She nodded. "Me, too."

He slid his hand across the table and she put hers into it. She had no idea what would happen between them once this case was solved—if it were solved—but she knew one thing. Griffin was her friend.

And she loved him.

She sat up straight and slipped her hand from his, the truth of what she'd just realized almost as frightening as feeling it in the first place.

I am in love with you, she thought, watching him watch her. She hoped one of his many talents wasn't the ability to read minds.

Obviously not, because he continued to eat his sandwich, every last bite, then had some of the chocolate pie she'd dished up. And then he returned his attention to his notes.

"I'm going to take a closer look around this place," she told him.

He nodded and smiled and she headed down the hallway, which led to the bedroom. It was a good size and beautifully decorated. It was a woman's room, she realized. The walls were a soft rose, and the dark wood four-poster bed, etched with rosebuds, was draped with white muslin and covered in a downy quilt and many soft pillows. Photographs of

Ivy as a child, as a teenager, as a young woman adorned the bureau. Ivy wondered if they had been her father's, or if he'd simply had them placed here after his death. It was a nice touch, in any case.

Griffin appeared in the doorway. "Nice room. I seriously doubt it looked this way when your father used this place."

"Why would he go to all that trouble to redecorate for me when he didn't even know if I'd marry Declan or not?" she asked.

"Maybe he had faith."

"He shouldn't have; I *was* going to marry Declan. If it wasn't for you—"

"Still, you didn't. You were stopped in the nick of time. The universe is looking out for you."

She smiled. "I sure hope so." She moved over to the photographs. "Want to see a picture of me as a gawky fourteen-year-old?"

He laughed and picked up the photograph, tracing her teenaged face with his finger. "You were as beautiful then as you are now."

"Oh, thanks a lot," she said with a laugh.

"I mean it, Ivy. I think you're absolutely beautiful."

She looked in his eyes; she could tell he was serious. He put the photograph down and lifted her chin with his finger, then kissed her. Gently. She wrapped her arms around his neck and he pulled her close, so close she could feel the strain of his erection against her thigh.

And then he kissed her over to the bed, where he lay her down and trailed his lips up her neck, then down.

"Make love to me," she whispered.

In answer, Griffin unbuttoned her shirt, slowly,

seeming to savor the moment when he would see her cleavage and the mounds of her breasts over her pale yellow lacy bra. He stared at her and a groan escaped his lips.

He took off her shirt and then her bra, bringing the scrap of lace to his face, inhaling her perfume. He leaned over her, caressing her breasts, teasing the taut nipples with his tongue until she arched her back and moaned. She grabbed a fistful of his hair as his tongue flicked and teased over the swollen peaks.

Slowly, he took off her pants and groaned again at the sight of her matching lacy yellow underwear. And then he took off his own pants and practically threw off his shirt. He slid a finger inside her panties and she almost let out a scream.

He smiled against her lips, then kissed her deeply as his hands wriggled her underwear down her legs and off. He was now completely naked himself and pulled her on top of him. She trailed her soft lips across his chest and down to his rock-hard stomach and lower, his groans becoming more hoarse.

And then she wrapped her hand around his erection, and explored the head with her lips, then teased along the shaft with her tongue, her hand moving up and down, down and up.

"Ivy," he groaned, grabbing her hair, reaching for her breast again.

She explored him until she thought he might explode, her lips tantalizing every inch of him. And when she kissed her way back up to his neck, her breasts against his rough chest, he flipped her onto her back and caressed every inch of her body with his own tongue—her breasts, her stomach, her belly button. And while he ran one hand over her breasts again and again, he slipped a finger inside her, sliding in and out, toying and teasing until she groaned. And groaned again. And then he followed his finger with his tongue until she cried out.

He took his time, alternating between teasing with a slide of his finger, a lick of his tongue and full throttle exploration of the depths of her femininity. When she moaned and writhed, he smiled and kissed his way to her breasts again, caressing and massaging one while he licked and suckled the other. And then he switched, all the while letting the rock-hard length of him press and poke against her.

"Griffin, I have to have you now," she breathed haggardly.

He couldn't seem to wait any longer, either. He raised up and leaned over her, meeting her beautiful blue eyes, and eased into her, slowly at first. She closed her eyes against the pleasure, moaning. He thrust, then eased out until she arched her back and grabbed his hips to pull him back in.

He thrust quickly into her, into the softness, the tightness, the wet-hot center of her. She was meeting his movements and moaning and crying out, her hands, her nails gripping his back. And finally, he exploded with a groan and collapsed onto her.

They lay there for a little while, in silence, their breathing and heartbeats the only sounds. And then Griffin reached for her hand and held it.

"What am I going to do with a secret apartment, anyway?" Ivy asked, her breathing still quick.

"I think we've made pretty good use of it," he said, turning onto his side to face her.

She laughed and held onto his hand, afraid for

this moment to go, for him to suddenly get up, revert back to detective mode.

"I'm glad the seashell wasn't destroyed," he said in almost a whisper. "I didn't have the greatest relationship with my father and I lost a lot of respect for him over the years, but he was still my dad. I have some of his things, things that meant something to him, and they help make me feel connected. So I think I understand what that shell means to you. What this place means to you."

Her heart squeezed in her chest, and she nodded around the sudden lump in her throat. There he went again, making her fall in love with him every five minutes. "Having some of your dad's things must have helped a lot when he was in the nursing home. That sense of connection, of memory, of having pieces of him."

He nodded and squeezed her hand, then closed his eyes, and Ivy had the sense that this kind of conversation was a lot for Griffin to take, that he didn't often *have* these conversations, except perhaps with Joey. And with the teen, he was probably able to feel less vulnerable since Joey was the kid, the one who needed *him*. Though Ivy was pretty sure Griffin needed Joey just as much.

She closed her eyes, too, hard as it was to look away from his face, his profile. *I love you, I love you, I love you,* she said silently over and over.

And then she yawned and curled up next to him, the sound of his heartbeat lulling her to a much-needed nap.

Chapter Twelve

"Hello, Miss Beckham," Griffin said into the telephone, tapping at the third name on his list of engaged "society" types in Manhattan. "I'm a reporter from *Manhattan Life and Times* magazine, and I'm doing a story on lavish wedding plans. I understand that you're recently engaged, and I'm hoping you'll answer a few questions for our piece."

Would she ever. In fact, she didn't stop talking for twenty minutes. Within the first two, she mentioned the name of her fiancé, Dean Markington.

Bingo. DM. Declan's favorite pair of initials.

In the next ten minutes, Griffin, plus one, was invited to a party tonight at Cornelia Beckham's Upper East Side town house.

There were four names on the list of "Declan's Possible Brides." Cornelia Beckham, Jane Faria, Elizabeth Ellsworth, and Paris Lamet. Jane and Elizabeth also went on a bit, both describing their fiancés as elderly. Declan could fake a lot, but being eighty wasn't one of them.

He would start with Miss Beckham.

Griffin stood up from the desk chair and stretched, then headed into the bedroom to check on Ivy. She was still fast asleep. After everything she'd been through so recently, she needed the catnap.

He watched her, watched her chest rise and fall. Her beautiful face was so at peace. He wasn't sure if bringing Ivy—they would both be in disguise, of course—to the party tonight was such a good idea. But he could use the extra pair of eyes, someone who knew Declan, knew him intimately in a way that only a woman who'd been in love with him could, someone who'd be able to spot him, even in the disguise Griffin knew his brother would be in. Dyed hair, colored contacts. Ivy had most definitely been in love with Declan. And Griffin had a feeling she would be able to pick him out right away.

Had been in love. Why was he so sure about the past tense? *Was* still in love? He couldn't imagine the heart still pining for someone who'd done what Declan had. Even if Declan wasn't the murderer—and Griffin was sure he was—Declan had surely killed Ivy's feelings for him. But maybe that wasn't the way the heart worked. There were countless true stories about women who'd fallen in love with convicted murderers—murderers who'd confessed—and even married them while they served life without parole. The mind, and more often the heart, believed what it wanted to, what it needed to, perhaps.

He tore his gaze away and headed back into the living room to call his captain and fill him in on the plans, then walked over to the windows and stared out at nothing in particular.

Samantha's face floated into his mind. Five years ago, she'd been a beat officer in his precinct when Griffin had fallen hard for her. She was tough, even a little gritty. And Griffin knew she would make a great cop, an excellent detective. They'd started dating, and Griffin had loved how easy it was to date within the force. Samantha understood him instantly; if he was quiet, she immediately—and correctly— thought it was because he'd been through the ringer on the streets, not because something was wrong with their relationship.

The first time she'd had to fire her gun was also the first time he'd seen her vulnerable side. And the way she'd opened up to him opened up something in him. He'd fallen in love.

And Declan, the bastard, was clearly watching. Waiting to pay his brother back for cutting off his freebies around the city. Griffin hadn't had a clue that Declan was romancing Samantha on the nights they weren't together. And this time he wasn't an MBA student or a resident. He was supposedly a special agent, FBI. And Samantha had always dreamed of going that route. And so she did him "little favors" that at first she didn't know were illegal. And even when she knew, when she knew that he was clearly a bad FBI agent, she still provided him with information that enabled him to bilk a civilian out of half a million dollars. When he had enough money, he was through with her. And he made sure Griffin knew exactly what his girlfriend had done. Sexually. Criminally. And otherwise.

And Declan had waited to see what the supposed big man of integrity would do. Turn in the woman he loved?

Past tense. His heart had turned cold against Samantha the moment he'd discovered what she'd done. But he'd long believed in hating the deed and not the doer, unless he could help it. And with Samantha, the strength she'd once had, that grit that had initially attracted him, had been rubbed away by a very talented con man with a special gripe against her—she was his hated brother's girlfriend.

Griffin hadn't had to worry about turning in Samantha or not. She'd killed herself the night she discovered she'd been had. That the life of lies she created for herself was precipitated on a bigger lie. She took two bottles of sleeping pills.

And it was Griffin who'd found her.

Those pretty brown eyes of hers, her long red hair, the dreams she'd had, all those memories faded from his mind as Griffin looked out at the city that had given him so much and taken so much away. He let thoughts of her fade away; he could barely take thinking of her, of what could have been.

When he thought of how he didn't hate Samantha, despite her betrayal of him and the police force, he thought of Ivy and how she might very well not be able to hate Declan.

Complicated, to say the least.

Forget trying to push thoughts of Ivy out of his mind. He couldn't if he wanted to.

Instead, he summoned up Declan's sinister face. Griffin would catch him and bring him in. That was all there was to it.

Come out, come out wherever you are, little brother.

* * *

Ivy's eyes slowly opened and a lazy smile stretched across her face.

Griffin.

He wasn't there in bed with her. Which meant she had a moment to lay there and remember every delicious sensation of their lovemaking. She traced her lips with her fingers, the imprint of his firm mouth still stamped.

She reluctantly got out of bed and dressed, then headed back to the living room, where Griffin was bent over the desk, furiously writing in his notebook, the computer whirring beside him.

"Hi," she said. Something about the tense set of his shoulders worried her.

He turned around with a quick, "Hey," then returned his attention to his work.

Okay. Something was wrong.

Just ask him, she told herself. *Don't be passive-aggressive and sulk on the sofa. Ask.*

"Griffin, everything okay?"

He didn't turn around. "Well, we have a murder suspect to bring in, one that happens to be your former fiancé and my half brother, so no, I wouldn't say everything was okay."

She stared at his back. *Jerk.*

She turned to head into the kitchen, to get away from him and whatever had set him off, which she naturally assumed was their lovemaking. Maybe they were getting too close for his liking.

"Ivy," he said, finally turning to face her. "I didn't mean—" Whatever he didn't mean he didn't finish. "Look, I've got to head over to the station and pick up some undercover wear for us. We've been invited to Cornelia Beckham's party tonight." He filled her in on their conversation. And that her fiancé's initials were none other than DM.

The thought of being in the same room—the same house—as Declan made her stomach twist. What would it be like to see him now? To stand before him? Would he apologize for what he'd done, the lies he'd told?

Would he confess to killing Jennifer Lexington?

Right. He would just up and confess to murdering one of his three former fiancées at his current fiancée's home. A party full of witnesses, no less!

And so they locked up the strange "secret property" and headed back to Griffin's apartment, where he simply deposited her inside. "I'll be back within an hour," he said. "Don't open the door to anyone. *No one.* Not even Joey if he should happen to come by. Okay?"

She nodded and tried to read his expression. Where was this strain coming from? This uneasy tension? How had they gone from the intimacy of making love, of being as physically close as two people could be, to this?

The moment the door closed behind him, she felt his absence. She sat down on the sofa and clutched a pillow to her chest, trying to give herself some time to think. More like to order herself not to get all worked up over Griffin's mood. His sudden withdrawal. It wasn't just his tone that had done unsettling things to her stomach. It was the very air around him, as if it had closed off.

You have better things to do than analyze the state of your relationship, Ivy Sedgwick. Ah. There was that word. Relationship. They didn't have one. Not in the traditional sense. They were working together.

Or more realistically, Griffin was utilizing her in the capture of a murder suspect. He was protecting her from said murder suspect. And one thing had led to another to the point that he was protecting her at very close range.

What are you doing, Ivy? she asked herself. Getting whooped upside the head by a con man was one thing. Setting herself up for heartbreak was another.

She forced herself to get to work, to go over the notes Griffin had shared with her about Cornelia Beckham. In her early forties, Cornelia was thrice-divorced from wealthy men and had no children. That would make her especially alluring to Declan. Pots of money and no children to deal with. Ivy wondered what Declan made himself out to be this time. Perhaps an independently wealthy playboy who'd fallen madly in love with Cornelia—Neely to her friends—the moment he laid eyes on her.

If he were Dean Markington, Cornelia's fiancé. Sure sounded like he was.

Her research for the party complete, Ivy got up and walked around, her gaze taking in the apartment. Not that there was much to take in. Griffin wasn't exactly a knickknack kind of guy.

She felt slightly guilty about opening the hall closet, but did so under the pretense of hanging up her coat, which she'd laid over the sofa. Just a closet and gave nothing away. Nothing out of the ordinary in there. A few pairs of sneakers. Dress shoes. Work boots. A wool overcoat and a trench coat. A couple of umbrellas.

As she headed back to the living room, she could just see Griffin confused and grumpy at Target, forced to buy a bath mat and shower curtain, a set of glasses, a microwave. The basic things you needed to set up an apartment. A woman certainly hadn't helped him shop or decorate. There were no extras in the apartment, except for one painting of a spare tree in wintertime. She wondered if that was how Griffin always felt.

The living room contained a brown leather couch with the requisite beige throw pillows and a beige throw. She smiled at the idea of Griffin at a furniture store, the saleswoman suggesting this or that, and Griffin nodding at whatever didn't make him cringe. There was a beige sisal rug on the floor and a glass coffee table, no bowl or vase or photos decorating it. Just a lone white coffee mug resting on top of today's *New York Times*, *New York Post*, and *New York Daily News*.

He was lonely, she knew. He'd led a lonely, solitary life, and she wondered if Declan had something to do with that. His brother was a grifter, a con man, and had been since childhood. And Griffin became a cop. He hadn't been able to stop Declan from a life of crime, but he'd been drawn to save the people he could.

She stood by the door of his bedroom, which was open. She wouldn't go in, wouldn't invade his privacy, despite having slept in there a time or two, but she couldn't help taking a look. It was the same as the living room. Same colors, same lack of personal touches. But there was a photo leaning against a stack of books on a shelf. It wasn't in a frame, and Ivy couldn't see well enough. She would take just a tiny peek, then hurry out.

It was a photograph of Griffin and Declan and their father. It was taken when the Fargo boys were children. Griffin looked no older than twelve or even thirteen, Declan around ten. Declan had actually shown Ivy some family photos—none of which included Griffin. Now, she was surprised he had. Usually con men kept their pasts completely a secret. Because they lived such lies, and told so many, they typically couldn't remember what was real or not. But Declan had spoken of his childhood in happy enough terms. As far as Ivy had known, the supposed estrangement with his "mean" half brother and his "uncaring" father had occurred during the past few years.

Naturally, Declan was as devilishly cute a boy as he was handsome a man. Smiling, of course. Whereas Griffin wasn't. Their father stood in the middle and had an arm around each of his boys. Mr. Fargo had a sternness in his face, an unkind quality in his dark eyes. But Ivy knew better than to judge a person by a photo.

"I don't know why I keep that out."

Ivy whirled around, her cheeks burning. She hadn't even heard his key in the lock.

"I—"

He came up behind her and picked up the photo from the shelf. "This was taken before Declan really turned, when he still could have gone either way, good or bad. He was eleven." He shook his head. "That was back when I still thought of him as my brother. When I tried to protect him from himself." He stared at that picture, then handed it to Ivy and walked out of the room.

Damn.

She glanced at the photograph again, at young Griffin, the way he squinted against the sunshine, the way he looked so directly at the camera. Declan's impish expression indicated that he might have been ready to stick out his tongue at any moment. And their father, despite the harshness Ivy saw in his expression, had his arms around his boys. Ivy was struck by the realization that the two people in the photograph were lost to him forever.

She placed the photo carefully back where it had been, then joined Griffin in the living room. He was busy laying out items from a small duffle bag onto the sofa. Wigs. Eyeglasses. Something that looked like a press-on goatee.

She wanted to say something, to apologize for invading his space, for entering his bedroom, touching his things, but he picked up one of the wigs from the sofa, slapped it on his head and grimaced, and she laughed and so did he. She supposed he was telling her it was okay. Or, perhaps, that he didn't want to talk about it.

A little part of Ivy believed he was telling her it was okay for her to be in his bedroom, that she was part of his life now, not just part of his all-consuming investigation.

"If you've ever wanted to try life as a blonde," he said, gesturing at the items on the sofa, "now's your opportunity."

She picked up the medium-length, dark blond wig with bangs. "I'm happy with my dark hair," she said. "But so was Declan. Have you noticed that he seems to go for brunettes?"

Griffin stared at her. "You're absolutely right."

"In this, he won't look twice at me," she said, slapping the wig haphazardly on her head. She smiled. "But in that"—she pointed at the shoulder-length, mousy brown one—"he would be offering to refill my drink."

Griffin smiled. "Then blond for a night, it is. For both of us." He reached in the duffel and pulled out furry blond stick-on eyebrows, then handed her less furry ones.

"Let me go adjust this thing," she said, pointing to her head. "And figure out how the heck to get these eyebrows on straight."

He nodded, his expression less strained than it had been when he'd gone. "Me, too." He picked up a pair of glasses. "Don't forget your specs. You know you can't see a thing without your glasses, dear."

She laughed as she took her bounty and headed to the bathroom. It was good to hear him tease again.

Ivy stood before the mirror above the sink, positioning the wig, easy enough considering her hair was short. She turned to the left and right, admiring the way she looked, actually. Not bad as a blonde. She looked like an entirely different person. The length and bangs and color strangely suited her, her pale complexion and her blue eyes. She never would have pegged herself for a blonde at heart.

Ivy added the glasses and smiled at her reflection. She sort of looked like a newscaster with the horn-rims.

For a good couple of hours she would be able to be this woman in the mirror, this blond reporter from the fictitious *Manhattan Life and Times*. She'd need a code name, of course, and would suggest a name she'd always liked: Anne. Or perhaps Lucy.

And for those couple of hours, she would get to be this completely different person, Anne or Lucy, a woman invited to parties by her handsome coworker—she wondered what name Griffin would choose—and whose only problem was figuring out which wealthy New Yorker had the most lavish of wedding plans.

She wouldn't be, say, a cop who had no idea if she had any business being a cop anymore. A woman who couldn't choose a fiancé to save her life. Literally. A woman who was staying with a homicide detective for her "own protection." Who was sleeping with said homicide detective and having no idea what they were doing.

A woman who just realized there was absolutely nothing in her suitcase that she could wear to a fancy party.

She poked her head out of the bathroom. "Griffin, you don't happen to have a cocktail dress in that duffel bag, do you? I'm afraid I'll stand out if I'm in slacks and a sweater."

"Already thought of and taken care of," he said, holding up a plastic dress bag on a hanger. "I estimated your size. We detectives are pretty good at that. And I got your shoe size from the pair in your room."

Did he actually go shopping for me? she wondered, eyeing the dress bag. A ratty old dress from the disguise bin at the precinct very likely didn't come wrapped in unmarred plastic.

He was blushing a bit, she realized, as he handed her the bag and the shoe box. Detective Griffin Fargo *had* gone shopping for her. Huh.

He stood staring at her for a moment, and she realized it was because she looked like someone who should be reading him the six-o'clock news. "Is that you under there?" he asked.

She smiled and nodded. "And thank you for going to the trouble of shopping for me," she added with a bit of a stammer.

He held her gaze, those dark eyes suddenly softer on her. Then in seconds, his usual unreadable expression was back.

She headed back into her room and pulled the plastic off the hanger. The dress was beautiful. Just perfect. The classic little black dress, but not too little. Simple, elegant, and very Audrey Hepburn. The shoes were satin pumps, sexy, but she could still walk in them.

She took off her clothes and slipped the dress on, then wiggled her feet into the shoes, which were surprisingly comfortable. Ivy rarely wore dresses like this; the parties she went to were pretty much limited to living room gatherings with those yummy pigs-in-a-blanket and platters of nachos. But it was nice to dress up, to feel so . . . sexy. Ivy added a touch of makeup, just a little mascara and some sheer lipstick.

One final fluff of her new bangs, and she was ready to check herself out in the full-length mirror attached to the closet. Whoa. She would not recognize herself in a room of *two* people. Would Declan, though? Would he see through the hair and glasses to Ivy underneath? He'd always made her feel as though he knew her so well.

Right. That must have been all her doing, projecting, wishful thinking. How could he possibly have known her? He wouldn't look twice at her in this outfit, despite how . . . pretty she looked. Cornelia had told Griffin on the telephone that the party would be very crowded and they might not even get a chance to say hello. But she would be thrilled to do the interview later in the week.

If it turned out that Declan was not the fiancé, Griffin thought it probable that he would be at a party like Cornelia's, hunting for his next victim.

So far, it seemed Declan had chosen younger women under the society radar, women like Jennifer Lexington, who were more involved with the artsy scene than "society parties." But, as Griffin had pointed out, it was impossible to tell what Declan—backed into a corner—would do, whom he would prey on.

There was a knock at the door. "Ready?" He froze and stared at her. "I'd say you are. You look—"

"Like someone else?"

He smiled. "Exactly."

"And you," she said, stifling a giggle at his curly blond wig and square tortoise-shell glasses, "look something like an absentminded professor."

"That's what I was going for," he said, winking at her.

Oh, how she needed that wink. That one-second-long gesture that told her they were a team again, conspiring against the bad, working together in the pursuit of justice. And flirting. Winking was always flirting. Except when it was just friendly.

"Before we go," he said, those dark eyes on hers, "I want to make sure you really want to go through with this. I can go alone, Ivy."

She shook her head, her silly musings gone in an instant. "I want him caught as much as you do."

He held her gaze, seemed to take measure of her, to decide right then and there if he could truly trust her, if she were on his side. Finally, he nodded.

"Okay, then. Hopefully, we'll get him tonight. But you have to promise me something, Ivy. You will not try to lure him into a trap and get him alone. Promise me you won't do anything that will jeopardize your life."

"Griffin, I'm a cop, too."

One who dealt primarily with the theft of wedding dresses and expired inspection stickers, but Griffin didn't need to know that. She'd been trained well and she had been in a few tough situations. "I won't do anything stupid," she assured him, and then and only then did he turn to go.

This is my father's world, Ivy thought, glancing around at the men and women at Cornelia Beckham's party. The three-story town house on the Upper East Side was crowded with the beautifully dressed. She didn't recognize anyone, but then again, she wouldn't. Her sister, Olivia, would probably know some of the people; Olivia had been an editor at a fashion magazine and probably hobnobbed with some of the society types in this elegantly appointed living room.

It was interesting to note that the conversations Ivy eavesdropped on weren't all that different from the conversations she heard all the time. Talk of children, of vacation plans to warmer climates, of celebrities making headlines. She'd always thought she wouldn't fit into this world, but perhaps all you needed was to *look* like you belonged. Certainly no one gave Ivy "What are you—a lowly police officer—doing here?" glances.

Griffin thought they should keep a low profile,

not be too chatty with anyone, and not introduce themselves as reporters from the phony magazine. If Cornelia even bothered to approach them to ask who they were, Griffin would introduce himself and Ivy as the journalists doing the wedding story, but he figured Cornelia wouldn't even bother. The town house was packed with people in several rooms and the lights were dim.

Which made it difficult to spot Declan, if he were even at the party. Ivy reminded herself to look for a tall, well-built man with either blond, red, or very dark hair, since he'd most recently had a chestnut brown color. He would also likely be in glasses, too.

Ivy glanced around, and each time her gaze settled on someone who *could* be Declan, her heart raced. Not with longing. But with fear, she realized. She was afraid. A man who was so slick, so without emotion or conscience that he could kill a woman— a woman he lived with—and then make love to another woman an hour later, was someone to fear.

"Let's take a walk around," Griffin whispered. "Check out the other rooms. We can split up, but if you see him, you come find me."

Ivy whispered that she would, and Griffin headed for the well-traveled stairs. Ivy turned toward the conversations that were coming from down the hall. She found herself entering a library, the walls lined with bookshelves and beautiful works of art.

"I just love the Renaissance period," a female voice said nearby.

Ivy surreptitiously glanced around a couple eating appetizers to see the voice belonged to a young woman she couldn't place, but whom she had seen before. Mousy brown hair, hazel or green eyes, late twenties, perhaps early thirties, average height, average weight. In a simple black dress, sensible pumps. Where did Ivy know the woman from?

It would come to her.

The brunette stood admiring a painting. Where had Ivy seen her before?

"I do, too," answered a voice she knew all too well.

She froze, then took a shallow breath to calm down. There was no mistaking the deep timbre of that voice.

Even though the voice was accented. Irish. And a decent fake.

Ivy waited a moment until her heart rate had slowed down enough so that color returned to her face. She turned slightly, slowly so as not to attract attention to herself, and stole a glance at whom the woman was talking to.

If she hadn't heard his voice, she very likely would not have recognized him. But now, all she saw was the profile she knew as well as her own face.

Declan.

She was dead sure of it.

He was in disguise, in thick-framed glasses that hid a good portion of his face, and he'd colored his hair very dark, almost black. He also had a mustache and beard, close-cropped. But it was him. It was Declan. And he stood around seventy-five feet away, several small groups of people between them.

She quickly turned around. *Go find Griffin,* she told herself. But when she turned back around, Declan was walking out the door. *Damn it!*

The woman he'd been talking to, the one she still couldn't place was now helping herself to a small plate of appetizers that a waiter was passing out.

She would have to follow Declan. She couldn't let him just walk away, disappear into the crowd, or worse—leave.

She would just follow him, not too closely, act nonchalantly, as though she were simply walking down the hall. And then she'd rush upstairs to find Griffin.

He was around a hundred feet ahead of her, and though the hallway was as dimly lit as the rest of the rooms, Ivy prayed over and over that he wouldn't turn around. She kept her eyes downcast, on the dark legs of his suit. Her hope was that he'd head upstairs. Then she could race up to find Griffin.

As her heels clicked on the polished marble floor, her heart hammered in her chest so loudly she was sure Declan would hear it. And *smell* her fear.

And then before she could even blink, he turned around so fast and was on top of her, pushing her into a utility closet with such force that her head cracked against the plaster of the wall.

Chapter Thirteen

The pain was so intense that Ivy saw white spots before her eyes, then black, then white and black dots. As her vision cleared she tried to stand, but Declan kicked an empty metal bucket at her legs and she slid down again onto the floor.

The smell of cleaning product emanating from the bucket, along with the pain on the side of her head, almost made her pass out. She tried to stand again.

"Do you want me to break your fucking legs?" he snarled, aiming a gun at her. "I will if you even attempt to get up again."

Ivy stared at the small, silver handgun. She recognized the silencer.

With the gun pointed at her chest, he leaned down and ripped the wig from her head. "Take off those stupid glasses," he ordered.

She did, and he laughed. "Did you really think I wouldn't recognize you?" he said.

"Why would you?" she asked, stalling for time as she got her bearings, looked around. The utility closet was maybe five feet by three feet and empty, save for the bucket. There wasn't even a mop to *attempt* to use as a weapon.

"Because I know your face, Ivy. Very well."

She was glad she didn't know this face of his, with the black hair and the beard. Glad that he didn't look like the man she'd known. Loved. Had been about to marry.

"Did you kill Jennifer Lexington?" she asked, trying to keep the emotion, the fear out of her voice. *Get him to confess,* she reminded herself. *Just keep your cool and get him to say the words.*

The smirk left his face. "No, I didn't. Not that I expect you or my big brother to believe that."

"Where were you at the time of the murder?"

He stared at her. "I was en route to Jennifer's. I spent the night . . . elsewhere. And when I came back to the apartment, I found Jennifer dead. I panicked and left."

"You panicked and left?" she repeated. "Are you forgetting the suicide note you forged?"

Anger lit his eyes. "Yeah, I *panicked.* I knew I'd go down for the murder. So I thought I'd just go to your place, we'd get married, go on our honeymoon, and I'd convince you to live abroad."

"Despite my not having a penny to my name," she said.

"I had other reasons for marrying you, Ivy."

"Such as?"

"Doesn't matter anymore," he said, his gaze running up and down her body. "Though you do look very hot in that dress. Not your typical style. I suppose my brother likes it, though." He moved even closer, standing inches from where she lay.

"If you didn't kill Jennifer, who did?" she asked.

And hoped she'd antagonize him enough not to touch her. But not enough to kill her, that was.

"Hell if I know," he said. "Jennifer was so annoying, anyone could have done it. She was coming into a fortune. Working on her mother to make sure she wasn't cut out of the will. Her father's due to drop dead any day." He smiled. "Though I suppose that doesn't interest me anymore."

"And Cornelia Beckham does?" she asked.

He let out a harsh laugh. "I don't do fatties."

"You're repulsive," she shot back without thinking. The man had a gun. Which he waved in her face at that comment.

"You want to know what's repulsive, darling?" He moved closer, the gun inches from her face. "Screwing brothers. *That* is repulsive. But trust me, Ivy, ole Griff is using you."

She ignored the bait, her eyes on the gun.

He inched back, seemingly very satisfied with himself. "I've taken every woman Griffin has ever liked, let alone loved. And he's just trying to pay me back by sleeping with you. As if I care now," he added with a harsh laugh.

Her brows rose. "Pay you back for what?"

"Ask him about Samantha," Declan responded without the slightest bit of expression.

Samantha. Ivy tried to remember if Griffin had mentioned a Samantha. She didn't think so.

Don't listen to Declan, she reminded herself. *He's a lunatic. Get back to the case. Get him talking about the morning of the murder.*

"Tell me something, Declan. Why did you take the letter from my father? And the cash from my wallet?"

"I wanted to make sure you'd marry me," he said. "And I couldn't be sure what that asshole father of yours wrote to you. The money I needed just in case."

"Just in case the cops managed to track you down?"

"And they did. Big Brother thought he finally got me. But, as usual, I am too smart and too fast for him."

"I still don't understand why you'd bother going through with the wedding if you thought there was a good chance I'd inherit nothing," she said. "That makes no sense to me."

"You're boring me, Ivy."

Oh, sorry, psycho! "Okay, then tell me this. If you really didn't murder Jennifer, why not just turn yourself in? Prove you didn't."

He laughed and waved the gun again. "You have that backwards, Officer Sedgwick. The police need to prove I did do it, not the other way around. And they'll nail me for it, regardless of the truth. I look too good for it."

That much was true.

She had no idea if he was telling the truth—if he killed Jennifer Lexington or not. She had no ability to read him, and he was a practiced liar. She needed to remember that with everything that came out of his mouth now.

"Here's what you're gonna do, Ivy," he said, now pointing the gun directly at her head. "You're gonna tell your boyfriend to back off and forget I exist. Or the next time we meet, and there will be a next time, I will kill you. And I'll kill him, too."

She took a deep breath. "You'd kill your own brother?"

"Half brother," he said. "And yeah, I would if I had to."

"I thought you said you weren't a killer," she threw out.

"I haven't had good enough reason to kill anyone," he said. "But if provoked, I'll put a bullet between your eyes faster than you could whimper 'please don't.'"

"Why were you going to marry me?" she asked again. "Just tell me."

"Wouldn't you like to know," he tossed back. And then he leaned down and grabbed the neckline of her dress, yanking it so hard that it ripped, revealing her bra and stomach.

"Don't you even think—"

"Just making it difficult for you to run right out of here," he said, laughing. "I don't do sloppy seconds."

God, he was vile.

"Remember what I said, Ivy. If both of you don't back off and stay out of my business, I will hunt you down and kill you. And Griffin. And if I have trouble getting to you, an associate of mine won't."

Ivy froze. "What does that mean?"

"It means that your pathetic little house won't be the only thing trashed next time. Your body parts will be, too."

"Who is this associate?" she asked. The woman he'd been talking to in the library?

"Jesus, Ivy, no wonder you haven't been promoted to detective yet."

With that, he straightened the tie of his expensive suit, then opened the door enough to squeeze through and backed out slowly, the gun still aimed at her. And then in flash, the gun was out of view and the door slammed.

Ivy jumped up, holding the front of her dress up, and tried to reposition the wig as quickly as she could. She sprinted out, startling a couple walking down the hall. She frantically searched the corridor for Declan, but he was gone. She raced toward the steps, colliding with a man.

Griffin.

"Damn it, Ivy, I've been looking everywhere for you," he barked in her ear. He glanced down at her dress. "What the hell happened?"

She let out the breath she'd been holding for so long. "Declan. He startled me in the hall and grabbed me into a utility closet." She told him everything that had transpired, leaving out nothing. Not even what Declan had said about "sloppy seconds."

"There's no way he's still here," he whispered, seemingly unaffected by all she'd told him. Including the mysterious Samantha. "I'm sure he's long gone, but I'm going to call it in, have them check the premises."

"And what about his threats? To kill us. Not just me, Griffin. You."

"I'm not scared of Declan, Ivy. Not for a second. And we can't let him win. He won't get near you again. I won't let you out of my sight."

As Griffin turned to call for backup, Ivy realized she was shaking.

"My partner and some uniforms will be here in a few minutes to take over," he said. "Let's go home."

"I'm fine," she said, her hands visibly trembling.

"Ivy, you were locked in a closet with a gun

pointed at your head by a suspected murderer. Who also threatened you. There's no need to be fine. Got that?"

Without meaning to, she slid her arms around his neck and he stood there and held her, not letting go even when the blaring of sirens could be heard.

Once Ivy was settled on the couch in Griffin's living room, the throw wrapped around her, Griffin headed into the kitchen to make her some tea. He hated even leaving her alone that long in his own apartment.

That bastard had really gotten to her. Literally and figuratively. She'd tried to appear cool and collected, but again he'd assured her there was no need to be; she could be herself, she could fall apart, and that was A-OK with him.

"It's not okay for a cop to fall apart when a murder suspect gets the best of her, Griffin. Gun in her face or not."

"Ivy, you weren't a cop in that closet. You were his former fiancée. You were a civilian."

She shook her head. "I was undercover."

"Ivy, you're not my partner."

Her gaze shot to his, and he realized too late that he'd said the worst possible thing that could have come out of his mouth.

And there was no easy way to fix it at the moment, without racking his brain to figure out, so he excused himself to make her a pot of tea. As he put the kettle on to boil, he still didn't know exactly how to rectify what he'd said. What it meant.

As he came back in the living room with two cups

of tea and handed her one, she said, "You must think I'm the worst cop."

"Ivy, I don't think that at all."

"I let him trap me," she said.

"You didn't let him do anything," Griffin pointed out. "You did exactly what you should have done, what I asked you to do. You were coming to find me. You couldn't have known he IDed you, Ivy."

"He could have so easily killed me," she said. "I just feel like I put myself in such a bad position, put everyone in that house, potentially, at risk."

He got up from the chair across from her and sat down next to her, taking the tea that she wasn't drinking anyway and placing it down on the coffee table. He took her hands in his and looked directly into her eyes. "Ivy, not only didn't he kill you, he gave you valuable information. Whatever you did in that utility closet was good police work. You saved your life. And you got him talking."

"Got him lying, maybe."

"No, talking. Maybe he didn't kill Jennifer Lexington. What he said is plausible. That he found her dead, that he panicked."

"Who else could have killed her?"

Griffin shrugged. "That's what we have to figure out. Maybe this mystery woman he was talking to at the party. Maybe Laura Frozier, though she has an airtight alibi for that night. Or maybe someone—perhaps someone who cares about you or someone who cares about Laura Frozier—discovered Declan was involved with Jennifer, went to her apartment to confront her, and Jennifer ended up dead."

"Someone who cares about me?" Ivy said. "Griffin, anyone who cares about me wouldn't be capable of murder."

He leaned back, putting his feet up on the coffee table. "Ivy, I can tell you story after story of ordinary people who resorted to murder because they were provoked."

"Well, isn't it more likely that it's someone from Laura Frozier's life? She was seen making out with Declan the night before the murder."

He nodded. "My partner has been sniffing around her friends and family. That's why he's been so scarce. And working other angles, as well."

"Such as?"

"Such as the fact that your mother doesn't have an alibi for the night of the murder. Neither does your friend, Alanna Moore."

Ivy rolled her eyes. "Griffin, please don't waste your time. My mother is not a cold-blooded killer. Neither is Alanna. Please."

"Ivy, Jennifer's murder didn't appear to be premeditated. Someone could have gone to talk to her, to tell her about you or Laura, get her to end things with Declan, and there's an argument, and in the heat of the moment, Jennifer ends up dead."

"Her head was bashed against the wall, Griffin. That's more than an argument in the heat of the moment. That's pure rage."

"And people can be driven to that, Ivy."

"And my mother's motive is?" Ivy asked, taking a sip of her tea. "It's not like my marriage to a Rockefeller or Kennedy was in jeopardy."

"But your mother did think Declan was old money. And she thought he was part of a world she always wanted you to be part of. A world she thought denied you."

Ivy shook her head. "She wouldn't kill over it."

"What about Alanna? She's been your best friend since middle school."

"It's more likely that Jennifer's killer is someone from Laura's world," Ivy said. "No one saw Declan making out with Jennifer the night before she was killed."

"We don't know that. Maybe your mother saw Declan with Jennifer. She lives in Manhattan. It's possible."

"Griffin, my head is about to explode."

Damn. He'd been so intent on getting her to accept the possibility that someone close to her could be the killer that he forgot himself. She'd been through hell tonight, and here he was, putting her through more.

"Can we just not talk about it, about any of it, for the rest of the night? Can we start fresh in the morning?"

He nodded. "Of course. If you want to turn in . . ."

"I don't want to be—" she stopped, glancing down at her feet.

"Alone?"

Her cheeks turned slightly pink.

"Ivy, you've been through so much. It makes sense that you wouldn't want to be alone."

He took her hand and led her into his room. He thought she'd feel safer, more secure in his bed.

"I'm sorry about the dress," she whispered.

"I'm just glad—" He stopped, anger boiling in his gut. "That he didn't lay a hand on you."

She lay down on top of the comforter and stared

up at the ceiling. He lay down beside her, on his side, and took her hand.

"It's going to be all right, Ivy. I'll check Cornelia's guest list to try to figure out the identity of Declan's mystery woman. And regardless, we'll catch him and bring him in for questioning. We'll bring in a number of people for questioning."

"Including my mother? And my best friend?"

"I thought we weren't going to talk about this anymore tonight."

She let out a deep breath.

"Is what he said true?" she asked. "Did he steal the woman you loved? Samantha?"

"That's a long story, Ivy. And for another time."

She glanced at him and nodded and looked wearier than he'd seen her look yet.

"I will tell you this, though, Ivy. I was wrong about what I said before. We are partners."

She stared up at him, then leaned forward and kissed him, gently, and traced his jawline with her finger. And then she lay down and put his arm around her waist, holding on to it.

Hours later, when he awoke, their position hadn't changed. She stirred, and turned, then settled her head on his chest, that beautiful face once again at peace.

His cell rang, but Ivy didn't wake. He grabbed it. "Fargo."

"Hey, brother. If Ivy didn't pass on my message, let me do it for her. Come after me again, and I will kill her. And I'll make it hurt."

Chapter Fourteen

Griffin checked and rechecked the deadbolt on the front door, then made sure the blinds on all the windows were drawn tight. Declan could hardly take a shot from the street, but Griffin wouldn't take any chances.

At close to two a.m., he lay down next to Ivy. She still wore her ripped dress. The flap was down, exposing her beautiful cleavage. He lifted it gently, then got up and walked over to his bureau and pulled out an NYPD T-shirt. He carefully unzipped the back of Ivy's dress and slid it off her body, no easy feat while she was dead asleep. He tried not to take advantage of the moment by looking at her gorgeous body, the swell of her breasts, the curve at her waist, the gentle flare of her hips. Her bra and underwear were black. He pulled his attention from the tiny scrap of lace between her legs, also no easy feat.

As carefully as he could, he slipped the soft T-shirt over her head, and she stirred, but turned on her side, which made it easier for him to draw the shirt down her body. It came to mid-thigh. At least she'd be more comfortable. Then he slid into bed next to her in his own NYPD T-shirt and sweatpants, then drew the down comforter over them. He listened to her breathe, the rhythm lulling him to sleep.

When he awoke it was past nine in the morning. And he was alone. Panicked, he bolted out of bed and ran into the living room. A deep breath of relief whooshed out of him when he saw Ivy in the kitchen, a carton of eggs and flour on the counter in front of her.

She's okay.

She's not only okay, she's making pancakes.

Ivy had slept fitfully, her arms and legs and head ending up on various body parts of his. Those times were pretty much the only times that Griffin actually felt okay, when she made that kind of contact, albeit in her sleep. Every time her arm flung across his stomach or her knee hit his hip, he was reminded of his job. Which for the forseeable future was to keep her safe.

He wouldn't tell her about the late-night phone call he'd received. There was no reason to tell her. The threat was against her, but it was for him. He pushed his brother out of his mind and concentrated on the woman in his kitchen. Not a sight he was used to.

Man, she looked sexy in his T-shirt. Now that she was standing, the T-shirt barely covered the middle of her thighs, and her long, shapely legs were quite a sight in his dull, beige kitchen.

"I hope you don't mind that I changed your clothes," he said, aware of the blush in his voice. "The dress seemed constricting."

"I appreciated it," she said. "So much so that I'm making you breakfast. My famous homemade pancakes. Famous for being a little lumpy and lopsided, but still delicious."

He smiled. "So you're okay? You woke up refreshed?"

"Not really. I still remember last night in that closet as though it happened five minutes ago. But I'm not going to let Declan control me."

"That's the spirit," he said. "And not easy. I'm impressed."

"You might not be after you try one of my world-famous pancakes." She flipped one, and it landed on the counter next to the stove.

Griffin laughed. "You can have that one."

She smiled. "But the next one might stick to the ceiling." She gestured at the coffeepot. "Fresh brewed. So where are we starting today?" she said, this time expertly flipping a pancake, albeit a lumpy one. "Questioning Laura? Her family, friends? Or perhaps we should start with Cornelia, get the guest list for her party and figure out who Declan was talking to. I'm trying to remember if I got the sense that they were together, or if they were simply just chatting there, you know the way people do about art or whatever when they first meet at a party. I can't seem—"

"Ivy, let's forget it for a couple of days. We need Declan to think we *have* backed off. Let him get comfortable again. Let him slip up."

"So what are we going to do with ourselves for two days?"

"Eat lumpy pancakes?" he asked with a smile.

"Any chance you want to take over the pancakes?" she asked. "I've got batter all over me and would love a fast shower."

He took the spatula and she squeezed past him in the small kitchen, the slight brush against him sending warm waves through his entire body. He did his best with the pancakes but burned a batch, and whipped up some scrambled eggs and bacon, too.

When Ivy returned to the kitchen, looking beautiful in jeans and a dark green wool sweater, he grabbed a slice of bacon and headed to the bathroom for a quick shower of his own. When he rejoined her, she'd just set down the platters of food on the table.

This is what it would be like to live with her, he thought, then had an instant "where did that come from?" moment. They sat and ate in companionable silence, also nice.

Nice. He hadn't had that feeling about being with a woman—thinking seriously about being with a woman—since Samantha. A long time.

The doorbell rang, and Griffin bolted up, gun drawn. "Go into the kitchen," he whispered to Ivy. "Stay hidden on the far side of the refrigerator."

He waited until she was in place, then headed to the door. "Who is it?" he asked, in position on the side of the door frame, as Ivy waited out of view in the kitchen.

Silence. And then, barely audible, came, "Joey."

Griffin put away his gun and opened the door. Joey dropped down to his knees in the doorway, sobbing.

Oh, Joe, he thought, bending down to slide an arm under the guy's arms. He prompted him up and helped him inside. The poor guy was crying hysterically. Ivy had found the box of tissues on the kitchen counter and put them on the coffee table. Griffin nodded a thank you at her, then led Joey to the sofa as Ivy went into her room.

Griffin knew that one of two things had happened: either Joey's father had passed away, or Julianna had dumped Joey. From the dark circles under Joey's eyes, it was clear the boy hadn't slept much last night. But he hadn't called Griffin, which told him Julianna was the problem. If his father had died, Joey would have called Griffin. He had made sure Joey knew he could call him any time, day or night.

"Let it out," Griffin said to Joey, his arm slung around the guy's shoulders.

And let it out Joey did. He sat there and sobbed for a good ten minutes, clutching tissue after tissue to his face, unable to talk. Finally, he said through his tears, "I just . . . don't . . . understand." He tried to catch his breath. "I thought . . . I thought she loved me." He broke down again, sobs wracking his body.

"Did you two break up?" Griffin asked gently.

"She dumped me," Joey said, swiping his large hands under his red-rimmed eyes. "We've been arguing for the past couple of days about my dad because I want him to come live with us, and Julianna was trying to change my mind, and then finally said there was no way she'd live with some 'crazy vegetable,' and that it was my father or her." He shook his head. "My father isn't crazy and he's not a vegetable." The tears came again and he buried his face in his hands.

Man, what a choice. Leaving his father in a nursing home, where he actually did belong, where he could receive the care and round-the-clock attention Griffin knew he needed, or the girl of his dreams.

And Joey had chosen his father. It was the right choice because it was about true love. And Joey's true love right now was his father. His beloved father who'd loved Joey like crazy. His dad came first.

Griffin would spend the next couple of hours explaining all this to Joey, and then he'd help Joey see that his dad was exactly where he needed to be. And once that was all settled, they'd shoot enough hoops for him to bring Joey to the realization that where *he* belonged was at home, with his mother and stepfather, and in school, finishing his senior year.

It was a good thing Griffin had the day's slate wiped clean.

"No. No. And no," Griffin whispered, those dark, dark eyes of his doing the shouting for him.

"Griffin, I'll be surrounded by cops," she whispered back, her chin up for emphasis.

The whispering was on behalf of Joey, who was now sitting at the dining room table, eating his second breakfast (apparently men were able to eat when heartbroken). Griffin and Ivy stood toe to toe in the kitchen, and Ivy was determined to get the toehold.

Griffin crossed his arms over his chest. "No. And that's final."

That's final? Ivy understood that Griffin Fargo felt oddly responsible for her safety. And she appreciated the extra protection he afforded her. But she was capable of taking care of herself (being pulled into closets by murder suspects notwithstanding).

And it wasn't like she wanted to traipse all over Manhattan alone; Alanna had called to invite her for an afternoon of "girlie bridal stuff." Her friend had finally paid for her wedding dress in full, was now ready for her first fitting, and needed Ivy's been-there-done-that advice. And it was also time to try on bridesmaid dresses.

Oddly enough, Ivy wanted to do this. Wanted to spend a few hours at Best Bridal in Applewood, going through racks of pastel taffeta creations with bows on the butt, oohing and ahhing at Alanna in her gown, obsessing over headpieces. That, at least, was normal. What a normal person did when her best friend was getting married. Much more normal than being afraid to leave the side of a detective because a lunatic had threatened her.

"Griffin, Joey needs you today. And I need my best friend. My BFF, as the kids say. I need to feel *normal.*"

He stared at her, seemingly understanding that his hands were tied. She couldn't stay in his apartment forever. "I'll be checking in with you every hour, Ivy."

She smiled. "Fine."

"Every hour," he repeated. No smile, of course.

"Every hour," she repeated.

We are partners.

They *were* partners. Every day Ivy saw more and more just how well Griffin knew the meaning of that word. He'd illustrated it beautifully as he'd comforted Joey earlier. As she'd listened, she'd thought: *This is the definition of partners. Someone who is there for you. Someone who lets you cry it out. Someone, in cop speak, who has your back.*

Griffin had Joey's back. And he had hers. What she hoped was that Griffin would let someone have *his*.

Why are bridesmaid dresses so hideous? Ivy wondered as she slid dress after fancy dress on the rack at Best Bridal. What was the need for two-foot-high puffs atop each shoulder? A giant bow directly on the butt? A band of white directly around the hips?

Ah, now this is more like it, she thought, removing a long, satin pale pink number with a halter-style top and delicate beading across the waist and hem.

"Find anything?" Alanna called out from her dressing room.

"A winner," Ivy said, holding up the dress to her in front of the wall of mirrors opposite the dress racks. "Perfect for your early summer wedding."

Alanna poked her head out of her room. "Love it. But I was really hoping you'd choose something mint green with multitiered ruffles."

Ivy laughed. "You are kidding, right? You never know with brides."

"No," Alanna said, her expression dead serious. She broke into a grin. "Totally kidding. Though it does describe the dress my cousin is making me wear in her wedding." Her face sobered again. "Ivy, you sure you're okay with being here, doing all this wedding stuff? Because if it makes you the slightest bit sad, just say the word and we'll go stuff our faces with pizza."

"That sounds good, actually, but no—I'm not the slightest bit sad. And I mean it. I'm past sad. What are the stages you go through when your wedding is stopped mid-walk down the aisle due to a runaway, criminal groom with multi-fiancées?"

"I think the stages are varied forms of relief," Alanna said. "With just about every possible other emotion." She popped her head back in. "So are you ready to see the dress I've been talking about for weeks?" she asked, parting the curtains.

Ivy gasped. "Oh, Alanna. You look absolutely stunning." The gown had an antique look, despite being brand new.

A short, stocky woman with a tape measure around her neck appeared from a back room. "Are you ready to be fitted? Whenever I hear a gasp like that, I know someone is happy with a dress."

Ivy stared at Alanna's reflection in the wall of mirrors. Her dear friend looked the way Ivy had looked on the day of her own almost-wedding. She could still remember sitting in the chair, fussing over her rhinestone barrettes, her sisters fluffing her train, Ivy marveling at the expression on her own face. The joy, the expectation.

It was a wonder Ivy still had expectations. At least Declan hadn't robbed her of her own hopes and dreams and aspirations.

While the seamstress was pinning Alanna's dress, Ivy stepped outside to call Griffin, as promised. He and Joey were on the way to Griffin's gym to play basketball and do some laps in the pool.

It was so good to hear his voice, that deep voice she couldn't get enough of. They spoke for just a few minutes, Ivy assuring him all was well, where she was, where she was headed next. And then he was gone, the phone silent, and Ivy again felt the sharp stab of absence.

When she returned to Best Bridal, the seamstress was done fitting Alanna's dress, and it was Ivy's turn to hop on the step stool and be pinned and poked in her pretty pink satin. Then, the two women spent a wonderfully long time choosing a headpiece and veil. *What luxury this is,* Ivy thought, discussing the nuances of lace and clips as though she didn't have a care in the world.

Twenty minutes later, they were seated in Luigi's Ristorante, awaiting a large pie with the works and a Caesar salad to split.

"Ivy," Alanna said, her expression serious, "I'm so proud of the way you handled yourself with Declan—when he attacked you and had you at gunpoint. You managed to elicit information out of him without antagonizing him. That's such good police work."

Ivy sipped her Diet Coke. "Thanks. I really need to hear that. Because I feel like the world's worst cop. Not suspecting a thing in all my months with Declan. My house getting destroyed. I might as well be our waitress or a bank president or anyone without a shred of police training."

"How could you possibly know Declan was living a double life?" Alanna asked. "You can't be so hard on yourself, hon."

"I might have suspected something if I'd been willing to look. Or think. Like Declan's interest in me in the first place. Come on."

"Ivy!" Alanna said.

"Wait—are you yelling at me because I'm doubting such a handsome man could have really fallen for me, or because I made Declan sound like he was anything more than pond scum?"

Alanna furrowed her brows. "Both."

"I didn't know he was pond scum," Ivy whispered. "I didn't know because I wanted his attention. I wanted a good-looking man like him to fall madly in love with me. So I ignored so many red flags."

"Name one," Alanna said, helping herself to a garlic knot from the basket the waitress set on their table.

"He was so in love that he spent only two nights a week with me. He was so in love that he never asked to move in with me, preferring to live in a dorm? With a roommate who supposedly snored? He was so in love with me that he managed to avoid most of my work functions—parties and dinners. Gee, maybe because he wanted to avoid a large group of cops."

"Ivy, based on what you thought—that he was a student—of course he could only spend a couple nights a week with you. A weekend night and one during the week. Totally normal. And of course he would live—supposedly—in a dorm. That's where students live. To be close to school. And what man enjoys his girlfriend's work or family functions?"

"So you really don't think my judgment is shot?"

Alanna took Ivy's hands. "No way. Not at all. And no one thinks so, Ivy. Except for you, maybe. So work on that, okay?"

Ivy smiled. "I'll absolutely try."

"And remember something. What you did in that closet, how you handled yourself as a police officer, kept you from getting killed. And you got the suspect to reveal vital information about the murder."

Ivy contemplated that for a moment, taking a sip of her soda. "You know, I really do think that if

Declan wanted to kill me, he would have. Right in that closet. No one would have been the wiser. No one had been in that hallway but me and him when he'd grabbed me."

Alanna visibly shivered, and Ivy suddenly had a vision of Griffin tearing the town house apart looking for her, finding her in that closet eventually.

"So what *does* he want?" Alanna asked. "What's with the threats and trashing your house?"

"He seems to want me and Griffin off his back so that he could romance his rich women, have a new group of fiancées, be a polygamist, and have several fat accounts—in addition to being the beneficiary of several fat life insurance policies."

The waitress appeared just then with their lunch, setting down a very large tray of pizza on their table.

"I can't believe I'm not dieting to make sure I fit into my gown on my wedding day," Alanna said. "But this looks too damned good."

Ivy lifted a gooey slice onto her plate. "Alanna, you're a size four and have been a size four since middle school. I don't think you're capable of gaining an ounce."

As they enjoyed their pizza and did a little reminiscing about high school and which of their old classmates Alanna was inviting to the wedding, Ivy was relieved to have a moratorium from discussing Declan and the case. But when neither of them could eat another bite, Alanna asked the question Ivy couldn't stop thinking about.

"Do you think Declan's telling the truth about not killing Jennifer Lexington?"

Ivy shrugged. "I really don't know. It's possible.

Maybe he really did come home, find her body, panic that he would seem the obvious killer once his double–triple life revealed itself, forge the suicide note, and then run."

"And it was your house he ran to," Alanna said. "If he were the killer, I'd almost think he would have tried to flee the country."

"So if he didn't kill her, who did? That's the burning question. One of his other lovers? Maybe he forged the suicide note because he knew who killed her. Laura Frozier. Or another of his fiancées that we have yet to uncover."

Or, as Griffin would have her believe, her own mother. Ivy knew her mom wanted to see her finally married to "good stock," but any scenario that led her mother to Jennifer's seemed so far-fetched. That her mother caught Declan kissing Jennifer passionately, followed Jennifer back to the apartment to confront her, and an argument led to her murder. It just seemed so unlikely. But then, so did Ivy's entire life at the moment.

"Is there any lead on the woman you thought you might have recognized at the party? The one Declan had been talking to?"

Ivy shook her head. "Griffin's partner was working on the guest list and questioning people, and so far, we have no idea who she was."

The waitress brought over their bill, which Ivy tried to pay, but Alanna snatched it out of her hand.

"This is my treat. For schlepping all the way out here today in the middle of everything going on in your life." She leaned over to hug Ivy. "I love you, my friend."

Ivy squeezed her back. "I love you, too. And honestly, Alanna, I want to hear every last boring detail of every detail—down to the garnish you select for your chicken entrée."

Alanna laughed. "Oh, trust me. I'll be happy to bore you with all that because no one else I know is remotely interested."

A moment later, they were on the street, the late March air holding a budding warmth that did wonders for Ivy. Soon it would be spring, a time to shed the weight of winter—and these heavy problems. With any luck, Declan would be caught very soon.

Alanna walked Ivy to her car, then glanced at her watch. "My monster-in-law is waiting for me at Richard's condo. Do you believe I have two hours of china-pattern shopping in my immediate future?"

Ivy laughed and hugged her best friend again. God, it felt good to hear her own laughter.

"Go ahead. I'll call you later."

Alanna blew Ivy a kiss as she hurried down the block. Ivy watched her as she rounded the corner, a bit bereft. Sometimes, there was nothing like girl talk.

She glanced at her watch. In ten minutes she'd need to call Griffin again, but she didn't want to call while on the road. She pulled out her phone. He answered before the phone even fully rang.

"I'm about to hop in my car and head back," she told him. "You'll meet me at the secret property, right?"

"Right. Call me when you arrive, okay?"

She assured him she would, and again, the moment their call was disconnected, she missed him. She envisioned him just then, his arm still slung around Joey's shoulders as they chomped down pizza. Joey was so lucky to have a friend like Griffin, someone who cared, someone so intelligent and insightful, someone with the rare gift of putting himself in someone else's shoes to see things from their perspective and viewpoint. Griffin was unusually nonjudgmental and—

"Oh, Ivy," singsonged a female voice.

Ivy turned around but didn't see anyone who was calling to her. There were many people walking up and down the busy main street of Applewood's town center, but not a one who was paying a bit of attention to her. Perhaps she was hearing things. She slipped her phone into her purse and got out her keys, only to hear her name being called again.

"Ivy, oh, *Iv-y.*" The same singsong. And then a head popping out from a doorway down the block.

Ivy strained to see who it was, but the woman had ducked back from view.

What the heck? Someone from the precinct, perhaps? The voice wasn't familiar.

Ivy hurried down the street toward the doorway, but as she got halfway down, the woman jumped out and stood there in the middle of the sidewalk. Ivy was so startled she froze.

She was even more shocked to discover it was the woman from the party. The one Declan had been talking to. And she looked exactly as she had at the party. Brown straight hair, medium length, early to mid thirties. Conservative clothing. A dark wool coat. She was too far away at this point for Ivy to see her face clearly.

Where the hell do I know this person from? she thought as her legs caught up with her brain and she started running to meet up with her. But the woman smiled and turned and sprinted away, rounding the corner.

What is going on? Ivy wondered.

As Ivy turned the corner, she saw the woman up ahead, running, turning around every few seconds to see how close Ivy was. Why was she calling to Ivy *and* running away?

"Stop!" Ivy called. "Just stop and talk to me!"

But the woman kept running. She made a right turn two blocks up.

Damn it. If I lose her . . .

Ivy turned the corner and stopped dead in her tracks. The woman was gone. Ivy whirled around, frantically looking all around her. Where did she go?

"No! Damn it," Ivy said aloud, bending down to catch her breath.

And then just as before, Ivy heard her name. In the same singsong voice. "Ivy. Oh, I-vy!"

Ivy ran down the block, frantically checking the doorways to see if the woman was hiding. This stretch of Morley Street was mostly apartment buildings, brick tenements, and walk-ups, and there was an auto body shop at the dead end. Ivy was familiar with this neighborhood. She'd twice been called to the auto body shop, once for a break-in and once because of a fight between two mechanics. And at the far end of Morley, she and Dan had been called in to investigate a call of domestic disturbance. But generally, this was a quiet neighborhood, working class, orderly.

Thanks to the dead end, the woman would not get past Ivy without being seen, unless she was Spiderwoman.

"Ivy. Ivy *Sedg-wick*."

Ivy stopped and turned around. She'd gone too far up the block. She stopped, straining to hear the slightest movement or intake of breath. *Where are you? Damn it!*

She saw a flash of black material from a doorway up ahead, the hem of the woman's coat sticking out. She was hiding in the doorway at the next tenement.

Okay, I've got you, lady. Whoever you are.

Ivy practically tiptoed up, preparing to pounce.

And realized she'd walked—run—right into a trap. And even though she thought herself a match for the strong arm that grabbed her into an open doorway, the hunting knife at her throat was another matter altogether.

Chapter Fifteen

"It's all your fault," the woman whispered into Ivy's ear as she dragged her down to the end of the hall. Her breath smelled of peppermint, as though she'd been chewing gum.

Ivy racked her brain to put the voice and face together, but got nothing. She drew a complete blank. She'd seen the woman somewhere, somewhere maybe just once or twice, like at a branch of her bank that she rarely went to. Someone she'd recognize only in context, maybe?

Keep your cool, Ivy girl, she told herself. *Just pay attention to the knife, and where it's pointing*. If she tried to jerk away in the slightest, she'd only slide right into the blade. And it was a sharp-looking knife.

"What's all my fault?" Ivy asked, ordering herself to keep her cool, keep her wits about her.

"Shut up," was the only response, the knife poking into her neck.

Ivy gasped as shooting pain and wet, sticky blood trickled down her neck.

They were in one of the apartment buildings, a tenement walk-up. Ivy wondered if the woman lived here. The heavy smell of frying onions was overwhelming. Ivy hated that smell. Strangely, her mother came to mind, an image of Dana Sedgwick cooking one of her favorite meals, liver and onions, which Ivy found beyond repulsive. Ivy also thought she smelled liquor on her assailant's breath. Whiskey.

A loud television could be heard coming from one of the apartments on the ground level. *A talk show,* Ivy thought dimly.

The woman dragged Ivy to an open black door on the far side of the stairwell. A steep staircase led down into the basement, Ivy assumed.

"It's all your fault, you rich bitch," the woman snarled at her.

Rich bitch? "What are you talking about? Who are you?" Ivy asked, trying to keep her voice firm but not antagonistic.

"What are you talking about? Who are you?" the woman singsonged back at Ivy, her features twisting with hate.

She stood behind Ivy, the knife poking into her neck once again before she shoved her down the gaping black hole. Ivy landed with a crack and then a thud on the cold cement ground, the whirring of the boiler the last thing she heard before everything went black.

As Griffin and Joey approached the Longmere Nursing Home on First Avenue, Griffin experienced the same tightness in his chest, in his throat, that always accompanied him on visits. If this place had that effect on him, he wondered what it must be like for a kid like Joey. Adult at eighteen or not, Joey was a kid.

Evidently.

A game of basketball at Griffin's gym, more food, a walk, and a round of ice hockey at an arcade they'd passed along the way had accomplished most of what Griffin had hoped for the day. Joey had come to realize—with a degree of self-pride—that his father meant more to him than anyone or anything. Including a woman. And since the particular woman didn't seem to put Joey's needs ahead of her own, Joey didn't have much trouble seeing that it was okay to put his ahead of hers. They'd both chosen themselves. And at eighteen and nineteen, they'd both made the right choice.

Whew. Only took two and a half hours to get there.

But the question of where Joey's father belonged, that hadn't been dealt with so easily. Joey still wasn't sure that his father was better cared for in the nursing home than he would be with Joey on the job.

Joey didn't quite get what the *job* was. Apparently, when visiting his dad every day for the past couple of months, he was more focused on the heartbreak of the situation, of the loss of who his father had been, than on the care his father required. Griffin figured Joey needed to see just how patients at Longmere were treated by the staff. And how it wasn't a matter of finding an apartment for the two of them and maybe a nurse's aid—which Joey wouldn't be able to afford anyway.

As they headed inside the building, Griffin glanced

at his watch. Ivy was due to check in with him in around ten minutes, maybe twenty at the most if there was traffic getting back into the city. That would give Griffin enough time to check in at the desk and give Joey a little time alone with his dad while Griffin spoke to Ivy.

She'd sounded good when they'd spoken. Both times. More than good. She'd sounded happy, actually, as if an afternoon with her best friend was exactly what the doctor ordered.

He'd realized then that he'd isolated her a bit too much. Protection was one thing, but keeping her from her friends and family on top of all she'd been through had likely caused more harm than good. Griffin had forgotten, that was all. He'd forgotten what it felt like to need family. To need friends.

To need anyone.

He still hated the idea of her so far away, a state away, even if it were just a twenty-minute car ride from midtown Manhattan. Once he had her safe and sound in his sights at her father's place—her place, he amended—he'd be loathe to let her go again.

As they neared the familiar reception desk with its posted rules and regulations, its big board of activities and the dining room menus and various announcements, Griffin was hit in the stomach with a sharp jab of memories of the last time he saw his father.

He was dead already, his broken body still on the scaffolding outside the building. It ran the length of the second floor; his father had jumped from the fourth and top floor and it had been enough to break his neck, which apparently had been Frederick Fargo's goal. As a doctor, his father would have known just how to throw himself, how to land, to achieve his goal. Had he been lucid at the moment, that was. His main doctor at Longwood thought his father had been lucid when he'd jumped; he'd had several such moments during the six months he'd been at the facility. Short-lived. A few hours. Once for two days.

Griffin had waited several hours afterward to try to reach Declan. He wasn't sure if Declan would receive the many messages he'd left at various numbers. And then a couple of weeks after, Declan had left a message on Griffin's home machine.

Glad to know the old jerk has been put out of his misery. That was it.

Griffin forced thoughts of his father, of Declan, out of his head as he and Joey signed in and then headed up in the elevator to his dad's room. Griffin was all too familiar with the floor, the way it would smell, a bit like Lysol, and Ace bandages, and medicine, and flowers. There were so many bouquets of flowers in the rooms, in the halls, that Griffin was surprised the place didn't smell like a meadow. People brought flowers when they visited. And cake. Griffin had always been sent home with slices of other people's cake. There had been something oddly comforting in that.

Joey's dad, Harry, sat in a wheelchair by the window, his favorite spot, and stared out. He turned when Joey entered and said, "Hey, Gramps," as he often did. Back when Griffin had first met Joey, the guy had been torn apart by that, but now, a couple of months in, Joey had almost come to rely on it for measure that his dad was *okay.* "Gramps" meant he wasn't agitated. Apparently, Joey's dad had been raised by his grandparents and had been crazy for his grandfather. And it was just fine with Joey now to be confused with that person, that connection.

Twenty minutes later, Griffin realized that staring at his watch every second would make Joey feel rushed, so he stepped out into the hallway. Ivy was late in calling. She should have arrived at the secret apartment ten minutes ago, even with traffic.

He called her cell phone. It rang five times before it went to voice mail. Which meant that the phone was on and wasn't picking up.

A chill ran up his spine.

She's turning in to the parking garage, he assured himself, *and just can't get to the phone at this moment.* He'd give her a minute, then try again.

Same response. She didn't pick up.

Two minutes and much pacing later, the same thing.

Something was wrong.

Griffin grabbed his wallet for the sheet of paper with Alanna's cell phone number. He called, and she picked up right away. She'd left Ivy at her car, just a minute before Ivy had last spoken to Griffin.

Where the hell is she?

Ivy opened her eyes, pain shooting from her ankle, from her head.

What the—?

And then she remembered. The woman. A basement. Stairs.

She was on the cement floor, her legs tied with

rope. The basement was dark, a dim bare lightbulb on a pull cord the only source of light.

Was she alone? Or was her assailant still here?

A sharp stab of pain made Ivy wince as she tried to sit up so that she could work on the knot around her legs. Why tie her legs but leave her hands free?

"Go ahead, exhaust yourself trying to undo that knot, Princess. You'll just make my job easier."

Ivy frantically looked around for the woman, but she was hiding or in the shadows. "Can you please tell me who you are and what you want?"

"Aren't we polite? I suppose that's what a top-notch education does. Even in a crisis, you say *please*." The voice dripped with venom. The woman hated Ivy, that much was clear. But why?

When Ivy had first seen the brunette at the party, she sensed that the woman was working with Declan in some capacity, his partner in con. Though how or in what capacity, she had no idea. But perhaps the woman was one of Declan's lovers? If she were, would she be calling Ivy a rich bitch? Rich women generally didn't throw that term around.

Resentful women did.

"I'm not surprised you don't remember me, despite how helpful I was to you." This was accompanied by a hard kick in the back of Ivy's thigh.

She yelped in pain. She hadn't even seen the woman come near. So she must be behind her, behind the boiler?

"But that's how you people are," the woman continued. "You don't notice *us*. People who actually work for a living."

"I'm a police officer, not Paris Hilton," Ivy said. If she could figure out how to talk to this psycho, how to gain her trust, she might get herself out of there alive.

A hard kick in the ribs was the woman's response. Pain shot through Ivy's torso and back.

"My name is Gretchen Black. But that wouldn't mean anything to you. I'm more than just the woman who trashed your pathetic little house and left you some threats on the walls and mirrors, by the way."

Well, *that* mystery was solved.

Ivy searched her memory. She couldn't remember ever having met a Gretchen before. *Gretchen Black,* she thought. *Think, Ivy. You must have heard that name somewhere. Where?*

"Keep thinking," the woman said. "It won't come to you."

"Then why don't you tell me," Ivy said, sick of the lunatic's games.

"Okay, I'll give you a really good hint. Listen closely now: Welcome to Sedgwick Enterprises. How may I assist you?" she said, her voice changing in an instant from mean and snarling to professional and crisp.

Ah. Of course. That was where Ivy had seen the woman! The one time Ivy had gone to visit Declan at the Sedgwick offices in Manhattan, this Gretchen Black person had been the receptionist for Declan's floor.

"You probably still don't remember me, though, Ivy Tower," she added. "You came looking for Declan McLean. And I told you he was in a meeting with the senior vice president of his division and would be out shortly. And you believed me, like an idiot. I kept you waiting for almost an hour. Idiot."

Ivy remembered. She'd been so nervous that day,

going to her father's offices, albeit a different floor than the chairman and president and chief everything officer or whatever her father's title had been. But as she'd gotten off the elevator, she'd realized that she was here for Declan, that he was completely separate from her father, and she'd relaxed.

She also remembered her exchange with the receptionist because it had been so awkward.

"Welcome to Sedgwick Enterprises. How may I assist you?" the receptionist had said in that same formal, professional tone.

"Good afternoon," Ivy had responded. "I'm here to see Declan McLean. He's expecting me."

"Your name?"

"Ivy."

"And your last name?"

It was then Ivy had faltered. It was very strange to say that you were a Sedgwick when visiting Sedgwick Enterprises. "Sedgwick," she'd finally said.

"Sedgwick? As in William Sedgwick?"

Ivy had nodded uncomfortably, and the receptionist had smiled and said, "I'll bet this is sort of how John F. Kennedy Jr. must have felt every time he traveled through JFK airport."

"Well, I'm hardly in John Jr.'s league."

The woman had smiled, somewhat tightly, Ivy recalled now, and informed Ivy that Declan was in a meeting and would be out shortly.

Declan had invited her to lunch in Manhattan; he'd thought it would be good for her to see her father's offices—see that it was just a business and not the castle with moats and forts that Ivy had expected. And he'd been right.

When Ivy had realized she'd been sitting in the

reception chair for forty-five minutes, she'd approached the receptionist, who'd said she would call the meeting room. The woman had spoken briefly to Declan, and apparently, he would be out in another fifteen minutes. Would she wait?

Of course she would. Another half hour, Ivy told the receptionist that she'd have to go. She was due back at work and the drive back to Applewood often took a half hour.

Declan had been so apologetic that night on the phone and promised to make it up to her with dinner that weekend, which he had, though now that Ivy thought about it, she had ended up doing the cooking that night because he'd sprained his wrist while playing racquetball with an important client.

Right. Right all the way.

"It was so much fun to see you waiting and waiting, squirming in that uncomfortable chair for an hour!" the woman said, laughing. "Oh, I so enjoyed that." She appeared from behind the boiler and stepped around Ivy. "You're such a dummy!"

Ivy chose to ignore that, instead focusing on the knife in Gretchen's hand. She had to keep her cool, had to keep herself in control here. "Was Declan even working there at that point?"

"Barely. Declan had no idea what he was doing. He was blackmailing one of the other junior analysts into doing his work for him for a while. But Declan could only fake his way through for so long."

"You helped, I assume."

The woman stared at her, her brown eyes narrowing. "Do you know what happens when you assume, Ivy Tower? You make an *ass* out of *you* and *me*." She laughed jovially but then immediately sobered up. "And I don't like being made into an ass."

God, she was bonkers. Off her rocker.

"But you assume correctly," she continued, pointing the knife at Ivy. "I did help. Do you want to know why?"

"Because you loved him?" Ivy said gently, hoping this was her ticket in. Or out, actually.

All her question earned her was another kick, this time at her lower leg. Ivy winced in pain. She was going to be very black and blue at this rate.

"*Love*, Ivy Tower. Not *loved*. Not past tense. What's past is *your* relationship with Declan."

"But you must know . . ." Ivy hesitated, unsure what would get her another hard kick or worse.

Gretchen stared at her. "I must know what? That Declan is involved with other women? So? He doesn't love them. All that matters is that I got rid of the one he did love."

Ivy froze. Did she just confess to killing Jennifer Lexington? *Keep her talking, Ivy*, she counseled herself. *And be careful.*

"So you killed Jennifer," Ivy said nonchalantly.

Confusion lit the woman's eyes. "Jennifer? That stupid slut? My God, she was as dumb as an ox. No, I didn't kill Jennifer. I planned to, but then someone accomplished that for me."

"Who?" Ivy asked.

Gretchen shrugged.

"Declan?" Ivy suggested.

That got Ivy yet another kick in the leg. "Stupid bitch. Declan wouldn't hurt a fly."

Ivy rubbed her shin. "So you don't know who killed Jennifer?"

"I don't *care* who killed Jennifer. But that little murder solved my problem."

"Your problem—of getting rid of the one he loved?"

She nodded. "I tried to set up a little catfight, but it ended up not working. But then, bizarrely, everything worked out according to plan. Funny how that happens!"

What?

"A catfight?" Ivy asked. "Between who?"

"Whom, dear. A woman with your advantages should really know how to form a grammatical question."

Oh, brother. "Between whom?" she tried again.

"That other slut Laura Frozier and Jennifer. I arranged for Jennifer to come across her fiancé with his tongue down Laura's throat."

Ivy gasped. "So he was in love with Laura? You were trying to get rid of Laura by having Jennifer confront her, maybe? You figured Jennifer would flip out right there and then, confront Dennis, as I believe he called himself, and therefore, ruin his good thing with Laura, who thought she was Declan's one and only?"

"You're too stupid for words!" Gretchen said, sneering, waving the knife for emphasis.

Okay, what was Ivy missing here?

"You. You are the one Declan loved."

Ivy's eyebrow shot up. "Me?"

"He was in love with you. He thought you were the salt of the earth, or whatever that stupid cliché is. Sweet and good and made of puppy dog tails. Or is that what boys are made of?" She seemed to think for a moment.

"I'm not following how setting up a catfight between Laura and Jennifer would get rid of me," Ivy said.

"My intention was to prevent the wedding. Your wedding to Declan."

Gretchen wasn't making any sense!

"If you wanted to prevent the wedding or destroy our relationship, why not just set me up to discover Declan was involved with another woman. Make that plural."

The woman's boot landed directly in the middle of Ivy's abdomen. Ivy clutched her stomach and bent over, vomiting blood. She fell over on her side, dizzy, nauseous.

Gretchen now stood right next to Ivy, then kneeled down and poked the knife at the side of Ivy's neck. "Don't you talk about Declan like that. You make him sound like he's a cheater." She dug the knife in enough to draw blood, and the trickle made its wet, sticky way around the front of Ivy's neck.

Because Ivy's hands were free, it would be so easy to try to wrestle the knife away, but her feet wouldn't get very far, and she'd risk being killed. This psycho meant business.

"Declan loved you," Gretchen said. "If I arranged to have you find out about Jennifer or Laura or the others he was working on as backups, you'd dump him. Or that's what I figured, given how goody-two-shoes he made you out to be."

"But isn't that what you'd want? Me to dump him?"

"And have him heartbroken?" she asked, shaking her head. "When you love someone, you don't want their heart broken. I figured if I arranged a catfight between the sluts, the heat would be on and he'd have to flee the country. He'd take me with him, since I'm his right-hand woman."

"But there wasn't a catfight," Ivy said. "So you went to Jennifer's apartment with the intention of killing her?" It still made no sense. It wouldn't accomplish what she wanted. Or at least Ivy thought not. She was beginning to think in circles.

"I thought if I killed Jennifer, he'd look guilty. He wouldn't be able to marry his precious Ivy Tower. He'd have to flee the country. And he would take me with him, as previously stated."

Ah. Okay.

"But you said you didn't kill Jennifer." *Tell me who did,* Ivy prayed silently.

"I don't know who did. As I was heading toward the building, someone was coming out. An older woman, I think. In sunglasses and a hat and a long white trench coat. Who wears a white trench before Memorial Day? I mean, really."

Ivy's blood froze. A white trench coat. An older woman.

Ivy's mother had a new white trench coat. A long one. And she'd worn it a few times, despite the still cold March weather.

Ivy's mother had killed Jennifer Lexington.

Oh God. No. No, no, no. Mom.

But it made sense. Her mother must have seen Jennifer and Declan together. Kissing, perhaps. And her mother had followed Jennifer to her apartment. The photos alone would have enraged her mother. But instead of racing off to confront Declan or tell Ivy what was happening, her mother had snapped and lunged for Jennifer, bashing her head into the wall.

No way. Her mother wouldn't have done such a thing. But the problem was that her mother did seem . . . capable of such a thing. She would do anything to see Ivy married to Declan, the supposed wealthy, accomplished son of her dear departed friend, who supposedly had left Declan oodles of money.

No. It was crazy. Her mother was not a killer!

Then why did it seem so possible?

Where was her mother the morning Jennifer had been killed? She'd called Ivy very early. At around seven. She'd wanted to come with Ivy to William's attorney's office to pick up the inheritance letter. And when Ivy had told her no, her mother had rattled on about the day of beauty she had planned for her daughter's wedding that evening. She was having her hair styled, and a manicure and pedicure. And she'd had all that done.

If she'd killed Jennifer Lexington in a rage, would she have been able to calmly sit and have her nails polished?

Maybe. Ivy could recall a time or two when her mother had been enraged. Even when Ivy had been in school, and passed over for this or that, such as the glee club or the lead in a play, her mother had threatened at least two of Ivy's teachers, promising to ruin their careers and lives.

"I could slit your throat right now," Gretchen said, tracing a line across Ivy's neck with the tip of the knife. "But I want you to suffer just a bit longer before I carve your perfect little heart up into food for my pit bull. Maybe I'll sic him on you just after I plunge the knife into your gut. Pumpkin just loves the smell of blood."

It was all too much for Ivy. She felt dizzy, white stars floating behind her eyes, then a strange flash of light burst out of nowhere in her mind. She felt so light-headed, but in a good way almost. Griffin's handsome face floated into her mind and she tried to smile, but couldn't.

And then she felt herself drifting . . . fading, the world turning black as she fell over.

Chapter Sixteen

When the seamstress at Best Bridal came back to the telephone and told Griffin that yes, a red Honda Civic with Ivy's plates was still parked outside her shop, he broke more than a few traffic laws to get to Applewood.

The car was locked and there were no signs of a struggle.

Damn it, where is she? Griffin thought, dread hitting him in the stomach. He headed into the shops that lined Main Street to ask if anyone had seen Ivy Sedgwick or anything out of the ordinary in the past hour.

No one had seen Ivy. No one had seen anything suspicious.

Ivy couldn't have just vanished into thin air.

He began questioning people on the surrounding streets. But the response was the same. He even stopped a group of ten-year-olds on their bicycles.

"Hey, kids, I'm a New York City detective," he said, showing them his badge.

"Wow," one said, looking at it up close and fingering the shield.

"Shut up, Conner," another hissed. "Or you'll get thrown in jail."

Griffin hid his smile. "Have you been doing something that might get you thrown in jail?"

"We didn't steal any cars," a red-haired boy said. "We just wanted to see if we could climb the fence. You know, at the auto body shop. Cuz when the mechanics are there, they chase us with these big wrenches."

"Well, you boys are not going to jail, okay?" Griffin said. "I used to climb a few fences when I was a kid, too. So, tell me, when you were riding around in the last hour, did you see a pretty woman with short brown hair, wearing blue jeans and a red coat?"

"You mean Officer Sedgwick?" Conner said. "She's always nice to us. Once she caught us jumping in Mrs. Stupidhead's flower garden and she didn't even yell at us or tell our moms or anything. Mrs. Stupidhead is evil."

Griffin kneeled down in front of the boy, his heart racing. "Did you see Officer Sedgwick a little while ago?"

"A long time ago, though. Like, maybe an hour?" Conner said.

"Yeah, she was running down Morley Street," the curly-haired boy said. "But she didn't have her gun out or anything. We were hoping to see her catch some bad guys."

"Were there bad guys?" Griffin asked, his mind racing.

The redhead shook his head. "Just some lady. Officer Sedgwick was running after her, but the lady was, like, hiding in doorways."

"They were playing hide-and-seek, I think," the freckled blond boy said.

"What did this lady look like?" Griffin asked. "Do you remember?"

"She sorta looked like Officer Sedgwick, but she wasn't like a babe at all," the little redhead put in. "Brown puffy hair, not long or short. I think she had a dark coat on."

"Where's Morley Street?" Griffin asked. "Can you show me?"

"Cool!" they all said in unison and sped two blocks down on their bikes.

Griffin ran after them. They stopped at the intersection of Morley Street and Applewood Boulevard. "Okay, guys, this is really important. Did you see Officer Sedgwick go into one of the buildings?"

Conner pointed to a brick tenement walk-up with a red door three-quarters of the way down the block. "I remember it was that one, cuz the screen's busted."

The redhead nodded. "Yeah, and—hey, look, there's the lady she was chasing."

Griffin slid his gaze to the woman walking out of a building at the far end of the block, then turned his attention back to the boys. "Thanks, kids," he said, handing Conner a twenty. "You split that between all of you. Okay?"

"Cool!" they shouted and sped off on their bikes.

The woman was walking directly toward him. He was at enough of a distance that he could pull out his cell phone and call 911 to request backup, while appearing to the woman to be making a simple phone call.

He'd make his move at exactly the right moment.

He didn't want to do anything that might spook her too soon and make her run. If she got away from him, he'd be screwed. As would Ivy. He didn't know this neighborhood.

As she got within one hundred yards, he adopted his most pleasant expression, adding a mix of confusion. "Excuse me," he said. "I'm lost. I'm looking for the auto body shop? I was told it was on Morley Street."

She turned to point down toward the dead end, and he grabbed her and had her prone on the ground in seconds. He cuffed her, and that was when he realized there was blood smeared on her hand.

"Where is Ivy Sedgwick?" he demanded.

"Wouldn't you like to know?" the woman sing-songed.

"Where is she?" he demanded again.

"She's dead, you pig," she said, turning to spit at him.

Griffin wanted to take his hands and wrap them around her neck, but he controlled himself with every fiber of his being. Within minutes, backup had arrived, two Applewood PD patrol cars stopping in front of him.

He explained the situation, and two of the officers led the woman away none too gently; the other two followed him down to the building the boys had indicated. One radioed their captain to inform him one of their own was in trouble.

As they burst into the vestibule of the building, Griffin found the inside door was locked. He pressed the intercom marked with SUPERINTENDENT. A man appeared and rushed over to open the door when Griffin flashed his badge.

"Ivy!" Griffin shouted. "Ivy!"

No answer. He ran the length of the first floor to check behind the stairs. No Ivy. But there was a door leading to the basement. Griffin tried it. Locked.

"That's the basement," the superintendent said, unlocking it.

Griffin called out Ivy's name again at the top of the steps. No response. He raced down, the uniformed officers trailing.

And then he saw her, lying in a pool of blood, a purple and black bruise on one side of her face. He ran over to her and checked her pulse.

Please, please, please, he prayed heavenward.

And was answered. She was alive.

The uniforms radioed for an ambulance, and within minutes, Griffin heard the sirens. He held on to Ivy's hand until the paramedics had her on the stretcher, and then they rushed her up the stairs and into the ambulance.

After he was assured that CSI was on its way to secure the site and investigate the crime scene, Griffin headed to Applewood General.

And there, for the first time since he was a boy, Griffin Fargo cried.

She was going to be okay.

Griffin sat by Ivy's bedside at Applewood General, half the local police department in the hallways and waiting room.

Alanna, sitting on the other side of Ivy's bed, was beside herself. "If only I'd stayed one minute longer to see her actually drive off, none of this would have happened."

"The psychopath would have trailed her into Manhattan and gotten her in the parking garage," Griffin said. "You wouldn't have been able to prevent it, Alanna."

Alanna's fiancé, a resident at the hospital, was assigned to Ivy, and that made for faster and more straightforward information. He stopped in to check Ivy's vitals, assuring them again that she would be as good as new with rest and recuperation.

Ivy would be able to go home tomorrow morning; her stab wounds were superficial, and despite the kicks she took to the legs and torso, she hadn't broken any bones or ribs. She'd been given a sedative and was still sleeping.

"Should I call Ivy's mom?" Alanna asked Griffin. "She's been vacationing in the Bahamas all week. She's due back tomorrow. Maybe I should just wait?"

"I think that's best," Griffin said. "She'll just be worried sick on the plane. And Ivy will be out of it for the rest of today anyway."

Alanna nodded, her eyes cloudy with tears and concern. She'd been sitting in the chair for over an hour, unwilling to let go of Ivy's hand for even a moment. Griffin knew how she felt. He'd been holding on to Ivy's other hand; even that slight physical contact was as necessary to him at that moment as breathing was.

Griffin was sorry he'd doubted Alanna, been suspicious of her. She was Ivy's best friend and her love for Ivy had been made clear to him in the past hour that they'd held their vigil at Ivy's bedside.

Griffin had never had many friends. He'd been unable to trust his own family—his brother, his father. And so he hadn't put much stock in friendships. It wasn't until he met Joey at Longmere that he learned about friendship, how completely innocent and unconditional it could be. How it meant simply giving a damn. And being there.

Finally, though, Alanna had to leave; her captain allowed her to take full part in the case, and Alanna thought she could do Ivy more favors by questioning Gretchen Black and investigating her background fully. Griffin assured her he'd call her when Ivy woke up.

One of the officers brought Griffin a large cup of strong black coffee, for which he was very thankful. He continued to sit next to Ivy, watching the gentle rise and fall of her chest. He hated the sight of her bruised cheek, the marks on her neck from where the knife had made contact. The weapon had been recovered from Gretchen Black's tote bag. It was very sharp. Ivy must have been scared out of her mind.

Because of the nature of the crime, Griffin had been allowed to remain in her room overnight as her protective detail. He'd been apprised of Gretchen Black's initial statement to police; apparently, the former Sedgwick Enterprises receptionist liked to speak in singsong, and she told officers that she would tell them only what she'd revealed to Ivy.

Such as the information about an older woman in a white trench coat, whom she'd supposedly seen leaving Jennifer Lexington's building as she'd been about to go in. Gretchen claimed she herself *hadn't* gone in. A crowd of people had gathered in front of the building to hail cabs, not quick on a Friday night, and Gretchen had been unwilling to risk being seen entering the building when she had murder on her mind.

So who was the older woman in the white trench coat? Witnesses he'd originally spoken to didn't recall seeing either an older woman in a white coat or someone matching Gretchen's description.

Griffin let out a deep breath as dawn broke, morning's first rays of light trying to make their way through the cheap metal window blinds.

When Ivy slowly opened her eyes, he was sitting at her bedside. She tried to speak, but her voice was groggy, and her eyes closed again. Griffin put a finger to her lips and told her to rest, that he'd been apprised of Gretchen Black's statement.

She began to cry. As tears streamed down her face, Griffin tried to gently wipe them away.

"You're okay, Ivy."

She shook her head. "Is my mother under arrest?"

"Your mother?"

She stared at him, then closed her eyes again.

He had a feeling he now knew the identity of their mystery woman. The lady in the white trench coat.

"Your mother is not under arrest, Ivy. She's still in the Bahamas, as a matter of fact. I was going to try to reach her at her hotel to let her know you were in the hospital, but I thought I'd just hold off since she's due back tomorrow."

Relief seemed to flood her face. "She couldn't have done it. She couldn't."

"Honey, don't even think about it right now," he said, tracing a finger down her cheek. "Or at least try not to think about it. Your entire body is going to be very sore for the next several days. I just want you to concentrate on healing. Emotionally and physically, Ivy. Alanna was here for hours, and now she's investigating Gretchen's past. And your entire department is in the waiting room."

She gave a little nod and squeezed his hand, then closed her eyes again. He leaned back in his chair, resting his head against its uncomfortable edge, and figured he'd try to get the hour or two of sleep that had eluded him all night.

Griffin opened the passenger side of his car, very gently scooped up Ivy in his arms, and carried her inside the vestibule of her father's secret home. On the way into Manhattan, he'd asked if she'd prefer his place or this one, and she felt they'd be safest here, since no one knew about it but them.

He opened door after steel door, finally entering the apartment. After laying Ivy down on the bed and covering her with the blanket, he went into the bathroom to draw her a bath. He found some pink bath beads and bubble bath in the medicine cabinet, and he poured some in, then set two thick towels on the rack.

When he returned to the bedroom, she was standing by the bureau, looking at the photographs of herself.

"Ivy?"

"My mother is not a killer," she said, tears falling down her cheeks.

"We'll get to the truth, Ivy. That's all we can do."

"My mother is not a killer," she repeated, and then her legs dropped out from under her.

Griffin was at her side in one stride, and he scooped her in his arms and carried her into the bathroom. "I thought you could use a hot bath."

She nodded, the tears coming faster. He undressed her, removing her sweater and her bra and then her jeans, underwear, and socks. He tested the water with his wrist and then picked her up again and gently set her down in the tub. She laid her head back against the plastic pillow and closed her eyes.

"I have no idea who I am anymore," she said numbly.

He sat down on the marble floor and leaned against the wall, drawing his knees up to his chest. "Ivy, you've just been through something traumatic. On top of everything else. You need to cut yourself a very big break. For the next several days, you're on couch rest. You're watching fun television shows and reading magazines. That's it."

"There's no way I can lay around doing nothing," she said. "Not when my mother might be—"

"Ivy, we don't even know if we can believe a word Gretchen said. She's clearly out of her mind."

Ivy nodded. "I know."

"How's the water?"

She offered a weak smile. "Feels good. And my entire body feels like a bunch of linebackers jumped on me." She was quiet for a moment. "I screwed up again, Griffin. I was chasing her, and all of a sudden, she had me. Just like what happened with Declan at Cornelia's party."

"You didn't screw up, Ivy. You were *set up.*"

She didn't seem to be buying that. But it was true. "I just don't even know where I'm supposed to be anymore. Between the debacle that was my wedding and what happened today, if I never stepped foot in Applewood again, it would be too soon."

"Understandable," he said.

"So what does that mean for my job? Do I even want to be a cop anymore? Should I be? I certainly can't be a cop under these kinds of circumstances— investigating my own mother for murder." Tears slipped down her cheeks.

Griffin's heart squeezed in his chest. He moved closer to to the tub, taking her soapy hand. "Ivy, hey," he said. "You don't need to figure anything out right now. And you know what? Your mother owns a long white trench. So do a lot of people. It's not so unusual. Manhattan's not a small town. The woman who Gretchen described could have been anyone."

"But it sounds a lot like my mom," she whispered. "I'm just so scared it is. My mother has her faults, Griffin, but I love her."

"So let's give her the benefit of the doubt, okay?" Griffin said. "Innocent until proven a suspect. Isn't that how it goes?"

She smiled. "I wish this were all over."

"And it will be over soon, Ivy. We can only investigate what seems plausible and try to waste as little time as possible on wild-goose chases."

"God, I wish I were more like you, tough, strong. A rock. I mean, here you are, hunting your brother and you're not falling apart."

"I don't love Declan, though. That's the difference."

"But you once did," she said. "So this has to royally suck for you."

He smiled ruefully. "It does. But my brother is an adult and made his own bad choices. I can't feel responsible for them. I can only do what feels right to me."

She nodded. "You must be so tired of babysitting me."

"Actually, I'm not."

She looked directly at him, then reached out her soapy hand again. He took it and held it and would be quite happy to never let it go.

She stood and rinsed off, and he tried not to look at her exquisite body, bruises and all, but she was standing a foot from him.

"You are so magnificent, Ivy," he said.

She smiled and stepped out of the tub, drying off with the fluffy towel he'd set out for her. She tucked it around herself, then took his hand and led him back into the bedroom.

She sat down on the edge of the bed and looked up at him, then wordlessly undid his belt.

He tilted up her chin with his finger. "Ivy. Are you sure?"

"I'm sure," she whispered and then unbuttoned his pants and slid them down his hips along with his Calvin Klein briefs.

She slid her hand around his rock-hard erection and then bent down to press her lips against his chest, her full breasts cocooning the head of his penis. She trailed her warm, soft mouth down his stomach until she found the hard tip with her tongue. She circled it, her hand moving in rhythm, and he groaned, his head back, his eyes closed, the pleasure so intense it took all his effort not to explode in her mouth.

He undid the towel and it dropped onto the bed, those creamy, full breasts magnificent before him.

He roughly massaged the heavy weight of them, toying with the sweet tips until they formed rigid peaks. She let out a moan, and he slipped his hands down her waist and pressed her very gently back onto the bed, afraid to press any of the areas where she'd been kicked.

He then got down on his knees and kissed the soft skin of her inner thighs, sliding a finger inside her hot, wet center.

She writhed and moaned and arched her back, her nails digging into his flesh, and he slid his tongue over her clitoris, the taut bud responding to his every lick. Ivy let out a scream and lifted up her legs so that they were around his waist.

He slid into her, hard, thrusting, his hands grasping her breasts. He then leaned down and moved her farther onto the bed, bending her legs up onto his chest so that he could reach even farther inside her. She was so tight, so wet, the center of her femininity pulsating around him. She met his thrusts and leaned up to kiss his chest, her tongue finding his nipples and then his mouth. They kissed in rhythm to their thrusts, the steady music of their lovemaking in perfect harmony.

"Griffin," she moaned, another little scream escaping her.

He grabbed her hips and flipped her over so that she was straddling him. He held her hips and rocked her against him, her head thrown back as she moaned so fast and so loud that he almost couldn't control himself. But there was no way he wanted this to end.

He slid halfway out of her to tease her while his mouth worked on each breast, and then he grabbed her hips and buttocks and rocked her hard against him, then lifted her up and down on top of his hard erection until she screamed her pleasure.

And then he flipped her over onto her back and lay down on top of her, pressing her hands over her head with his. He looked at her beautiful face, at those blue eyes, and he kissed her gently, then thrust into her, over and over and over until he let out a harsh groan, unable to control himself any longer.

He exploded inside her, then collapsed on top of her, his breath slowly returning.

"You really know how to make a girl forget a bad day," she whispered into his ear.

And then he laughed, so hard that he couldn't stop. He couldn't remember the last time he'd actually laughed like that, so spontaneously.

"That was amazing," he whispered into her ear, the scent of bubble bath on her sweet skin. *We're amazing*, he wanted to add, but he couldn't, so he didn't.

He just closed his eyes, glad her heart was beating in rhythm with his own, making it seem that all was okay in the world.

Chapter Seventeen

Ow.

Even the slightest movement sent a rippling of pain through Ivy's entire body. Her torso felt like it had been someone's punching bag. Kicking bag was more like it. And her face was sore from where she'd hit her cheek on the way down the stairs of that basement.

Griffin had drawn the curtains tight over the blinds to keep out the harsh glare of the morning sun. *He is that kind of guy,* Ivy thought, her gaze on his chest, rising, falling as he slept.

Ivy froze, which once again sent a series of "ows" through her body. Griffin was sleeping next to her. Sleeping. Most of the times they'd lain together, whether or not they'd made love, she'd woken up alone. He'd be either making breakfast or taking notes. But he wouldn't be sleeping. That was way too vulnerable a position for Griffin Fargo.

Yet here he lay. The realization brought a smile to Ivy's lips. He trusted her. Finally. And he cared about her. That she could read on his face, in those dark, dark eyes, the moment she'd opened her eyes in the hospital and seen him. When she'd awoken in that uncomfortable cot with its standard issue blankets (hospitals needed to think about down— or at least down alternative—blankets), the first thing she saw was Griffin Fargo's face. Unmasked. And she'd known he'd gone from doing a job to caring very deeply about her.

Whether he loved her was another story. That wasn't so evident on that handsome face of his.

His chest was incredible. Built. Muscular. And those shoulders. Those arms. Those biceps, triceps. She could go on.

I love you, she said to his sleeping form.

At seven a.m. on the dot, Ivy's cell phone began its nonstop ringing for the morning. Her captain. Her partner, Dan, who still managed to put his foot in his mouth while expressing "his condolences." She let him know she wasn't dead. And her coworkers, a steady stream of well wishers. Her sisters were next; Griffin had called both of them the afternoon she'd been brought in. They'd left messages at the hospital, but she'd been too weak to call anyone back.

And very touching to Ivy was the stream of calls from various people of Applewood who'd heard about her "bravery" and what she'd endured in that dank, dark basement with the "psychopath." They'd each shared a story from their own experience with Ivy the police woman or Ivy the Applewood resident. Ivy rarely stopped to think about those smaller everyday events of police work in a small community, what made a town feel like home, what made people true neighbors. Mrs. Hattie O'Malley told Ivy how thankful she was for how Ivy stopped at her house every day for three months after her hip surgery, just in case she needed anything. Elizabeth Deckler reminded Ivy of how she'd gotten through those scary first few weeks of single motherhood because Ivy had stopped by every day on her way home from the precinct to check for prowlers, as the house had been broken into recently.

The calls and stories deeply touched Ivy. She'd been so sure her dream was to become a detective, to be promoted, but the Mrs. O'Malleys and shop owners and curious kids of Applewood, such as the ones who'd basically saved Ivy's life by being kids and climbing over fences to be able to spy unseen on adults "playing hide-and-seek," was what she really loved about her job. The give and take of community, of small town. Applewood wasn't the enemy. Declan McLean and his band of one mentally unbalanced helper was.

When her cell phone rang for the thirtieth time that morning—and it was only eight o'clock—Ivy turned it off to let her voice mail take messages. Griffin was wide awake, showered and dressed, *deliciously,* in faded jeans and a navy sweater.

She suddenly had a vision of him kneeling before her as she sat on the edge of the bed. She closed her eyes as sensations managed to rock her again. Just thinking of Griffin Fargo and his amazing body, his amazing skill as a lover, had that effect on her.

Ow. Some of her more acrobatic movements last night had made certain sore parts of her anatomy even more sore. But oh, how she'd forgotten her time in that basement while Griffin had worked his magic. A little extra soreness in her side was well worth it.

As Griffin made coffee and sliced some of that scrumptious Portuguese bread for their breakfast, Ivy headed into the bathroom, ready to take stock of her bruises. She'd avoided mirrors until now. From the sore spots on her neck, she apparently had a nick-necklace.

She stood naked before the full-length mirror on the back of the bathroom door. One side of her torso was badly bruised where she'd been kicked repeatedly. As were both of her legs. The left side of her face was boxer material. And her neck wasn't as bad as she'd expected. Just a few minor puncture wounds.

She was alive. That was what mattered. And if she stayed in the bathroom, say, for the next few hours, she wouldn't have to deal with the concept of her mother as a potential murder suspect.

That was all she was at this point. A potential suspect.

Ivy still wasn't sure if her mother could really have murdered anyone. What she was sure of was that a tanned and rested Dana Sedgwick, who'd planned her Bahamian trip for months, was due into LaGuardia airport early this afternoon.

Griffin had assured her that a fleet of police wouldn't be waiting to pick her up for questioning the moment she stepped off the plane. Instead, he and Ivy would go to her apartment to talk to her. Not even question her, Griffin had said. Just talk.

Finally, Griffin knocked on the door. "You okay in there?"

"Just procrastinating from rational thought," she responded.

He chuckled. "Well your bread is getting cold. Stale, I mean."

Ivy smiled. She grabbed the soft baby blue bathrobe that Alanna had bought for her as a going-home-from-the-hospital gift, tying it gently around her sore middle. She opened the door, and there stood the man she loved.

Over breakfast, he filled her in on his afternoon with Joey, then made her laugh as he told her that the mayor of Applewood had promised to honor the "bicycle boys" with special medallions for aiding in the investigation of the disappearance of an Applewood Police Officer. Those boys would never have to worry about being thrown in jail for climbing fences again. They'd be local heroes and would get away with all sorts of flower-stomping from now on.

After breakfast, Ivy checked her voice mail. Seventeen new messages awaited. While Griffin poured over his secret notebook at the desk in the living room, Ivy headed into the bedroom to return quite a few calls.

Dana Sedgwick lived in an Upper East Side apartment building in one of the last great rent-stabilized, two-bedroom apartments. She'd had it since Ivy was born.

"So this is where you grew up?" Griffin asked as they exited their taxi. "Fancy."

"I still went to public school," she said.

"So you went from New York City to tiny town,"

he commented as they entered the building. "Usually it's the reverse."

"Unless you grow up in the city," she pointed out. "Then you crave a small town. Though in some ways, New York neighborhoods are like small towns—you go to the same deli for your bagel and newspaper every morning, the same dry cleaner, the same drug store, the same coffee shop. There are just more people."

"Yeah, like eight million of them," Griffin said. "And you know what, I'll bet more than one 'older woman' has a long white trench coat."

He was being kind. Who, as Gretchen Black had noted, wore a white trench before Memorial Day? If at all. It was just so unpractical. Unpractical was her mother's middle name, though.

As they rode up in the elevator to Apartment 12B, Griffin squeezed Ivy's hand.

Her mother was expecting them. She wasn't expecting the ambush that might follow the first round of questions about her vacation, though. Griffin had told Ivy on the way over that approaching this in a straightforward manner was best. Avoid subterfuge, avoid trying to elicit information. Best to just tell her exactly what Gretchen had told them.

If she weren't involved in the crime, her mother might even enjoy the drama of being a "potential murder suspect" and milk it for all it was worth with her friends and neighbors. She could just see Dana now. *Who knew my stylish designer trench coat would get me into so much trouble!*

Ivy took a deep breath in front of Apartment 12B. Then finally she rang the bell.

"My baby!" her mother said theatrically as she opened the door. Dana Sedgwick, tanned and elegant in a celadon pants suit with a ruffled cream-colored shirt peeking out of the jacket, wrapped Ivy in a hug. Then when Ivy turned slightly, Dana froze, her gaze on Ivy's bruised cheek. "What happened?" She reached out a hand to gingerly caress Ivy's purple and black face.

Ivy took a deep breath. "Declan's hench-woman."

Dana Sedgwick's face crumpled and then she burst into tears. She ran over to the sofa and sat down, burying her face in her hands.

Ivy and Griffin shared a glance. *That* was an unexpected reaction. "Mom," Ivy said. "I'm all right. It's just a bruise. It'll fade with time." She wouldn't mention the worse bruises on her torso and legs.

"It's all my fault. All my fault!" Dana said between sobs. She gestured wildly at the box of tissues on the kitchen counter, and Griffin got them for her. "Thank you, Detective Fargo," she said, sniffling into a Kleenex. "It's nice to see you again. I think."

Again, Ivy and Griffin shared a glance. Was her mother worried about something in particular? Feeling guilty at something she might have perpetuated?

"Please call me Griffin," he said.

After all, I may be investigating you for murder, but I am sleeping with your daughter. Badumpa.

"Mom, what's all your fault? What do you mean?" Ivy asked, sitting down beside her and rubbing her shoulder.

"I'm the one who set up the introduction between you and Declan. I invited him to that party so that you two could meet. And I ruined your entire life in the process!" She broke down into sobs again.

"Mom, my life isn't ruined."

"Of course, it is. You were mortified in front of a hundred people. Everyone knows you chose a criminal to marry. Your boss probably fired you, right? I mean, how could he trust your judgment?"

Ivy's mouth would have dropped open were she not used to her mother by age twenty-seven. This was typical. "Mom, no one thinks any less of me. I mean, everyone knows you're the one who introduced me to Declan, pushed for us to get together. You were under the impression he was a wonderful person, and wealthy to boot."

Griffin shot her a sharp glance, which Ivy took to mean: *Do not antagonize the potential murder suspect. Take your jabs and don't dish any out!*

But she could barely help it.

Dana's expression soured. "Well, no one's talking, are they? No one could possibly fault me for thinking Declan was anything less than a wonderful match for you. He's the ultimate con artist, isn't that right?"

"Right. So everyone just figures we all got taken."

Dana nodded. "He has a hench-woman? What does that mean?"

"It means she attacks women who get in Declan's way," Griffin put in. "Her part in Declan's life of crime is to slip in to various locales and set things up for him. For example, she gets part-time employment in places where it would benefit him to have access to files and data and phone numbers."

Dana shook her head. "This is all so upsetting." She turned to Ivy and took her hands. "Ivy, honey, you know I love you to pieces. I just wanted you to finally have happiness, finally know a man's love.

Know what it's like to live as husband and wife with an up-and-coming captain of industry. I was so happy as your father's wife. My marriage to William Sedgwick changed my life, Ivy. Opened the world to me."

You were married to him for one week! And he cheated on you the next morning!

"Mom, I know. But I wasn't marrying Declan because he was 'an up-and-coming captain of industry.' I'm a police officer, remember? I get my hands dirty. I was marrying Declan because I thought I loved him. That's why people should get married, Mom."

"Mrs. Sedgwick," Griffin said, sitting down across from her and Ivy. "As you know, there was a murder on the morning that Ivy was to marry Declan. A woman named Jennifer Lexington. Declan was living with her. In fact, they were engaged and planning to marry two weeks later."

Dana bolted up. "Yes, yes, of course, I know that. Terrible. Just terrible. It's why Declan ran away when he saw you, right, Detective? Declan McLean, a murderer. Who would have thought? I remember him as a sweet teenager. His mother and I were old friends. She would come into Manhattan to visit with me, and occasionally I'd go out to that little town where Ivy lives now, and Declan was just a delightful young man."

Her mother was nervous. Very nervous.

"Mom, I need you to answer this honestly. Did you happen to see Declan and Jennifer together in the days before the wedding was to take place?"

Dana twisted her hands together and walked over to the windows, her expression tight. She turned to face Ivy and Griffin, her eyes flashing with anger. "That piece of shit! I saw him kissing that young woman with the long brown hair. Kissing her, right in the window of a Starbucks. Do you believe his nerve?"

Ivy's stomach rolled over. She sat down on the sofa, unable to breathe. Unable to accept what was coming next. The question Griffin would ask. The answer her mother might give.

"Mrs. Sedgwick, on the morning of March twenty-first, did you go to Jennifer Lexington's apartment building?"

Dana pursed her lips. She glanced at Ivy, then turned her attention back to Griffin. "You bet your butt I did."

Chapter Eighteen

Ivy closed her eyes, waves of nausea turning in her gut. She felt Griffin's gaze on her, felt his concern for her. She even felt the *I'm sorry* she'd bet anything he was telepathically sending to her.

"And can you tell me what happened?" Griffin asked.

"Well, I wasn't even planning to go there," Dana said, heading back to the sofa and sitting down. "I mean, what's a little dalliance, right? That's what men do. They have affairs. They can't keep their zippers up. Men are simply not monogamous creatures. Trust me, *I* know."

Ivy glanced at Griffin. His expression was the typical detective's detached compassion, conveying to the suspect that *yes, of course, who wouldn't have felt that way?* while not actually commenting on anything. Doing so could lead the suspect off course, on tangents, and away from confessing. He would let her mother tell the story in her way in her own time.

"But the hair salon where I was having my hair, nails, and makeup done for the wedding was actually just two blocks from that girl's apartment. So I went there."

"How did you know where she lived?" Ivy asked.

Dana turned to Ivy, seeming surprised, relieved, really, that Ivy had spoken to her. "I . . . well, I followed her. She and Declan had come out of the Starbucks and gone in separate directions. I knew better than to confront Declan, since it's not like he could help seeing other women. Men, as I've said, are men, after all. I wanted to confront the woman, let her know that Declan had a fiancée so that maybe she'd dump him. Women are much more moral than men."

"And did you confront her?" Ivy asked, stunned that all this was going on behind her back. While she was testing lipstick colors for her wedding, thinking that was her biggest problem, her fiancé was making out with his other fiancée in Starbucks, and her mother was chasing down the "other woman." Unbelievable.

"Well, I followed her for a couple of blocks, planning my big speech, but then she went into an apartment building, so I didn't get the chance. I stood there in front of the building for a few minutes, and when a man came out, I asked him if he knew the name of the woman who'd just gone in. I told him I thought she was an old friend but wasn't sure. He told me her name was Jennifer Lexington, and I told him that she wasn't who I thought she was, and hurried away."

"And then you went back, the morning of Ivy's wedding?" Griffin asked.

Dana nodded. "As I said, I didn't plan to. I'd washed my hands of the whole matter. My concern was that the wedding go off without a hitch, that Ivy marry such a catch. But I just couldn't pass that building without telling her to leave my soon-to-be son-in-law alone. So I marched across the street, ready to tell that slut to keep her hands off Declan."

"Mom," Ivy said, realizing full well she was stalling for time, for anything to keep her mother from saying the words that were surely to follow. "Can you tell me what you were wearing that morning?"

"Wearing?" Dana repeated, her brows furrowed. "Let's see. It was such a warm morning. Remember? Fifty degrees at seven in the morning. So I put on my gorgeous new Donna Karan white trench. Oh, do I love that. I wore it every time it rained in the Bahamas, and oh, the compliments I got!"

Ivy took in a very deep breath. Again, she felt Griffin's gaze on her, felt him telling her to be strong, to just listen. Felt him assuring her that he was there for her.

"And then what happened?" Griffin asked.

"Well, I was about to march right up to the intercom and press that thing really hard, to make sure it was extra loud, and wake up that slut and tell her to find her own man. But then Donovan, my stylist, called me over—he'd just gotten out of a taxi on the corner." Dana looked at Ivy's hair. "I wish you'd gone to Donny, Ivy. He would have talked you into going blond for the wedding. Or at least a lighter brown, with chunkier highlights. I think yours are way too subtle."

"So Donovan called you over to him?" Ivy prompted, about to implode.

"Yes, he called me over, and I said up to the windows, 'To hell with you, slutty. My baby is marrying

Declan. And that's all that matters. Karma will get you.' And then I ran across the street to meet Donny and he opened up his salon. Isn't that wonderful that he opened at seven-thirty just for me? Just so I'd have perfectly freshly colored hair on the day of my baby's wedding? I gave him some tip, too. And you're not even supposed to tip the owner of the salon. He took me two shades lighter than normal, and I think it suits me. I hope the Bahamian sun and surf didn't make it too brassy. What do you think, honey?"

Ivy stared at her mother, a joyful relief bubbling inside her. "Mom, are you telling me that you didn't go into the building? You didn't go up to Jennifer's apartment? You didn't speak to her?"

Dana shook her head. "What was more important? Wasting my breath or making sure I had a good six hours to have my hair cut and colored and styled. Color takes a while, dear. And I needed to have my nails and makeup done, afterward, then a good few hours to dress and accessorize. I wanted to get to the church a couple of hours early to meet and greet. It's not every day I get to be mother of the bride." Tears came to her eyes. "Of course, I didn't get to be, after all. Oh, thank God I planned that vacation. It restored my sense of self."

Ivy smiled and hugged her mother so tightly that she winced in pain. What mattered right now was that unprompted, her mother had fully admitted to being in front of Jennifer Lexington's apartment, in the outfit described by the witness, albeit a psychopath witness, and then stated that she did not go inside the building. And a much more credible witness, the owner of the hair salon, could corroborate her story and the exact time.

Of course, it was still possible that her mother had run into Donovan after going into Jennifer's apartment, after bashing her head into the wall. But would her white trench coat be so white? Wouldn't it have been splattered with Jennifer's blood? She couldn't possibly have come out of Jennifer's apartment at seven-thirty and gone straight to Donovan. She would have been freaked out, surely, not to mention bloody.

Her mother did not kill Jennifer. And from the look on Griffin's face, he'd come to the same conclusion, as well. Or, at the very least, she was much lower on the suspect list than she'd been a half hour ago.

"So you're okay, sweetie?" Dana asked Ivy. "The good detective here will catch Declan and that awful hench-woman and your life will go back to normal?"

Ivy nodded. "Yes." As normal as could be expected.

"You'll meet someone else, Ivy. Someone wonderful. In fact, why don't I introduce you to Poppy Harway's nephew? He's a dentist. And let me tell you, dentists make a good living."

Ivy smiled. "That's okay, Mom. But thanks." Ivy stood up. "Detective Fargo, can I speak with you for a moment?" She led him into the kitchen. "Okay?" she whispered. "Is she off the list?"

"That'll take verifying," he said.

"I'd like to stay here with her, have lunch. I'm just so relieved, Griffin. You have no idea. I feel like I've been given my mother back. And now all I want to do is spend some time with her."

He stared at her. "The last time I let you out of my sight . . ."

"I know," she said. "But Gretchen Black is behind bars. And Declan isn't after me, Griffin. If he was, he would have killed me when he had the chance."

He let out a breath. "I'll go verify what your mother said and meet up with my partner. Are you absolutely safe here, Ivy?"

She nodded. "She might talk my ear off, but that's the worst of it. Can't be more painful than my shin at the moment."

He reached up a hand and caressed her bruised cheek, those dark, dark eyes intense on hers. But intensely emotional.

I love you, I love you, I love you, she said silently. Clearly they had some telepathic ability—aka amazing chemistry—so maybe he did know what she was thinking.

She didn't mind anymore. She loved him like crazy and she wanted him to know. But she wouldn't say it. Wouldn't put that on him right now . . . just in case he didn't feel the same way. And Ivy honestly didn't know if he did or didn't.

"Listen, Ivy. I will meet you back at the secret apartment," he whispered, "at exactly six o'clock. Triple check that you have your cell phone if you go anywhere with your mom, okay?"

"Six o'clock," she repeated, squeezing his hand.

When the door closed behind him, her mother said, "Handsome. What do detectives make these days?"

Ivy laughed. "Mom, don't be so focused on money."

"Money does buy happiness, Ivy. This past week,

what were you able to do for yourself? You probably couldn't even afford a massage."

"I have a pretty good nest egg, Mom. It's called working hard and saving money for the future."

Dana waved her hand dismissively in the air. "It's just as easy to marry rich as to marry a schlub." She then launched into a long story about her friend Ellen, who married a high school math teacher and was now forced to vacation only once a year in Florida. That actually sounded very nice to Ivy, but she knew better than to even try to open her mother's mind.

With a smile, Ivy settled down on the sofa as her mother made a pot of coffee. She'd almost forgotten that the best way to forget her troubles was to spend a little time in her mother's fantasy world.

After an hour at the precinct and a meeting with his partner and captain, Griffin headed to Donovan's Salon.

Nice place. Marble floors, a huge arrangement of fresh flowers on the reception desk, and some New Age music coming from the speakers. Griffin showed the woman at the front desk his badge, and in moments, Donovan appeared.

"Detective, what can I do for you?" the young man asked, his greenish snakeskin pants so tight Griffin wondered how he breathed. The man eyed Griffin's hair. "I'd say just a trim, really. You have great hair," he added, his hands suddenly on Griffin's head.

"Whoa," Griffin said, stepping back. "I'm actually

here to ask a few questions about a murder that occurred nearby."

He grimaced. "Oooh, yes, we all heard about that." He gestured to a black leather chair. "Well, hop on, and we can talk and get you groomed at the same time."

Griffin eyed himself in the mirror. He could use a trim, he supposed. He usually went to an ancient barber who had one of those old-fashioned joints with the swiveling pole, but while he was here, he might as well save time.

You want to look good for Ivy, he chided his reflection as Donovan settled a black cape over him. Yup, he did. *Nothing wrong with wanting to look good for the woman you love.*

He bolted up.

"Buddy, you are damned lucky I'm not giving you an old-fashioned shave, or you would have been sliced. Ever see those old Clint Eastwood movies where the barber sharpens his razor on a hanging strip of leather? Man, I love those classics. And the Dirty Harry ones, too. 'Go ahead, make my day.' Hey, ever say that to a perp?"

No wonder Donovan and Dana Sedgwick got along so well. Griffin settled back down on the chair, putting aside his very startling thoughts about his feelings for Ivy, and got to the matter at hand: her mother and the morning of the murder.

By the time Griffin was settling his tab at reception, he had both a good haircut and the corroboration he'd hoped for.

Ivy would be happy. And that made *him* happy.

* * *

After lunch at the trendy new vegetarian restaurant her mother had been dying to try, Ivy and Dana headed back toward her mom's apartment. After a cloudy, cool morning, the sun had come out, and Ivy slipped her arm through her mother's, feeling very much at peace. She'd told her mom about the first letter from William Sedgwick, and after a few choice words for her husband of one week, Dana had again swiped dismissively at the air.

"You're doing just fine without his stupid money," her mother had said over their soy and seitan lunches. And coming from her mother, that was one hell of a compliment.

"So what do you have planned for your first day back?" Ivy asked as they walked up Madison Avenue, naturally her mother's favorite walking zone.

"Oh, I just remembered," Dana said. "I need to go to Tiffany's to buy Georgia Davenport an engagement gift. Not that she even invited me to the engagement party, which I think is tonight. Or maybe tomorrow. Bitch. But do I love Tiffany's. Come with me, honey."

"Tiffany's makes me feel poor," Ivy said. "I can't afford a key chain there."

Dana laughed. "But if you don't come with me, how will you pick out the engagement ring of your dreams?"

"Mom, I don't think any engagement rings are in my future."

"Oh, I do. I saw the way you and that handsome detective were looking at each other. And do you think I wasn't spying on you in the kitchen? I saw him touch you."

Ivy smiled. "There might be something going on between us."

Dana squeezed Ivy's shoulders. "I must say, dear, you do look happy. Happier than I've ever seen you look. And you have every right to look very happy after all you've been through. So I'd say you're in love."

Ivy blushed.

"So do detectives make a decent living?" Dana asked, and then began chattering nonstop about Georgia Davenport's engagement ring, an heirloom passed down from her grandmother. This would be the second time Georgia gave *herself* the ring.

"Georgia scored herself a real catch," Dana continued. "Young, too. Early thirties and handsome. And she's pushing *fifty*. And not exactly a beauty, either. But apparently, it was love at first sight between her and David McKeren. According to Georgie, he's the son of an oil magnate. A Texan. With a drawl and everything. What do you think I should get them? I don't know Georgie very well. A candy dish, maybe?"

Ivy stopped dead in her tracks.

David McKeven. DM.

It could be just a coincidence. As Cornelia Beckham's fiancé's initials had been. Ivy was sure it was. But a little casual snooping into Georgia Davenport's life was how Ivy was going to spend the rest of her afternoon.

As Griffin headed back to his apartment to pack a bag for tonight, he could have sworn someone was following him. That nagging feeling wouldn't go away, despite no one being behind him on Sixty-second Street but an elderly couple.

And then he was shoved from behind with such force that his head hit the parked car in front of him. Griffin bolted up. Declan stood at the corner, grinning.

"Loser!" Declan shouted, then ran.

Griffin chased him down the street toward Central Park. Damn. There were too many hiding places in the park. He'd lose him.

Just keep your eyes on him the entire time, he cautioned himself.

He kept chase, Declan about five hundred feet ahead. Just as he'd thought, Declan ran into the park. Griffin had no doubt Declan was baiting him, leading him into a deserted area where he'd try to either kill him or knock him out as a lesson.

Payback for Gretchen, maybe.

Griffin chased after him, for the first time wishing the park didn't have so many of those damned boulders.

Where the hell is he?

"Oh, brother, you looking for me?"

Declan's head poked out from behind one of the boulders. Then he ran again, and Griffin leapt from higher ground, tackling Declan.

It was then that he realized Declan had something in his hand. A brick.

And before he could even blink, the brick came crashing down on his head. Again. And again.

Chapter Nineteen

It was a good thing that Ivy's mother was such a fount of knowledge about Georgia Davenport. Ivy knew where she lived, whether or not she preferred the Food Emporium or Gristedes supermarket, that she wore her slacks hemmed too low as though she were Madonna, and where her engagement party was being held. Apparently, Dana didn't run in Georgia's much wealthier social circle, and she was spitting mad that the Sedgwick name didn't open up more doors for her. After all, her mother had argued, it was the name that should matter most.

Ivy had refrained from laughing.

But she did learn that Georgia had inherited over three million dollars from her late husband, who'd died two years ago. And that the engagement party was being held at Fritz's, an elegant restaurant in midtown.

Ivy glanced at her watch. It was now five o'clock. She'd need to meet Griffin at six, and then they'd disguise themselves much better than they originally had, and crash the party. This time, Ivy would not leave Griffin's side. She wasn't taking any chances.

She stopped to call Griffin. No answer. That was unusual. Perhaps he was in conference with his captain? She'd try him again in ten minutes.

Fritz's was located just a few blocks up. Ivy figured she'd check it out, survey the entrance and exits, note the surrounding buildings and stores. As Ivy neared the restaurant, she noticed several well-dressed couples going in, one of the women in a full-length fur coat, despite the warm temperature. Could the party have started already? It was five o'clock, so not *that* early.

A sign on the glass door said: CLOSED FOR PRIVATE PARTY. Ivy glanced down at her outfit, grateful she'd worn a skirt for the sake of her mother. Her tights and knee-high flat leather boots weren't exactly fancy-party wear, but she would likely get away with appearing to be part of the catering staff. She slipped inside the crowded entrance. People were just arriving, giving their coats to a woman inside a walk-in closet.

Ivy slipped past, keeping her head down, and walked toward the swinging doors of the kitchen, which were down a hallway. Inside, chefs were bustling at stations, and the waitstaff, wearing red aprons, were hurrying with trays of hors d'oeuvres. Ivy saw a coatrack with several aprons hanging and grabbed one, slipping into it nonchalantly.

"Hey, you!" snapped a voice.

Ivy whirled around. A man wearing a red apron marched up to her. "You're late, first of all. And second of all, all waiters, including ones from the catering place, must wear these red hats." He reached into a box and placed one on Ivy's head. It was like a mini fedora, but without the feather.

And would do well to disguise her, if she kept her head down.

"Jesus, what are you waiting for?" the man said. "Take a tray and go. We have enough staff at the front. Head to the back area. And I don't want to see any empty plates lying around. If you see empty plates on the tables, you're to bus them immediately."

Ivy nodded. "Will do." She headed back down the hallway carrying a heavy tray of what appeared to be chicken satay. The smell of the peanut sauce in such volume so close to her nose was making her a little sick.

She weaved her way through the crowd. Several guests stopped her with an "Mmm, that looks delicious," but eventually Ivy made her way to the back of the room, where there were fewer guests mingling. The bar was toward the front, but a three-piece jazz band was in the back. There was a decent-size dance floor, which Ivy imagined would be filled with shaking hips in about a half hour, when guests finished their first drinks.

"Ooh, Miss, I'd like to try that," a man said.

Ivy stopped and smiled and fixed him a plate.

"They say the third time's the charm, right? I hope this one lasts."

"I'm an optimist," Ivy said. "So, I think it will."

"Crazy, though. They were just dating for a couple of months, then whammo, they get engaged. Georgie was pressing him for a commitment, to give up the other women who were undoubtedly in his life, and finally, he popped the question. I've never seen her so happy. Well, except at her first wedding, of course."

And just where is this question-popping groom? Ivy wondered.

She smiled. "Did you like the chicken satay?" she asked, using the opportunity to stand slightly behind the man, who was on the large side, and look around.

"Delicious," he said, then looked Ivy up and down. "Just like you. I wouldn't mind seeing what's under that apron. After the party, we could—"

"I'd better serve the rest of the chicken before it gets cold," Ivy said. She leaned closer. "If my boss catches me chatting with the guests, I could get fired."

He smiled and patted her on the butt. "Off with you then."

What a jerk!

Her head down, Ivy walked around with her tray, stopping to place the appetizers on little plates and picking up empty plates with half-eaten chicken flesh.

And just as she was about to ask the couple in front of her if they would like to sample the chicken satay, she stopped dead in her tracks.

Not fifty feet away, laughing loudly at something an older man had said, was Declan McLean. He wore a tuxedo, a rosebud pinned in the button-hole. His hair was white blond and he seemed to be wearing light blue–colored contact lenses. He wore silver, square-shaped eyeglasses and had a bit of a goatee. He looked erudite. And very handsome. And totally different.

"Congratulations, David!" a middle-aged woman

said to Declan. "It's such a pleasure to meet you. Georgia was just telling me all about you."

"The pleasure is all mine," he drawled in a reasonable Texas accent.

Ivy noted the way he looked into the woman's eyes, a hint of seduction, of masculine appreciation of her charms. She watched as he slid his gaze to her ample cleavage, then back up to her face. *So that's how he does it,* Ivy thought.

And the woman seemed delighted, as though she were in on a little secret. That the groom found her hot.

Ivy turned around and began loading her tray with empty plates. She needed to slip outside and call Griffin right away.

"Ladies and gentlemen," a voice called from the front of the restaurant. "My treasured guests."

Ivy stayed behind a group while straining to see. A very thin, forty-something woman in a very ornate white dress stood next to Declan; they each had a glass of champagne in their hands. Based on what her mother told her about Georgia, who was too thin, blond, and tanned for her mother's liking, Ivy was looking at the bride-to-be.

"I have a very special announcement," Georgia said. "You have been invited here this evening to celebrate our engagement, but also to witness our wedding." The guests began buzzing. "Yes, David and I are to be married this evening. Surprise!"

"This is how we Texans like to do things," Declan–David said to a big laugh and applause. He then gave Georgia one hell of a kiss, including a dip.

Unbelievable, Ivy thought as she weaved her way

around the far side of the crowd, her tray held up to block her face. She hurried to the kitchen and set down the empty tray on a stack of others, then hurried back out.

And ran smack into a very angry-looking Declan McLean.

"You just can't stay out of my business, can you?" he whispered. He grabbed her and pushed her out a door. It was the garbage area. He threw her on the ground on the far side of the Dumpster, her head banging into it.

"Declan—"

He reached inside the pocket of his jacket and withdrew a small silver handgun. It glinted in the gathering darkness. "I told you when I last saw you that if you butted into my business again, I'd kill you. See the silencer, Ivy?" he asked, standing directly over her. "You're dead, baby. But first, I'm going to have a little fun. If I have to screw that old hag tonight, I might as well get a tight piece of ass right here."

"If you lay one hand—"

He laughed. "You'll what? Scream? Yell for your boyfriend? Well, he can't help you, Ivy. I got rid of him today. That's right. I bashed his fucking head in."

Ignore him, Ivy told herself. *He's lying.*

"Don't believe me?" he asked, unzipping his pants and leaning down to press the gun at her temple. "Call him. He won't be coming to the phone for days, Ivy. And if he does, you won't be able to understand a word he says. Not with his brains all over his face."

"What are you talking about?" she said, her blood freezing in her veins.

"Let's just say that your boyfriend won't be coming to your rescue." He laughed. "Tsk-tsk, Ivy. I don't think Dead Daddy Dearest would have approved of Griffin, either."

Griffin is fine, Ivy told herself. *He is fine and on his way to the secret apartment right now. Don't let Declan distract you.*

"What did my father have against you?" she asked.

"Not much," he said. "He caught me fucking Gretchen on his desk one night. For a major corporation, you'd think your father would have had better security. I had more sex in his office than he did."

"I'm surprised my father didn't give you a raise and a promotion instead," Ivy said.

Declan laughed. "He might have, but I told him if he said one word to you—if you ever found out from him or any of his lackeys—I'd kill you and your sisters."

Ivy gasped. So that was why her father wouldn't state his reasons.

"So go ahead, sweetheart," Declan said. "Call your boyfriend. I'll bet he doesn't answer his phone." Declan handed her his cell phone with a smile.

Ivy's heart hammered in her chest. She pressed in Griffin's number. No answer. After five rings it went to voice mail.

Declan laughed, then used the gun to lift up her skirt. "Thanks for wearing a skirt. You made this so much easier for me, hon." He lay down on top of her, the gun at her temple.

Ivy squeezed her eyes shut. She felt Declan's erection pressing against her thigh. His hands went under her apron, under her shirt, and he grabbed her breasts hard. He rubbed against her, groaning, the gun never wavering from her head.

He was moaning now, his hands reaching up her skirt and roughly pulling aside her underwear. And when he reached inside his pants to pull himself out, Ivy took the one chance she had.

She kneed him as hard as she could between his legs. She nailed him. He shouted in pain and fell off her, the gun clanking to the ground.

She scrambled to get up, but he grabbed her around the ankles and she went down, her head hitting the rough pavement hard. For a second she saw white spots. Then black. And then her vision cleared. And this time she was in a more vulnerable position. Declan lunged at her from behind, pressing her down on her stomach with his body.

"Let's try this again," he said, hitting her hard on the temple with the butt of the gun. She felt dizzy. So, so dizzy. "You know I prefer it doggie-style anyway, baby."

Griffin came to, his head pounding. He pressed his hand to his temple and it came away sticky with blood.

Ivy. He had to get to Ivy.

His cell phone was ringing. Griffin managed to get it out of his pocket, but didn't recognize the number and it stopped ringing by the time he flipped it open. He tried to sit up, but got such a stab of wincing pain that he lay back down, squeezing his eyes shut against the throbbing in his head.

He called Ivy's cell, but it rang and went to voice

mail. He tried the phone at the secret apartment but there was no answer.

He tried her mother's apartment and after simply saying who he was, he got a nonstop earful about lunch and Bloomingdale's and then a woman named Georgia Davenport, who was engaged to an oil magnate named David McSomething and who had the nerve to not invite Dana to some party at Fritz's tonight, despite it being so close to her apartment.

David McSomething.

Declan.

"Dana, did you tell Ivy about this?"

"Why, yes, of course," Dana said. "I tried to get her to come with me to Tiffany's to buy a gift, but she said she had some police business to take care of."

Shit. No. No!

Griffin tried to stand, but his legs buckled, and he went down. *Get up,* he told himself. But when he tried again, almost making it to a kneeling position, he fell back down again, and this time, everything went black.

Chapter Twenty

"Yum, I can't wait to have this delicious ass," Declan said into her ear. "I really did love you, Ivy. I was going to marry you even though you had nothing. No money. Nothing coming in ever. That's how much I loved you. But then that stupid bitch Jennifer gave me a hard time about seeing me with Laura. And I thought she was talking about you at first. She kept saying she was going to tell you. So I bashed her head into the wall. And then I find out she was talking about that skank Laura."

Oh, my God, Ivy thought. *He is most definitely a murderer. And he has a gun. Be careful.*

"I killed her for nothing," he continued, "and ended up losing you anyway. I would have left you alone. Even though you were fucking my brother. But then you wouldn't leave me alone, would you?"

Ivy kept quiet. Anything she said would antagonize him. She'd have to think. Think her way out of this alive.

"You just can't keep away from me, can you?" he murmured into her ear, his tongue following, to

Ivy's disgust. He pulled her underwear down, and she took the opportunity to kick her leg back. He grunted and fell back, and she scrambled to the far side of the Dumpster.

"You stupid bitch," he said. "After I rape you, I'm going to blow your brains out, just like I knocked the brains out of your boyfriend."

Ivy frantically looked around in the dusk for something, anything to use as a weapon. And then she found it. A broken piece of pipe. There were several of them, she saw, under the Dumpster. She grabbed one and waited.

When he came around to her side, she whaled the length of pipe as though it were a baseball bat and his head were the ball. And down he went.

Ivy fell to her knees. She was in the first throes of shock. She had to get out of there.

But as she bolted up, his hands reached out and tripped her, and she fell. This time he stood over her, blood dripping from the gaping wound in his head, the gun pointed at her chest.

"Bye-bye, bitch," he said, and leaned down to put the gun between her eyes.

I love you, Griffin, she said silently. Then said a prayer.

She heard the shot but didn't feel any pain. *That's loud for a silencer,* she thought numbly, wondering if she were dead.

And then Declan, a bullet hole to his chest, fell down next to her.

Ivy whirled around.

Griffin stood there, a bloody mess, his gun dangling at his side.

A crowd had begun to form. Ivy heard someone

say, "Oh my God, someone call the police!" And then there was screaming.

Griffin's legs seemed to give out and he dropped down to his knees. Ivy raced over to him.

"Griffin, stay with me. Stay with me. Please. You got him. It's over. Stay with me!" she said over and over, her pleas drowned out by the sound of the wailing sirens.

Now it was Ivy's turn to sit by Griffin's hospital bedside. She held on to his hand and sat and sat until the morning light broke, unable, unwilling to let go.

"I killed him, didn't I?" he said.

Ivy jumped up. "Griffin."

"Did I?"

She didn't know how he'd take the news. But who else to tell him but her? "Yes. He's gone."

He took a deep breath and winced in pain.

"You saved my life, Griffin," she told him, leaning her head gently on his chest.

"So does that mean you owe me a favor for life?" he asked, those dark eyes on hers.

"Absolutely. Anything."

"Marry me."

Tears sprang to her eyes. "I thought you'd never ask."

He smiled and squeezed her hand.

Chapter Twenty-one

Three months later . . .

Once again, Ivy sat before the mirror at the dressing table in the back room of the church in Applewood, scowling at the rhinestone-studded barrette holding her veil in place.

That was where the similarity to the other wedding she'd planned ended. Well, except for her attendants and some of the guests.

Her sisters fluffing her train and arranging her veil, her mother out doing the meeting and greeting, Ivy stared at her reflection and laughed. She was never so happy to be sticking a girlie barrette in her scalp. She'd never been so happy before, period.

There was a knock at the door, and Ivy shouted a "Come in."

"Excuse me, Miss Sedgwick."

Ivy turned around to find her father's attorney, George Harris, standing before her. Had she invited him?

"Please forgive the intrusion," he said. "However,

in the event of your impending marriage to another, your father left instructions for this letter to be delivered to you on your wedding day. The instructions call for you to read the letter aloud with your sisters present."

Ivy and her sisters stared at each other. She took the letter from Mr. Harris, slit open the envelope, and pulled out one piece of paper. Handwritten, this time.

> *Dear Ivy, Olivia, and Amanda,*
> *I've always wanted to say I'm sorry. For not being the father all of you deserved. In my own way, a way I know wasn't close to being good enough, I did love each one of you. And I wish you all the best. You will soon learn from my good attorney that I've left you three the bulk of my estate, to do with as you please. I know money doesn't buy happiness. Trust me, I know. But it's what I have to give at this late point. And it's yours.*
> *P.S. Ivy, I knew you'd end up with a good man.*
> *With love, your father, William Sedgwick*

Ivy, Amanda, and Olivia stared at each other, tears in all of their eyes. They stood and held hands and observed a moment of silence for their father. They had each made their peace with him.

"Ivy! Yoo-hoo! Showtime!" her mother called, poking her head through the door. She eyed their solemn, yet happy faces. "What I miss?"

"And now," the bandleader called. "I present to you, for the first time, Mr. and Mrs. Fargo!"

Griffin blushed and Ivy beamed as they entered the ballroom hand in hand. They stood in the center of the beautifully decorated room, tiny twinkling lights above them, and danced to their song, "You're My Best Friend" by Queen, which just so turned out to be a favorite song of both the bride and the groom.

And then Ivy danced the night away, including a slow dance with Joey, who'd brought his new—very appropriate and very sweet—girlfriend as his date.

Dan, still her partner, unfortunately, jitterbugged up to her, a full glass of wine in his hand, which he sloppily sipped. "Hey, Ivy, good thing I didn't spill my beer on you. You might need to let someone else borrow this one."

Ivy smiled. She hoped so. Because if dresses did hold the promise of the future, this one would surely last a lifetime.

If you enjoyed *Shadowing Ivy*,
don't miss the other two novels in the trilogy
that tell the romantic and suspenseful stories
of Ivy's half sisters, Amanda and Olivia.

Read on for special excerpts from
Janelle Taylor's

WATCHING AMANDA
and
HAUNTING OLIVIA

WATCHING AMANDA

Chapter One

A beautiful dark-haired woman wearing an ankle-length fur coat and matching earmuffs was throwing a temper tantrum—complete with foot stomps—in the lobby of the Metropolitan Hotel. While her two children played tug-of-war with a silk flower plucked from a previously lovely display, the woman wagged a manicured finger in Amanda Sedgwick's face.

Amanda, one of the Metropolitan's many front desk clerks, sat on her uncomfortable little stool behind the mile-long, granite reception counter and resisted the impulse to jump up and grab the woman's finger. She forced herself to smile "the Metropolitan way" and checked her computer monitor again. "I'm sorry, Ms. Willington, but your reservation is for only one room and we're completely booked. I can have a porter send up two cots for your—"

The woman narrowed her cold blue eyes. "Did you say *cots*? I don't think so. You are to find me two suitable rooms—my usual suite and an adjoining double with two full-sized beds for my children. *Immediately*. And it's *Mrs*. Willington. Not *Ms*."

Amanda mentally referred to the Metropolitan Hotel Handbook she'd received when she began working at the hotel eight months ago: *Metropolitan Hotel front desk clerks are Guest Specialists. Metropolitan Hotel policy is that the guest is always right—even when he or she appears to be in the wrong or is exceedingly difficult*. To Amanda it seemed that "exceedingly difficult" was a euphemism for obnoxious.

Hmmm, so since there was no suite with an adjoining double room available anywhere in this entire huge, thirty-two-story hotel, how exactly was Amanda to produce one?

"I wish there was—" Amanda began.

Mrs. Willington stepped closer, removed her earmuffs, and slid the band around her wrist. "Clerk, I don't care what you wish. I want two suitable rooms, adjoining, *now*."

How dare you, you pompous prima donna! Amanda yelled back—silently, of course. *I want this, I want that! Well, I want my baby boy to wake up healthy tomorrow. I want to be home with him right now instead of arguing with you. I want so many things . . .*

Amanda said none of this. It wasn't the Metropolitan way. The Metropolitan was one of the most expensive hotels in Manhattan. And as a "guest specialist," Amanda's job was to make Mrs. Willington happy.

The problem was that there weren't two adjoining rooms available. Mrs. Willington could have a double for herself and a double across the hall with two twin beds for her children, or she could have the one suite she reserved for all of them. The Metropolitan was hosting three different conventions this weekend, and the annual Christmas tree lighting at Rockefeller Center—just blocks away and a major attraction in a city full of attractions—was scheduled for this Tuesday. The hotel was booked.

Period.

Amanda forced another smile and explained to Mrs. Willington that she had two options: the one suite or the two non-adjoining doubles.

Was that steam coming out of Mrs. Willington's ears? *Yes, I do believe it is,* Amanda thought. The full force of the woman's anger was about to be let loose on Amanda, but luckily, Mrs. Willington's children had chosen that moment to chase each other around their mother, grabbing her fur coat to stop themselves from falling.

Mrs. Willington let out a shriek. "Stop that right now!" she yelled to her children, who stuck out their tongues at each other but listened. The woman smoothed the ruffled fur and turned back to Amanda. Or, rather, she turned back to Amanda's counter and began pounding on the call bell next to Amanda's computer monitor.

Amanda could feel her cheeks burning. The lunatic woman banged on the bell with unnecessary force. People in line and milling about the marble and glass lobby stopped and stared. Even Mrs. Willington's own children stopped throwing jelly beans at each other to stare at their mother—and they had to be used to her by now.

Amanda counted to three (one of the Metropolitan employee handbook's suggestions for dealing with "exceedingly difficult" guests). "Mrs. Willington, if you'll—"

Ding! Ding! Ding! Ding! Ding!

She pounded on the bell with all her strength.

"Mrs. Willington! How lovely to see you again!"

Uh-oh, that was the voice of Anne Pilsby, the front desk manager. Amanda's boss.

Amanda glanced behind Mrs. Willington to find Anne rushing up to the woman. Anne's mouth was drawn into a tight coral line as she shot Amanda a withering look.

"Mrs. Willington," Anne gushed, smoothing her fitted tweed jacket, "I do hope everything is to your satisfaction this afternoon."

"It most certainly is not," enunciated Mrs. Willington, who launched into a tirade about Amanda's lack of skills, initiative, hospitality, and diplomacy, especially when dealing with the wife of F. W. Willington.

Amanda had no idea who F. W. Willington was. And it was a shame that his wife seemed to think she had no other identity.

"Step aside, Ms. Sedgwick," Anne snapped, practically pushing Amanda out of the way to ease behind her computer. A few minutes and clicks of the keyboard later, Anne smiled. "Ah, I have found the perfect set of adjoining rooms for you, Mrs. Willington. Miss Sedgwick should have known there is always a set of rooms on reserve for our treasured guests. A suite for yourself, as always, with an adjoining double room with two full-size beds for your beautiful children. How big they're getting!" Anne added, smiling at the kids, who were now taking turns flying the silk flower through air as though it were an airplane.

"Ow!" yelped a woman, whirling to see what had poked her sharply in the back. The flower dropped

to the floor at her feet. She glared at the children,
now giggling and hiding behind their mother's
legs. The woman waited for the mother's apology.

There was none.

"Brats," the woman muttered and stalked away.
Anne ignored the incident, so clearly the injured
party was not a wealthy repeat guest of the Metropolitan Hotel.

"I expect to be compensated for having to ring
this bell so hard," Mrs. Willington said. "My hand is
hurting now."

Oh, brother! Amanda thought, rolling her eyes.
Was she kidding?

"Of course," Anne replied with a consoling smile.
"A complimentary hand massage in our spa should
do the trick."

No, she wasn't kidding. Neither was Anne, who
lied about "on reserve" rooms. Yet she'd done some
fast and clever guest reassignment.

Satisfied, Mrs. Willington grabbed her children
by the hands and headed for the elevator. Anne
snapped her fingers high in the air, and a porter
rushed to help Mrs. Willington with her luggage.

Anne turned to Amanda, the bright white smile
now replaced by a frown. "Amanda, I'm very disappointed in the way you handled one of our
best—"

The phone rang at Amanda's station. As any of
the front desk clerks could answer the ringing line
from their stations, Amanda decided this wasn't the
time to interrupt her boss's *That Wasn't the Metropolitan Way* speech.

"Well, answer it!" Anne barked, shaking her
head.

I hate this job. I hate this job. I hate this job, Amanda silently chanted, picking up the phone.

"Metropolitan Hotel, front desk," Amanda said in the Metropolitan way—which meant with forced good cheer.

"Amanda, thank God I got you," came Lettie Monroe's panicked voice. "Tommy is burning up with fever. It's over a hundred and four! And he's so listless. I'm worried, Amanda."

Oh no. Lettie, Amanda's neighbor and her eleven-month-old son's babysitter, wasn't prone to exaggeration. Amanda squeezed shut her eyes for a second and tried to will the panic away. "Lettie, take Tommy to the emergency room in a cab right now. I'll meet you there."

"I'm on my way," Lettie responded. "See you soon."

Amanda hung up the phone. "Anne," she said to her boss, "I'll need to lea—"

Anne put her hands on her hips and surveyed Amanda. "You've needed to leave early two other times this month. Babies get sick, Amanda. It's what they do. I've raised two of my—"

Babies get sick. It's what they do. . . .

"Tommy was a month premature, Anne," Amanda interrupted through gritted teeth as she gathered her purse and checked her wallet for cab fare. "He's prone to—"

Anne dismissed her with a wave of her own manicured hand. "Maybe if you'd breastfed, you wouldn't have such a sickly child."

Amanda recoiled as if slapped in the face. How dare she! "For your information, not that it's any of your business, I did breast—"

"I'm not interested in your personal life,

Amanda," Anne said, raising her chin in a show of dismissal. "If you abandon your post, I'll have no choice but to permanently relieve you of your employment at the Metropolitan Hotel. Your frequent absences leave us short-staffed without proper notice, per the Metropolitan Employee Handbook."

No. Amanda couldn't lose her job. No job meant no health insurance. And Tommy's frequent ear infections and high fevers meant constant trips to the pediatrician.

There was no way Amanda could afford COBRA on what meager savings she had.

"Anne, please." Amanda abandoned her indignation and flat-out pleaded. "Tommy is very sick. He has a fever of a hundred and four, and he's—"

"And it seems your babysitter is fully capable of taking him to the hospital," Anne interrupted. "If I ran home every time my child got a cold I would not have achieved the position I hold now."

Amanda refrained from taking the glass of cold water on her desk and throwing it in her boss's face.

"Tommy doesn't have a cold," Amanda said. "He could be seriously ill and—"

Anne held up her palm in Amanda's face. "I've now wasted ten minutes of my own day and this hotel's time in dealing with you, Amanda. Enough is enough. This was the third time I've had to warn you about your attendance record. Pack up your locker, return your name pin and uniform, and see payroll about picking up your final paycheck. I'll alert them that you're coming. You're fired."

Who are you, you monster? Amanda thought numbly. This wasn't happening. This couldn't be happening.

"The only place I'm going is to the hospital," Amanda told Anne. She took off her name pin and thrust it into the woman's hand.

"Ow!" Anne yelped. "You pricked me."

The phone rang at Amanda's desk. Amanda grabbed it, praying it wasn't Lettie with more bad news about Tommy.

It wasn't. It was a guest wanting information.

"It's for you," Amanda told Anne and shoved the phone at her before running across the lobby, praying she could get a cab.

Only when she was outside in the chilly December air did she realize she forgot to get her coat and hat.

Amanda frantically raised her arm to hail a taxi in front of the hotel. *Please, please, please,* she prayed to the fates of the universe.

As if this is my lucky day, she thought, letting out a frustrated breath as occupied taxi after occupied taxi sped past. Finding a cab in midtown Manhattan was never easy, let alone at the start of rush hour and during the holiday season. The streets were crowded with New Yorkers and tourists coming and going in every direction

Amanda shivered in her thin uniform. If a taxi didn't come soon, Amanda would have to waste more time running back inside for her coat, which was on the basement level in the "hourly employee" locker rooms.

Please, please, please, she prayed again, extending her arm as far as it could go, her eyes darting to check for available cabs.

Yes! A taxi was pulling to a stop right in front of the hotel and right in front of Amanda. *Thank you,* she whispered to the darkening sky. She rushed over to the cab and claimed it by holding on to the door handle, prepared to pull it open the moment the slowpokes inside appeared ready to emerge.

Hurry up, please! she silently shouted at the occupants of the backseat, who were taking their sweet time. The man had his hand in his wallet, and the woman, who was facing the other way, had a silver cell phone pressed to her ear.

As she watched the male occupant pay the driver and await his change, she decided she would try to talk to Anne tomorrow, when she went back for her coat. Maybe Ms. Scrooge would be in a better mood. Or find an ounce of holiday season compassion in her heart.

Come on, Amanda urged the couple silently. Finally, the man turned to open the door, and Amanda pulled it open for him. *Out, out, out!* she coaxed mentally. He was yakking into his own cell phone while extending a hand into the taxi to help the woman, also still gabbing on her phone.

Finally, the woman emerged. And Amanda froze. It was her sister.

Her half sister, actually. Olivia Sedgwick.

Without looking in Amanda's direction once, despite the fact that Amanda was standing a foot in front of her sister, Olivia dashed onto the curb, saying something into the phone about a "layout." As Amanda stood there openmouthed, her hand barely still touching the cab's door, the man pressed something into Amanda's hand, then joined Olivia on the curb and escorted her into the hotel.

Amanda opened her fist to find a five dollar bill.

Well, isn't that humiliating, Amanda thought, darting into the taxi and giving the driver her destination.

Olivia's companion clearly took Amanda, dressed in uniform, for a front-door valet, whose job it was to greet arriving guests.

As the driver flipped the meter and pulled away from the curb, Amanda glanced out the window just in time to see Olivia and the man greet some well-dressed people who were seated at a grouping of plush sofas in the lobby. She watched Olivia smile and laugh and shake hands, and then as the taxi swerved into a lane that was actually moving, she lost sight of her sister and turned back around.

Whoa. Olivia Sedgwick in the flesh. She felt a stab of envy and longing that startled her. She thought she had accepted the very different lives her sisters led and put them in their proper perspective years ago.

When was the last time I saw her? Amanda wondered. *When was the last time I saw my other half sister, Ivy? Or the only person we all have in common: our father, winner of the I-Can't-Be-Bothered-To-Be-A-Father award, William Sedgwick.*

It had been years since she'd spoken to her father, but Amanda could pinpoint the exact day she had last spoken to her sisters: eleven months ago, on the day her son, Tommy, was born on a snowy January morning.

Because he'd been premature, she barely had a look at him before he was whisked away to the neonatal intensive care unit. And while they were separated for that short while before she could go see him, she was so overcome with longing for her family—and overcome with longing to provide her newborn son with family—that she picked up the phone in the room and called Olivia and immediately got her answering machine. Amanda had left a message, informing Olivia that she was a brand new aunt and that mother and child were doing well at Lenox Hill Hospital.

Amanda had left the same message for their other half sister, Ivy. And then she called her father's office, which was the only number she had for William Sedgwick. Though it was only eight o'-clock in the morning when she'd phoned, William's secretary had answered. William had been in, but in a closed-door meeting and had asked not to be disturbed for any reason. Amanda didn't want to reduce the birth of his grandson to a message on a While You Were Out pad, but she wasn't sure William would call back if she didn't leave a message of magnitude. The secretary, a very pleasant-sounding woman, congratulated Amanda heartily, and assured her she'd let William know the great news the moment the conference room door opened.

It must have been some long meeting.

Chapter Two

From the beginning of her pregnancy Amanda knew that Tommy's extended family would have to come from her side; there was no other side. Tommy's father wanted nothing to do with her or their child.

Don't think about him, Amanda cautioned herself. But of course she did. Too often. Paul Swinwood's good-looking face, his warm brown eyes, that one dimple in his left cheek, appeared before her mind's eye. And as always, she had to blink back the sting of tears that accompanied any thought of him.

She'd loved him.

She'd known him only a few months, but she'd been crazy in love with him.

"I can't, Amanda," he'd said when she told him she was pregnant with his child. "I'm sorry, but this isn't what I want. I am so sorry."

That was it. She'd told him she was pregnant, and five minutes later he'd left her apartment. She never saw him again. She'd tried to call him during her pregnancy, and when Tommy was born. His phone had been disconnected. And her letters had come back marked "Return To Sender."

Amanda had always considered herself a smart woman, a good judge of character. She'd truly believed that Paul had loved her, too.

Yeah, so why did he abandon you the minute you told him you were pregnant? Why did he change his phone number and flee his apartment? Yet she had refused to phone or visit him at his company.

"Maybe he was just too scared," her best friend, Jenny, had said. "Jerk! Coward! I don't care if the two of you were only dating for a few months. So what? A decent human being doesn't run away from something like that! Jerk!"

Jenny sounded off on the issue of Paul Swinwood for days, weeks, months. Finally, right before she had given birth, Amanda told Jenny to let it go. Paul was gone, and that was the only issue on the table. Amanda's future and her baby's future were what Amanda had to focus on. Not the merits or lack thereof of a man she didn't know as well as she thought she did.

And so, with no father handing out cigars the moment Thomas Sedgwick came into the world, with no grandmother knitting baby booties—Amanda's beloved mother had passed away several years ago—with no family in the world other than her long-estranged father and her long-estranged half sisters, Amanda wanted desperately for her son to have the family that Amanda had never had.

And so she'd called her half sisters. And she'd called her father.

And she'd received the same response from all three.

A "Congratulations On Your New Baby" card, inside which was a check. One thousand dollars from William Sedgwick, and one hundred dollars each from Olivia and Ivy. In addition to the checks, her father and sisters had also each sent flowers and a stuffed animal. A plush teddy bear from William and one from Olivia and an adorable giraffe from Ivy.

Tommy loved all three.

Neither sister visited Amanda in the hospital or asked to see Tommy, their nephew. They had both called back the day Tommy was born, each congratulating her, and each with a reasonable excuse as to why she couldn't come to the hospital. Olivia, a features editor of a national women's magazine, was going on location somewhere for an important photo shoot with a supermodel. And Ivy, a police officer in New Jersey, was working around the clock on a stakeout.

And Amanda's father, the venerable William Sedgwick, simply sent another check, this time for two thousand dollars, when Amanda left a second message telling him she would love to see him, would love for him to meet his grandson.

Amanda had sent back the first check, hard as it was to turn down a thousand dollars. Perhaps he'd thought its return meant Amanda was saying a thousand bucks wasn't enough. Perhaps the second check, which she also returned, was simply "please leave me alone" money.

Amanda didn't know. Couldn't know.

Because she didn't know her father at all.

The wealthy William Sedgwick, a man her mother never married and a father Amanda barely saw her entire life, had never been interested in Amanda or any of his daughters as far as Amanda could tell. If he were a true father to her, as she always dreamed, she might have kept the first check and opened a college fund for Tommy. But to accept what seemed like guilt money, not that William Sedgwick appeared to feel guilty for anything, was just wrong to Amanda.

She'd hoped the birth of an innocent child would sway her sisters into forging a new relationship. But neither Olivia nor Ivy seemed interested.

Born to different mothers, only one of whom had been married to William, the three Sedgwick sisters led very different lives. Amanda's mother, a former secretary of William's until her pregnancy and lovestruck gazes got her transferred to another office, also refused his "keep quiet" money and raised Amanda single-handedly in Queens. Olivia's mother, a wanna-be socialite, furious when William wouldn't marry her when she became pregnant, famously sued him for millions in child support and won a comfortable living. Ivy's mother, who often bragged that her daughter was the only legitimate one, had her marriage annulled by William within a week of their wedding. She too made out handsomely financially, and was able to raise Ivy in style.

William never married again. A brilliant businessman with no interest in family life, William rarely saw his three daughters except for a two-week summer vacation at his cottage on the southern coast of Maine. The mothers were not permitted on the property, and as each woman had her own motive for wanting her daughter invited back every year, the mothers complied.

Despite her negative feelings about William, Amanda's mother felt it was important that Amanda get to know her sisters. Olivia's mother wanted to make sure her daughter was exposed to her father's rich-and-famous lifestyle. And Ivy's mother wanted to make sure the other Sedgwick daughters, *illegitimates* as she called them, received no more, preferably *less,* than Ivy.

Over the summers, Amanda got glimpses of goodness in both her sisters, but generally, the three girls treated each other as rivals.

And grew up as strangers.

What different lives we lead, Amanda thought as the taxi sped through the Midtown Tunnel toward the New York City borough of Queens, where Amanda lived. Olivia was as glamorous as her job—beautiful, stylish, and very well-off in her own right. Ivy, much to her snooty mother's dismay, was a policewoman in a small New Jersey town and was also beautiful, but in a different way than Olivia. Ivy was earthy and natural, preferring jeans and sweaters to Olivia's cashmere and gold.

And then there was Amanda, who could hardly make ends meet, but whose son, Tommy, was worth the heartache his father had caused. If Amanda let herself think about it, the parallels between her own situation and her mother's love affair with William Sedgwick so many years ago would be particularly painful.

The family's lack of interest in getting to know Amanda and her baby was also painful, but Amanda was so fulfilled by motherhood that she stopped feeling so alone in the world.

I have my son. I have good friends. I have a roof over my head, Amanda told herself.

Well, I have a roof over my head if I can convince Anne not to fire me, she amended as the taxi bumped and swerved its way along.

Tommy was going to be all right. He'd been admitted to the hospital and had been kept overnight for observation and treatment, but it was just a bad virus.

As Amanda watched him sleep in his crib, which was against the wall in her bedroom, Tommy stirred and pressed his tiny fist against his cheek. Her heart squeezed in her chest.

I love you, my sweet boy, she whispered. *I love you so much.*

Leaning against the crib, on the baby blue round rug on the floor, was the big giraffe Ivy had sent and sitting next to it, the bear from Olivia. The sight of the stuffed animals sitting side by side made Amanda happy, made her feel as though her sisters were almost in the room, in spirit, if not physically. When she looked at the giraffe and bear she believed her sisters did care about Tommy, did want to know him, did want to be his aunts.

There was simply too wide a gulf between them for her sisters to put aside years of estrangement simply because a child had been born. But if not a child, an innocent baby, a new Sedgwick, then what?

Amanda bent over Tommy's crib and kissed his forehead, which was cooler now. He was still wheezing a bit, but at least his cough didn't sound so dire,

Amanda thought as she watched his little chest rise and fall under his blue-and-white pajamas.

Amanda glanced at her watch. It was almost eight-thirty. Anne worked until nine on Fridays. Perhaps if she called her boss now, begged—yes, begged—for her job back, Anne could be swayed. This was busy season at the hotel, and perhaps Anne needed Amanda at work tomorrow more than she needed to train a new hire.

Amanda picked up the phone and dialed. A receptionist transferred her to Anne's direct line.

"Metropolitan Hotel, front desk manager Anne Pilsby speaking."

Amanda took a deep breath. "Anne, it's Amanda Sedgwick. I wanted to tell you how sorry I am for what happened yesterday. I understand how important it is for your staff to be reliable, and I want you to know I'm taking new steps to ensure that I won't have to leave work again."

That was true. Even if those steps were baby steps. Lettie, her neighbor and Tommy's sitter, felt terrible that Amanda had gotten herself fired.

"I feel so guilty!" Lettie had said. "I should have just taken Tommy to the hospital and left you alone. The result was the same, whether you had been there or not."

But it wasn't. At the sight of his mother, Tommy had stopped crying and had sagged into her arms. If Tommy had had a bad cold or a mild fever, Amanda would have stayed at work. But a fever of one hundred four was dangerous, as was dehydration. And besides, Lettie had children in school; it wasn't fair of Amanda to ask Lettie to bring home Tommy's illnesses to her own kids.

Amanda had assured Lettie that she'd work on her boss or try to find a job that would pay the rent and allow her more flexibility. She'd yet to find one of those, though.

Please be understanding, Amanda prayed into the phone. *I need the benefits. I need the week's vacation I have coming to me.*

"I'm sorry, Amanda," Anne responded without a shred of feeling in her voice. "But I have already replaced you. Please empty the contents of your locker within a week or they will be removed and discarded. You may pick up your final paycheck, which will include your vacation pay, docked from the extra personal days you've taken this year. Human Resources can tell you how to extend your health insurance. Good-bye."

Amanda listened to the click and the buzzing dial tone for a few moments and then finally replaced the phone. She stared up at the ceiling, mentally subtracting the four extra personal days she'd taken.

Well, one day's vacation pay would still cover the electric bill and a few small Christmas gifts.

I'll get through this, she told herself. *I'm a resourceful person. If I nursed my mother through the final stages of cancer, I can do anything.*

That was hard. And at least her mother had still been alive, her warm hand still able to hold Amanda's. Her mother had been sick for over two years, and Amanda had dropped out of City College after only three semesters in order to care for her mom and also work full time. She'd never built up any kind of longevity in one industry because she needed flexibility to deal with the fluctuations of her mother's treatment. Once, she'd wanted to be a nurse, but the requirements were more than Amanda could sign on for at the time. And then her mother lost the battle and Amanda got pregnant. On her own in every sense of the word, she couldn't very well afford to go back to school for any kind of career training.

The phone rang, and Amanda jumped to answer it. Perhaps it was Anne, calling back to say she didn't want to be such a Scrooge, after all.

"Amanda Sedgwick?" asked a male voice she didn't recognize.

"Yes, this is she."

"My name is George Harris. I'm an attorney at Harris, Pinker and Swift."

Was Anne suing her? For being a bad employee?

"We represent your father, William Sedgwick," the man continued. "I'm so sorry for bothering you at this sensitive time, Ms. Sedgwick, but I do need to inform you that the reading of the will is scheduled for—"

Amanda blinked. "Excuse me?" she interrupted. "The reading of the will?"

Sensitive time?

"Your father's will," Mr. Harris explained.

"My father's will? I don't understand," Amanda said.

Silence.

"Ms. Sedgwick," the man continued, "I am very sorry. I was under the impression that you knew that William—that your father—had passed away."

What?

Amanda gripped the phone. "My father is dead?"

"Yes, unfortunately," Mr. Harris said. "He died

last night. Late-stage cancer was discovered some months ago—he didn't want anyone to know. I'm so sorry."

As the air in Amanda's lungs whooshed out of her, she dropped the phone. She sat numbly, blankly staring at her lap, where the receiver lay.

"Ms. Sedgwick?"

Amanda picked up the phone and put it to her ear, but all she heard was the rushing beat of her own heart.

My father is dead.

My father is gone.

The father I never really knew is now gone forever. I'll never have the chance to know him. Tommy will never have the chance to know his grandfather.

Tears welled in Amanda's eyes. "I'm here," she told the lawyer.

"Ms. Sedgwick, do you have a piece of paper and a pen? You'll need to jot down our address and the date and time of the reading of the will."

Amanda picked up the notepad and pen on the side table and numbly wrote down the information the lawyer gave her. He offered his condolences again, and for the second time in fifteen minutes, the phone buzzed in her ear.

She glanced down at the address in midtown Manhattan, on the East Side. She shouldn't have bothered writing it down.

There was no way she was going to the reading of her father's will.

HAUNTING OLIVIA

Chapter One

The moment Olivia Sedgwick entered the playground, the dream boy and girl flitted through her mind as they always did, the girl's light blond hair bouncing on her thin shoulders as she skipped. The boy, holding a frog, gently cupped it in his hands as he held it out to Olivia before both children faded away.

Visits to the playground always brought the children to mind, their images as real as they were in her dreams, which were more frequent now.

Olivia sat down on a bench near the wrought-iron bars separating the playground from the busy city street, her lunch, a salad in a plastic container, on her lap. Her appetite was gone.

The last time she'd come to this playground, just two days ago, the dream boy, three or four years old, had been marveling over a daddy longlegs making its way up his little arm. The girl, the same age, in a yellow tutu, twirled along a meadow filled with wildflowers, despite it being January in New York City. Like now, the images were fleeting, a moment, maybe two. But they were as vivid as a photograph. Sometimes the boy and girl were very young—but never infants—and sometimes they were older. Like thirteen.

"What you're doing is illegal, you know."

Olivia turned at the unexpected voice of her coworker, Camilla Capshaw. *Glitz* magazine's assistant beauty editor, one of her only friends at the office, waited for a group of moms pushing strollers to pass, then sat down next to Olivia, pulling her own salad from a bag onto her lap.

"Sitting on a bench is illegal?" Olivia asked.

"Entering a playground when you're not accompanied by a kid is illegal," Camilla explained, tossing her shiny, straight dark hair behind her shoulder.

Olivia glanced at her. "Really? We could be arrested for just sitting here?"

Camilla nodded and speared a cucumber. "Don't you remember reading about that woman who got a ticket last year for doing the same thing?"

Olivia shook her head and swiped a cherry tomato from Camilla's salad, her appetite returning. Camilla's presence always made Olivia feel better. "No, but I guess I understand the reasoning behind it. Especially in a city like New York."

"Why would you spend your precious lunch minute watching a bunch of tiny screaming lunatics, anyway?" Camilla asked. "We work with enough screaming lunatics." She sipped from her water bottle. "I've seen you sitting here many times. How can you stand the noise?"

Olivia made a show of glancing at her watch. "We'd better get back to the office. Our lunch minute is up."

Camilla raised an eyebrow. "One day you're going to tell me all your secrets, Ms. Private. But you're right: if we're a second late for Bitch Face's two o'clock staff meeting, she'll probably fire us."

Their boss was definitely a nightmare to work for, but at least she'd saved Olivia from having to answer Camilla's question.

"Motherhood ruins your life," Camilla whispered into Olivia's ear. "Case in point—your boss."

Olivia followed Camilla's upped chin at her supervisor, Vivian Carl, senior features editor of *Glitz* magazine. Vivian, sitting at the far end—the executive end—of the conference room table, was nine months pregnant, due three days ago, and looked very uncomfortable, both physically and otherwise.

"Vivian, we've reassigned your celebrity interviews for the upcoming months," the editor in chief, Desdemona Fine, announced, without looking at Vivian. "Olivia will now interview Nicole Kidman for our June issue and take over your feature article on the best spas in the country."

Vivian sent Olivia a withering glance, then turned to the editor in chief. "I'm sure I can handle all my work. I'm planning only a three-day maternity leave, and—"

"Moving on to personnel matters," Desdemona interrupted, pushing her poker-straight blond hair behind her shoulder. "As representatives of *Glitz* magazine, one of the most influential and popular beauty and fashion journals in the country, I expect you to dress *appropriately*. For example"—she slid her cold gray gaze on an editorial assistant—"Uggs are out. And *mock* Uggs were never *in*. Additionally, we at *Glitz* magazine do not support the counterfeiting of designer goods." The editorial assistant turned red and slid lower in her chair. "If you are unsure about the image you are projecting as a *Glitz* staffer, please see our fashion director or one of our stylists."

Olivia glanced at *Glitz*'s fashion director, whose cropped blazer was made entirely of sparkling black feathers. Olivia tried not to stare at her hat, a bizarre silver cone that reminded her of an art project for preschoolers.

"Bitch Face chewed me out over the length of my skirt yesterday," Camilla whispered to Olivia as the editor in chief droned on. "'An inch higher would completely change your look,'" Camilla mimicked. "'You really should invest in a full-length mirror, dear.' I hate her guts."

Olivia shot her friend a commiserating smile. "I love the way you dress," she whispered back, taking in Camilla's thrift-store glamour ensemble. The editor in chief often commented that vintage and "send to Goodwill" were not synonymous.

Olivia had worked at *Glitz* for five years and had never been taken to task by the editor in chief.

Because you have a great sense of style, Camilla had once said. *That's all Bitch Face really cares about. And because you have the bucks to buy great clothes. And because you're a Sedgwick. You can do no wrong.*

First of all, Olivia wouldn't say she had a great sense of style. She was attracted to understated, classic clothes in pale, muted shades or black. She hated to stand out. And she didn't have big bucks. As the associate features editor of *Glitz*, Olivia could barely afford the rent on her Manhattan apartment.

It was the *Sedgwick* that gave the impression of money and glamour and grandeur. Olivia's father, William Sedgwick, who'd passed away only one month ago, had been a regular on *Forbes* magazine's Wealthiest in America list.

In fact, magazines and newspapers provided Olivia with most of her information about her father; the rest came from gossip—which might or might not be true—from her mother.

Olivia hadn't even known that her own father had been dying of cancer.

If he hadn't named Olivia in his will, she had no doubt she would have found out about his death from the *New York Times* obituary section. As it was, she'd learned of his death from his lawyer.

Olivia forced herself to focus on the editor in chief, who was sitting at the head of the long, polished table, still cutting staffers down with a word or even just a glance.

"You're not related to *the* Sedgwicks, are you?" the editor in chief had asked five years ago at Olivia's interview—her fifth and final for the magazine.

The Sedgwick, Olivia had wanted to correct. But she'd rightly sensed you didn't correct Desdemona Fine, whose real name—according to office gossip —was Mona Fingerman. There was no family of Sedgwicks, past or present. There was William, *the* Sedgwick. And his three daughters, each born of a different mother, none of whom were society page material or remotely well-off, let alone living in luxury.

Olivia's mother berated Olivia on a daily basis for not living up to her name. *You're a Sedgwick! If*

I had the name, I'd milk it for all it's worth. And it's worth millions.

Olivia's mother had never married William Sedgwick. She'd famously sued him for millions in child support and had been awarded a very comfortable settlement. Of Olivia's half sisters, only Ivy was a "legitimate" child, only Ivy's mother had been married to William. Briefly, of course. According to legend, Dana Sedgwick had gotten a young William dead drunk during a trip to a luxury casino in Las Vegas and sweet-talked him into marrying her at a drive-through wedding chapel. He had the marriage annulled within the week. When anyone asked Dana how long she'd been married to William, she often said they'd had many good years together.

Olivia's mother had had a fling with William. She'd been his flavor of the month twenty-nine years ago, and when Candace Hearn told him she was pregnant with his child, he ended the relationship. She won her settlement and had tried to foist Olivia on her father since the day she was born. William had never been interested. Fatherhood wasn't among his interests or priorities.

Except for the summer she turned sixteen. A summer she never allowed herself to think about.

"Those staffers on the associate level would do well to emulate Olivia Sedgwick's style," Desdemona said, smiling at Olivia.

Olivia felt her cheeks burn. She also felt the eyes of her coworkers and her immediate supervisor, Vivian, narrow on her. Thanks to being Desdemona's pet, most of Olivia's coworkers hated her. Those who took the time to get to know her, like

Camilla had, realized that Olivia wasn't the affected snob they thought she was.

"I can handle the Nicole Kidman interview," Vivian said to Desdemona. "It's the cover story, so—"

Desdemona held up a hand. "So *Olivia* will handle it for you. Do you really think you can represent *Glitz* magazine with leaky tits and baby spit-up on your blouse?"

Vivian burst into tears. Hormonal, I-can't-take-another-minute-of-you tears.

Olivia closed her eyes and shook her head. This was so unfair. Desdemona was so unfair. But instead of threatening the editor in chief with a discrimination suit, Vivian simply sobbed, then ran out of the room. No one would ever back her up anyway. Desdemona was too powerful.

"Waddling doesn't become anyone," Desdemona said under her breath with a tsk-tsk tone, then returned her attention to the meeting minutes.

And Olivia thought Desdemona couldn't possibly get any more vicious.

"Do yourself a very big favor," Camilla whispered to Olivia. "Never get pregnant."

Too late, Olivia thought. Not that she was pregnant right now. But she had been once. A long time ago.

As Olivia settled herself in bed with an article to edit (how many pieces on Botox was *Glitz* going to run?), a boy's face flitted into her mind, a good-looking face with intelligent, kind hazel eyes. This was not the dream boy, though once upon a time, he had been Olivia's dream man. Not that Zachary Archer at sixteen had been a man, of course.

Olivia could still see the way Zach's sandy brown hair fell over his forehead. She could still see him so clearly.

It had been so long since that summer—since that lonely fall and winter and heartbreaking spring— that thinking of Zach and what she'd gone through had lost its power to send her to her knees. She had no idea how she'd managed to get through that time and then immediately afterward, college, as though she'd graduated from a regular high school like every other incoming freshman. Her mother had used the Sedgwick name and legacy to get her into her father's alma mater. Olivia would be walking across campus, forcing herself not to think of Zach, but his face would appear before her mind's eye and the pain would whoosh the air from her lungs.

She'd spent her college years either studying or crying, which didn't allow for friends. And then after college she'd come home to New York City, where she'd grown up just off Park Avenue in a small apartment her mother had managed to buy with her settlement from William. Her mother had a contact at *Glitz,* and Olivia, still numb, had come back to life just a little. Working for a fashion magazine like *Vogue* or *Glitz* had always been her dream. Olivia's relationship with her mother had improved in those early months, when Olivia had had something else to think about other than Zach.

Other than the pregnancy. The birth. The news that had come so cruelly.

"Why isn't it crying?" sixteen-year-old Olivia had asked the nurse, still unsure whether she'd had a boy or a girl.

"Because it's dead," the nurse had said flatly. *"Stillborn."*

She'd fainted then and had woken up alone in a small, airless room. When the nurse's words had come back to her, she'd gasped and dropped to her knees and then screamed. The same nurse had come rushing in and told her to "stop making such a racket," that it was the middle of the night.

Her mother was all she'd had after that. Her father couldn't stand the sight of her after that summer. Her sisters had no idea that Olivia had been pregnant and shipped off to a home for unwed mothers hours up the Maine coast. They had no idea that she'd been forced to put the baby up for adoption. Or that the baby hadn't taken a single breath. And so Olivia had distanced herself from her sisters even more. Her mother had been an only child, so there were no aunts, no cousins to turn to. Just Olivia and her memories.

Her father's name had gotten Olivia the job at *Glitz*, and she'd been there ever since. Five years. She'd started as an editorial assistant to Vivian and had been promoted twice. Desdemona had often hinted that Olivia could count on having Vivian's job, too.

Tears burning her eyes, Olivia set the article aside and glanced out the window of her skyscraper apartment building; flurries blew around in the January wind. Despite the warmth of her apartment and her cozy down comforter, she shivered. The idea of stealing her boss's job while Vivian was on maternity leave—a weeklong maternity leave— made her sick to her stomach. Sometimes Olivia thought about leaving *Glitz*, but crazy as it sounded, she liked her job very much; she was suited to it, and she adored Camilla. Despite the bitching and backstabbing, *Glitz* had provided Olivia with work she loved, structure, a life. And with a mother like Candace Hearn, Olivia had learned to tune out bitching. Backstabbing was another story. Her mother might have had a shrill shell, but inside she was something of a marshmallow. Desdemona Fine, on the other hand, was a shrill shell inside and out.

Out of the corner of her eye, Olivia noticed the red light blinking on her answering machine. She'd been so wrapped up in memories and work when she arrived home that she hadn't even thought to check her messages.

She padded out of bed and pressed Play.

"Livvy, dear, it's Mother. I ran into Buffy Carmichael. You remember Buffy, darling. She chairs so many charity events. Anyway, Buffy mentioned that her son, Walter, is recently separated, and of course I gave Buffy your number, so expect a call, dear. He's very wealthy. She showed me a photo and he's no Orlando Bloom, but at your age you can't afford to be picky about looks—only about income. Bye, dear. Oh—I'd really like you to consider changing your mind about tomorrow. I'd really like to be there when you find out what your father left you in his will. Ta-ta!"

Olivia rolled her eyes at the phone. She'd gotten out of bed for that? And why couldn't her mother talk like a normal person?

At your age . . . Please. Olivia was twenty-nine! Young. And she couldn't care less about a man's looks or income. Once she'd moved back to New York and started working at *Glitz*, Olivia had numbly dated many different men—grad students, CEOs, a plumber (whose pants did not hang down), a chef, a mechanic, a shrink. The list went on and on. She dated. She had sex. And that was about it. She tried—really tried—to fall in love with several of the men she dated; she tried to develop real relationships with them, but a piece of her— the most important piece, the deepest piece—just didn't come out of its hiding place. It had once. With Zach. Maybe you loved like that only once.

She hoped not. She'd last loved like that when she was sixteen. If that was her last hurrah—her *only* hurrah—she was in big trouble.

And no, Mommy Dearest, you can't come with me to-morrow. Tomorrow, Friday, January thirtieth, was the day she was to receive her father's letter from his lawyer. An envelope with her name on it. To Be Opened No Sooner or Later Than January 30.

Olivia had no idea what the date could possibly mean. Why January 30? It was just an arbitrary day, but perhaps it meant something to her father.

Her sister Amanda had already received her inheritance letter a month ago (also on a specific day); it had stated that Amanda would inherit their father's million-dollar brownstone on the Upper West Side—*if* she followed a bunch of ridiculous and arbitrary rules for a month, such as not looking out of certain windows or going in certain rooms. Her father had even arranged for a watchdog to ensure that Amanda followed his rules to the letter—literally. That watchdog ended up becoming Amanda's husband. The happy couple—who donated the brownstone to a children's charity—was now on an extended honeymoon.

Olivia was so happy for Amanda. She was still getting to know Amanda and Ivy, her other sister, who was engaged. *Both my sisters are getting on with their love lives, and I'm stuck getting fixed up by my mother.*

She had no idea what her father had in store for her—or if she'd bother jumping through his hoops. He owned only two other properties: a cottage in Maine and an old inn in New Jersey. He wouldn't leave her the Maine house. Not after what happened there.

The summer she had turned seventeen, Olivia had gone back to her father's cottage for her annual summer vacation with him and her sisters. It had taken so much out of her to agree to the trip. But Zachary hadn't been in town. His family had moved away, she'd heard. No one knew where. She kept hoping she might hear something of what became of him, but no one knew. And no one really cared. Zach Archer, whose father was famous for falling down drunk in the middle of the street during the day, and whose mother was famous for sleeping with other women's husbands for small favors, didn't have much of a chance in Blueberry, Maine, a coastal town of wealthy year-rounders and summer tourists. When Olivia had known him, people liked to shake their heads and say, "That poor kid." Zach had hated that.

Perhaps William left me the New Jersey house, Olivia thought, heading into the bathroom. She'd never thought of her father as "Dad"; she'd always referred to him as her father, or William. She had called him Dad just once, thinking it might soften him, make him see inside her, listen to her, but it hadn't.

Anyway, she was sure the bequest would come with some silly rules about doors to open and windows not to raise. Maybe she'd accept the terms of the will and donate the house to a charity close to her heart, as Amanda had done with her inheritance. Olivia would probably have to spend a month at the house—and the idea of spending a month in her father's world made her faintly sick—but she could always commute to Manhattan from New Jersey. She'd need more time to handle all her boss's work while she was on maternity leave anyway.

Olivia headed into the bathroom, opened the medicine cabinet, and took out the jar of $100-an-ounce cucumber nighttime moisturizer that Camilla had swiped for her from the beauty department's goodie bags (the magazine got so many expensive freebies). She breathed in the fresh scent and looked at herself in the mirror. At times like this, when her face was fresh scrubbed and her hair was down (she liked wearing chignons at work) and her elegant out-fits were replaced by an old *Buffy the Vampire Slayer* T-shirt and her comfiest yoga pants, she could still see the sixteen-year-old girl she was before her life changed forever. Before she began spending a part of every day in a playground—sometimes just a few minutes, sometimes hours—just to imagine what her baby might have grown up to be like at every stage, every age.

2013

Nail-Biting Romantic Suspense
from Your Favorite Authors